Holy Water

Rule of Capture

ISBN: 978-1-68313-096-3

First Edition
Printed and bound in the USA

Cover art by Yuuji at ThinkStock.com
Cover and interior design by Kelsey Rice

Book IV in The Sacred Journey Series

Holy Water

Rule of Capture

Karen Hulene Bartell

P
Pen-L Publishing
Fayetteville, Arkansas
Pen-L.com

Other Books by Karen Hulene Bartell, PhD

The Sacred Journey Series

Sacred Choices, Book I

Sacred Gift, Book II

Lone Star Christmas: Holy Night, Book III

The Sacred Messenger Series

Angels from Ashes: Hour of the Wolf, Book I

Christmas in Catalonia

Belize Navidad

Sovereignty of the Dragons

International Cookbooks

Fine Filipino Food

The Best of Korean Cuisine

The Best of Taiwanese Cuisine

The Best of Polish Cooking

To Peter Bartell, my husband and best friend.
With deep respect for water, nature's driving force.
In memory of the lives lost during the 2015 Memorial Day flood.

Contents

Drama and Drizzle

We can say that the earth has an organic soul, that its flesh
is the land, its bones are the structure of the rocks . . .
its blood is the pools of water . . .
its breathing and its pulse are the ebb and flow of the sea.

– *Leonardo da Vinci*

Angela steadied herself on the granite incline. Near the highest of the three peaks, she gazed down at the changing landscape. Climbers starting out at the base looked like beetles. Below them, hikers on the loop trail looked like ants.

Suddenly dizzy, she lurched against the solid rock, regaining her balance, grounding herself. She breathed in the Hill Country's fresh air to collect herself. Inhaling, she filled her lungs with the subtle scents of bluebonnets mixed with mountain laurel.

"Fresh, isn't it?" asked Tulah, her college roommate and weekend hostess.

Wearing rappel gloves and hiking boots, Tulah gripped the rock like a weathered mesquite. Her shoulder-length blonde hair was swept back in a ponytail and tucked through a baseball cap. Blue eyes smiling, her tanned cheeks rosy from the climb, she grinned, apparently unfazed by the steep slope.

Angela nodded as a stiff breeze blew her shoulder-length dark hair into her eyes. Brushing her hand across her high cheek bones, she finger-combed the errant strands of hair behind her ear when she heard Tulah's younger sister, Kelby.

"Ozone." Kelby lifted her nose and drank the wind. "Yup, rain's on its way."

"Nothing in the forecast." Shrugging, Tulah turned back to the climb, leading them toward the top of the dome. Minutes later, she called over her shoulder. "How're y'all doing?"

"Okay." Kelby grunted but continued to inch her way up.

"What about you?" Tulah glanced behind her at Angela.

"I'm taking it one toehold at a time."

"Cautious is good. This climb isn't as easy as it looks."

"I'll second that." Twisting her mouth into a crooked smile, Angela compared the two sisters' styles. Tulah scaled the slope like a mountain goat, literally jumping from niche to perch. Kelby clung to the granite with both hands and feet, seeming to crawl, not walk, up the rocky surface.

They continued to climb Enchanted Rock, following the sun's ascent, but instead of the sky getting lighter, a bank of clouds obscured the sun.

Suddenly, a streak of lightning flashed in front of them, temporarily blinding Angela. She heard the peal of thunder a moment later as it echoed against the rock. From nowhere, a light smattering of rain began falling, dampening their hair. Then it turned into a downpour, drenching their clothes, making the smooth granite dome slick as ice. Another flash of lightning stuck nearby, branching in several directions.

With a shriek, Kelby teetered as she lost her footing, scrambling, slipping on the wet rock. Arms spread wide, she dug in with her fingernails, grabbing anything to break her fall. The only plant hardy enough to sprout in sheer granite was a prickly-pear cactus, and she screamed as her bare skin connected with its spines. Though it slowed her descent briefly, the cactus pad broke off in her hand as Kelby began sliding down the dome on her belly, gaining momentum.

Angela watched as Kelby approached the edge and then suddenly changed course, veering toward a granite outcrop. With a sickening thud, she heard Kelby crash into a boulder below. Tulah scrambled after her sister, calling to her. Angela carefully backtracked to Kelby, vertigo slowing her descent.

The girl lay moaning as Tulah took off her own jacket and placed it under Kelby's head. "Call nine-one-one!"

Angela held up her cell. "Just waiting for them to answer." Then she spoke into the receiver. "There's been an accident on Enchanted Rock, about thirty feet below its peak. Am guessing it's a compound fracture. The bone's sticking out of her leg."

"Don't move her," said the dispatcher. "Keep her stable until the helicopter arrives."

After giving the details, Angela hung up and turned toward Tulah. "They're on their way."

Within minutes, they heard the whir of blades. They watched as the helicopter hovered overhead and two medics rappelled down a line toward them. One wrapped Kelby's leg in a splint, while the other guided a rescue basket and helped load her.

The medic glanced from Kelby to the rocks below them. "You're one lucky lady. If you hadn't slammed into this boulder, nothing would have stopped your fall for two hundred feet."

Tulah took a deep breath. "It could've been worse."

"It can always be worse." Angela raised her eyes to the figure only she could see. *Thank you,* she mouthed.

Dressed in buckskin, his hair in braids, the Native American acknowledged her with a solemn nod.

Oblivious to the figure, Tulah stared through him, asking the medic, "Where are you taking my sister?"

"HC Memorial Hospital, Ma'am. By the time you arrive, we should have her leg set—"

"Don't forget these cactus spines." Kelby held up her right hand, her fingernails bloody, her hand a puffy, red pincushion.

The medic gave her a sympathetic smile. "And the cactus spines will be tweezed out."

"Some people will do anything for attention." Tulah hugged her sister gently. "Don't worry. You'll be good as new. We'll meet you at the hospital as soon as we climb down. Not everyone can be air-lifted." She glanced at Angela. "Some of us have to get down the old-fashioned way."

"At least it stopped raining." Kelby gave her a crooked smile. "All drama and drizzle, no measurable precipitation."

"Yeah, no rain in weeks, and today we get a trace, just enough to make the rock slick."

Tulah called her parents with the bad news.

"They just left Midland," she told Angela, "and should be in Fredericksley in about five hours."

Tulah in the lead, Angela clambered down the rock face as fast as vertigo and smooth, wet stone allowed. Then they hopped in the car, and Tulah careened along Ranch Road 965. "Not enough rain to even wash off the surface oil. All that drizzle did was make the road slick."

By the time they arrived at the hospital, Kelby was being wheeled back from an MRI scan. She looked pale and appeared to be sleeping.

Tulah caught her breath. "Is she all right?"

"She's been examined and X-rayed," said the nurse, "but she's drowsy. You can talk to her for a few minutes until the doctor arrives, that is, if she can stay awake."

Leaning over her sister, Tulah took her hand. "Mom and Dad are on their way. They're bringing Brooke back with them."

Kelby's eyes fluttered. "What?"

"Mom and Dad will be here in a couple hours. They said to give you their love."

Kelby's eyes closed, and a moment later Angela heard light snoring.

"Don't worry," said a man entering the room. "We've given her something to ease the pain, and it made her sleepy." Smiling, he transferred the chart to his left hand and shook hands with Tulah. "I'm Dr. Franks, and you're . . ."

"I'm her sister, Tulah Bankhead, and this is my roommate, Angela Brannon. How is she?"

"The X-rays show no other bones were broken. They're still interpreting the MRI images to determine if there are any hairline fractures or broken pieces. Once we have the results, we'll wheel her into surgery to set the bone."

"How long will that take?" Tulah watched him with anxious eyes.

He shrugged. "It depends on whether or not we need to insert pins, screws, or plates."

Tulah's eyes opened wide. "It's that bad?"

Reacting with a sympathetic smile, he said, "Let's not borrow trouble, but you can expect surgery to last from two to six hours. In the meantime, why don't you and your friend get something to eat and try to relax?"

"And fill out the paperwork," said the nurse.

Angela took out her cell phone. "While you do that, I'll update your parents."

An hour later, they pushed open the hospital doors and breathed deeply. The sun was shining. Surveying the robin's-egg-blue sky, Tulah grimaced. "Why couldn't it have been like this for the climb?"

"It was, all except for a passing shower."

Tulah glanced back at the hospital. "And look what that caused. No precipitation in weeks, and that tiny rain cell cost Kelby her broken leg."

Angela shrugged. "It could've been worse."

"How?"

Angela tried to read Tulah's eyes, debating how much to share. "Did you notice how Kelby's fall seemed to suddenly change course?"

Tulah narrowed her eyes and gave a delayed nod. "Now that you mention it."

"She didn't slide down the rock in a straight line. Didn't it seem odd, that at the last minute, she veered toward a granite outcrop?"

"Why?" Tulah watched Angela closely. "Do you know something I don't?"

"Let's just say someone was looking out for her."

Tulah's eyes opened wide. "What *are* you saying?"

"It could've been much worse."

Tulah's forehead wrinkled. "You sensed something?"

"I *saw* something." Angela took a deep breath. Still debating, she peered into Tulah's eyes and made her decision: *I can trust her*. "Actually some*one*, I saw a Native American man in braids and buckskin catch her arm, change the direction of her fall."

Tulah nodded slowly. "For years, I've heard legends about a 'Guardian of the Rock,' supposedly some shaman named Wind Spirit that protects climbers, but that's all I thought it was, stories and legends." She exhaled quickly. "I don't know what to say."

"Let's just say Kelby's guardian angel was watching out for her." Angela smiled. "Come on, let's get something to eat. I don't know about you, but I'm starved."

"Now that you mention it, so am I." She returned a grin. "Like German food?"

They found an outdoor table in a beer garden just off Main Street. Ancient live oaks shaded them from the sun, while a balmy breeze caught their hair.

Angela looked over the menu. "I'm not familiar with German cuisine. I don't know what to order."

Tulah's taut face relaxed into a smile. "Try the sampler. It's got a little of everything."

Angela read the description: "Bratwurst, knockwurst, and pepperwurst served on a bed of sauerkraut, red cabbage, and sweet and sour potatoes." She looked up at Tulah. "Sounds delicious."

She grinned. "Just wait till you taste it."

"What can I get you?" asked the waitress, pen and pad in hand.

Angela noticed her outfit: white apron over embroidered black jumper. "I'll try the sausage sampler."

Tulah said, "I'll have the wiener schnitzel and a flight of beer."

Angela cocked her head. "What's a flight?"

"It's a sample of six seasonal brews, like that." The waitress pointed to six tiny glasses at the next table.

"This isn't just a pub," said Tulah. "It's a microbrewery. They make about two dozen seasonal beers each year. A flight gives you a taste of each, and it's different every time."

"You talked me into it." Turning toward the waitress, Angela added, "I'll have a flight, too."

The woman hesitated, assessing her. "I'll need to see some ID."

Angela felt her cheeks burn as she reached for her purse and handed the waitress her driver's license.

Tulah grinned as she turned toward Angela. "That's what you get for looking so young."

"The day will come when you'll be glad to look underage." Their waitress laughed. "Be right back with your flights, ladies."

Tulah's cell phone rang, and she quickly answered it, speaking low. "Hi, Mom." Whispering, she gave an update on Kelby. Apparently responding to a question, she glanced at Angela. "I'm trying not to annoy the other diners. Angela and I are having lunch." She listened silently for a few minutes, her expression getting more serious, and then said, "Okay, see you in about an hour. Love you."

The waitress brought their flights. "Start with the pale ale on the left. It's the lightest flavor, and work your way to the dark stout on the right. That's the heartiest." She smiled. "Should have your orders out in a minute."

Tulah lifted the tiny glass on the left. "*Prost.*"

Angela followed her example. "*Prost.*"

"Not bad." Tulah set down her glass, seeming lost in thought. Then she became silent, her stare unfocused.

Angela watched her friend. "You seem a million miles away. What's wrong?"

Tulah started. "What?" She shook her head. "Sorry, something my mother said."

"What was it?"

"She's worried about Kelby, first and foremost."

"But . . ."

"The family business needs all of us to help out at the winery. Now that Kelby's out of commission, she's worried about finding someone to take her place."

"What does Kelby do at the winery?"

Tulah absently sipped her beer. "She drives the tram, takes guests on tours through the vineyards to the winemaking complex. Then she finishes with a private tasting, where guests can sample and compare wines."

Angela mulled it over. "Does it pay anything?"

"That's the problem." Tulah gave a mirthless grin. "It's a competitive market. Especially during this drought."

Angela squinted as she raised her shoulders. "What do you mean?"

"We can't afford to hire anyone. The whole family pitches in just to keep the winery open. With Kelby on the sidelines . . ." Tulah grimaced. "A salary could make or break the business."

Angela mentally rewound the past semester. Catching her breath as she recalled the pain of her mother's sudden death two months earlier, she remembered how Tulah's family had opened their home to her over weekends and now Easter. "What if . . ."

Tulah sat up straight, watching her. "What's going through that beady little brain of yours?"

"What if I fill in for Kelby this summer?"

Tulah shook her head. "The job doesn't pay anything."

"How about room and board?" Angela looked hard at her friend. She raised an eyebrow. "Would that work?"

Tulah's eyes lit up, and then sighing, she shook her head. "It wouldn't be fair to you."

"Actually, you'd be doing me a favor."

Tulah scoffed. "How do you figure that?"

"You knew my adviser had helped me get an internship at Enchanted Rock."

"Yeah . . ."

"She said I'd earn credit for the experience and could graduate in August."

"What's wrong with that?"

"State Parks barely pay interns. I'd have had to turn the job down because I couldn't afford living expenses." Angela stared at her friend. "See? You'd be helping me, not the other way around."

Tulah took a deep breath, seeming to think it over. Then she met Angela's eyes. "But if you're working at Enchanted Rock, when would you have time to help at the winery?"

"That's easy." Angela smiled. "It's a shared internship, which means I'd only have to work twenty hours a week at the park. The rest of the time, I'd be free to help with the winery tours and tastings."

"But—"

"Careful, they're hot." Handling the plates with a towel, the waitress set them on the table.

"Thanks, this smells wonderful." Angela breathed in the piquant aromas of her steaming sampler.

"How's the beer?"

Angela glanced at their nearly untouched glasses. "We've been too busy talking to find out." She caught Tulah's eye and winked. "But something tells me I prefer wine to beer."

As the waitress left, Tulah's blue eyes looked gray as they focused on Angela.

"Despite your making it sound like we'd be doing you a favor, you're the one who'd be helping us. You don't want to spend your last summer in school working two jobs. The winery isn't your problem."

Angela shook her head. "You're wrong. It is my problem. You and Kelby wouldn't have taken me climbing today if I hadn't been considering this internship and wanted to see Enchanted Rock. In a way, it's my fault she fell and broke her leg. The least I can do is take her place."

Tulah scoffed. "It was the freaky weather that caused it, not you." Then her eyes homed in on Angela's. "What about Kio?"

Angela glanced at her engagement ring. "He's in Fort Davis, working nights, trying to establish himself. We knew our time together this summer would be limited." She looked up at Tulah and smiled. "That's what phones are for. From my point of view, it's all settled." Angela held out her hand. "If your parents agree, do we have a deal?"

Tulah shook on it.

By the time they finished lunch and walked back to the hospital, Tulah's family had arrived, and her mother was busy signing the paperwork.

Tulah hugged her father and then threw her arms around her sister Brooke. "Look at you!" Holding her at arm's length, Tulah ran her eyes up and down her sister's bloated frame. "Eight months' pregnant, when are you due?"

"Eight months next week." Brooke corrected, deadpanning. "But who's counting? I'm due in five weeks."

"Wow, a baby in the family, it's hard to imagine you a mother and me an auntie."

Their father smiled. "Or imagine your mother and me grandparents."

"Proverbs 17:6," said Mrs. Bankhead. "The crown of the aged is their children's children."

Turning toward Angela, Tulah introduced her to Brooke. "This is my obviously pregnant sister, Brooke. She's going to stay with us until after the baby comes."

"My husband works on oil rigs," said Brooke. "We've been moving from boomtown to boomtown across west Texas. Noah works days, nights, weekends, and holidays, rotating his schedule between forty and a hundred and forty hours a week. He's never home." Brooke gave Tulah an affectionate wink. "I need to be with family when our baby's born."

"Wouldn't have it any other way." Holding out his arms, their father drew her toward him in a bear hug.

"And this is my friend and roommate, Angela. She's spending Easter with us and will be . . ." Noticing Angela's high sign, she broke off mid-sentence.

"Will be what?" asked her father.

Tulah took a deep breath as she glanced at Angela and told him their idea. "What do you say?"

Angela gave Tulah an anxious smile as they waited for his answer.

He drew a deep breath and ran his hand through his hair. "I'll have to talk this over with your mother, but as far as I'm concerned, Angela, consider yourself one of us." He put his arm around her shoulders and hugged her. "Welcome to the Bankhead family."

"What's this?" Tulah's mother walked over in time to hear the punch line.

Tulah explained, filling in her mother on their idea. "So what do you think?"

"*What do I think?!*" She put her arms around Angela. "I think you're heaven-sent, pure and simple. Welcome to the Bankhead family."

Absorbing their warm hospitality, Angela swallowed hard to control her trembling bottom lip. Their affection was overwhelming after the loss of her mother. Before she could speak, Dr. Franks approached them, and Tulah introduced him to her family.

"How is she?" asked Mrs. Bankhead.

"The MRI indicated there were no head injuries, and it was a clean break, no hairline fractures or broken pieces. We've set the bone, put on the cast, and your daughter's ready to be released." He spoke to the nurse and rejoined the group. "Kelby will be out shortly."

A few minutes later, they watched a nurse wheel Kelby toward them. Tulah grimaced when she saw the size of her sister's cast. Then she put on a bright smile and took a pen from her purse.

"Let me be the first to autograph it."

Kelby's mouth lifted in a half grin. "Sure, first up the rock, first to sign my cast, competitive to the bitter end."

Tulah chuckled as she signed and read aloud. "Kelby Bankhead, Best in Free Fall Class." Then she handed Angela the pen.

Angela read aloud as she wrote. "The last shall be first," she looked up with a grin, "at least down the hill."

"Two comediennes, just what I need." Kelby looked at her cast and bandaged hand, still swollen from the cactus spines. Then she rolled her eyes. "I should've known something would happen today. It's new moon."

Easter Sunday dawned sunny and bright. As Tulah drove to church, Angela looked out at the hillsides of bluebonnets, their hues seeming to blend into the Texas-blue skies. She rolled down her window to breathe in their subtle fragrance.

"They're gorgeous." Angela leaned out to get a better view of the blue fields.

"This is part of the Willow City Loop," said Tulah, "thirteen scenic miles of blue, red, pink, white, and yellow flower-filled valleys and meadows. It's one of the Hill Country's prettiest springtime spots."

"I believe it."

"We got a good crop of bluebonnets this year despite the drought. Even though sprinkles like yesterday's showers don't do a thing to recharge the aquifer, they seem to be enough for the wildflowers to bloom."

"What are those reddish-purple flowers?" Angela pointed to a patch near crushed granite.

"Those are wine cups," said Tulah. "They're native Texan. In fact, we're picturing them on our newest label."

Angela glanced at her with a smile. "Wine cups. Clever marketing, which reminds me. When do you want me to start at the winery?"

"The tourist season's already heating up. The Wildflower & Wine Trail happens over the next three weekends."

Angela squinted, trying to understand. "What do you mean 'trail'?"

"They're events where all the wineries participate in tastings. Tourists can sample the wine and enjoy the wildflowers all along the trail from Austin to Fredericksley."

"So the 'trail' is basically Highway 290," said Angela.

"For the most part," Tulah grinned, "but small family wineries like ours also take part. Since we're off the beaten path, it helps attract new customers."

Angela nodded. "It makes good business sense. So it looks like tourist season's already begun, and next Saturday's my official first day on the job."

They met the rest of the family outside the church. With Kelby hobbling on crutches, they slowly made their way up the steps and down the aisle. Just as they took their seats, the organ began playing the entrance hymn: *Rain Down.*

"How appropriate," Kelby whispered.

After the opening prayer, the priest said, "Let us renew our baptismal promises." The choir sang *Water of Life* as he and the deacon sprinkled the congregation with holy water.

The first reader addressed them from the lectern. "A reading from Isaiah 43:16-20. Thus says Yahweh, who made a way through the sea, a path in the raging waters . . ."

"Water again," whispered Kelby.

"I am making a road in the desert and rivers in wastelands . . ."

Soon after, the priest stood up and smiled. "How fitting our first reading was about water and deserts. During this drought, water is on everyone's mind."

Kelby made a sour face.

"As Lent came to an end, some of us might have felt we'd stumbled through a spiritual desert. Easter may have seemed a heat mirage along our journey, always appearing just beyond the horizon. We started Lent intending to use its forty days to grow closer to God, to grow more self-disciplined. But instead, maybe we found ourselves straying, drifting, wondering what had happened to our noble intentions. Drudgery, not devotion."

He paused as he looked at the congregation.

"Maybe this is why Lent lasts forty days. It gives us enough rope to hang ourselves. Forty days gives us time to reflect on our weaknesses. By Holy Thursday, we were parched, thirsting for living water.

"Not just during Lent, many times, we find ourselves starting out with high hopes, meaning to get it right this time. We end up staggering instead of striding, dehydrated with a spiritual thirst, waiting for God to send 'rain' to continue our journey.

"Maybe you've seen a nature documentary, or seen arroyos, dry riverbeds, and dusty ground where plants and animals wither as they wait for rain. Suddenly, water that fell as rain many miles away gushes in a torrent, turning the dust to mud, then into a lush wetland where all life thrives.

"Maybe this was what Isaiah had in mind when he wrote 'water in the desert.' In ancient times, as now, parts of Israel have seasonal rainfalls that bring the desert to life. The desert's a good parallel to a Christian on a pilgrimage. We all rely on God's outpouring of blessings, especially when we're plagued by doubt and spiritual drought. We pray God will rain down the grace to continue.

"Like spring showers, Easter's the seasonal 'rain' for us, bringing us rivers in our spiritual desert after our Lenten journey. As the Israelites wandered through the desert on their way to the promised land, they relied on God to sustain them each morning. They longed for the time the deserts would be true oases of living water, when life would triumph over death.

"Easter, that glimmer at the end of the Lenten journey, is not a mirage. It's not an arroyo or intermittent stream. It's the river in the desert that sustains us throughout the year."

On the way home from church, they crossed a bridge over choked, bone-dry land. Angela stared at the rock piles and crushed granite below.

"Seems like an odd place to build a bridge."

Tulah glanced at her. "What do you mean?"

"There's no water."

"That's because it's an arroyo. You should see it when it rains. Water gushes through here fast enough to wash away a car. Then a day or two later, the swollen stream shrinks to a slow-moving creek and then to a trickle. Tadpoles and minnows hatch in its shallow waters. After a week or two, it stops flowing. All that's left are evaporating pools of water."

"What about the tadpoles and minnows?" Angela watched her closely. "What happens to them?"

"The tadpoles sprout legs and hop away as frogs. Raccoons and birds eat most of the minnows—"

"Just like fishing in a barrel."

Tulah nodded. "But a few escape downstream and survive. Finally, the pools dry up, and the river becomes the dusty arroyo you see now."

Angela shook her head. "Seems like a short life cycle."

"It's enough to hatch a new generation of frogs and fish to spawn the next. In Texas, nature has to catch its opportunities when it can."

Angela knitted her brow as she scanned the dry landscape. "Without water, how does nature survive?"

"Good question." Tulah took a deep breath. "Every river, every lake, every drop of water in Texas is allocated. Until recently, nothing was reserved for wildlife."

"What's it used for?"

"Over half the water's used for irrigation. Municipal use accounts for a third of it. Ranching, mining, and manufacturing use the rest."

Angela narrowed her eyes. "You mean, no water's allocated for fish or wildlife?"

"Technically, the people of Texas own all surface water—streams and rivers." Tulah took her eyes from the road to glance at Angela. "Aquifers are another topic altogether. Texas gives out water permits, but until recently, not a drop of water was set aside for the environment."

"What?" Angela looked out the windshield at the miles and miles of dusty land. "How can fish and wildlife survive without water?"

"Texas started introducing environmental flow protection in 1985, but only on *new* permits. Most permits were issued—"

"Before then." Angela finished the sentence for her.

"Exactly." Tulah nodded. "Less than ten percent of all permits have been issued since 1985. Many river basins are over-allocated."

"Meaning . . .?"

"Texas has issued rights to pump more water than exists."

"So if the permit owners use all they're legally allowed, some rivers and streams would run dry in a drought. Wow." Angela took a deep breath, letting the idea settle in. "That is so sad."

She thought of the internship paper she had to write. *Maybe I could write something about water for wildlife.*

Suddenly Angela felt the car swerve as her seatbelt tightened. "What happened?"

Pulling over, Tulah parked on the shoulder. "Just missed hitting a turtle. It must be looking for water."

Angela glanced around as they stepped out of the car. "I haven't seen any water in miles. Is there a spring around here?"

"Not that I know of. Am guessing instinct told this guy to head for the riverbed." She surveyed the parched landscape and sniffed. "Which is dry as a bone."

Angela picked him up and noticed the red stripes on his neck. "He's a red-eared slider, a water turtle."

"He won't find any water around here."

Angela looked at her friend. "Is there a pond or creek nearby?"

Tulah scratched her head. "There's a stream that runs near the cabin."

"Is it nearby? Could we drive him there?"

Tulah looked at her watch. "Mom's having the family over for Easter dinner." Then she looked at the dusty turtle. "Sure, it's only a couple minutes out of the way."

As they started back to the car, a red convertible sailed past them. Both girls watched the clouds of dust billow behind it as it sped out of sight.

Angela held up the turtle. "Good thing we happened along when we did, or this guy would have been history."

Tulah turned off the county road onto a caliche ranch road. Then she parked in front of a rustic log cabin with a built-on porch. Baskets of petunias hung from its rafters.

Angela noted the porch swing was gently rocking. "Who lives here?"

"This is one of the B&B cabins we own." Tulah led the way along a crushed granite path, where red Turk's Caps and purple Mexican Sage grew wild. "Good, it's still flowing."

Immense cypress trees, hundreds of years old, lined the stream's banks. As Angela stared, she saw their beauty twice. Once as the aged sentinels standing guard, and a second time reflected in the narrow stream. Their feathery green fronds, lacy in the dappled light, simultaneously gave the image of timeless strength and ethereal vulnerability.

She noticed the wide rocky shores on either side of the stream and marveled. "Is this whole area ever under water?"

Tulah nodded. "When we're not in a drought, this river's filled from bank to bank."

Slowly turning, Angela took in a panoramic view. "Even this small stream is lovely, but I wish I could see it in its full glory."

Tulah gave a dry laugh. "If it ever rains, maybe you will."

Angela walked onto the dry riverbed along the brook. Then she set the turtle on the sand and watched him run toward the water. "It was a short drive, but how far was it from where we picked him up?"

"A mile or two," said Tulah, "but a long walk for his little legs."

"And that's if he knew which direction to take." Angela smiled. "Thanks for taking the detour. It was probably the difference between life and death for this guy."

Tulah raised an eyebrow as they started back to the car. "Could be."

As they approached the cabin, Angela looked at its limestone chimney and tin roof. "You said your family owns this place?"

"Yeah, my parents installed electricity and converted it into a B&B a year or so ago. It's even got its own rainwater collection system." Tulah pointed toward the cistern.

"Is anyone renting it?"

Tulah stopped in her tracks and turned toward Angela. "Why?"

"It's adorable, but I don't see any car here." She shrugged. "Just wondered."

Tulah hesitated for a moment and then sighed. "It was booked for this weekend . . ."

"But . . ."

She grimaced. "The couple cancelled. In fact, they were the sixth cancellation we've had. People stay a night and then leave."

Angela's ears perked. "Do they say why?"

Tulah smiled sheepishly and then hunched her shoulders. "They say it's haunted."

"Really?" Angela looked at the gently rocking porch swing. "So then this cabin's available?"

"You might say that," Tulah chuckled, "since no one's ever stayed here more than a night."

Angela looked at the surrounding grounds. "Is this place very far from your house?"

"Five minutes away by car, two if you're walking."

"Really?"

"We took Hall Road, the back way here, but it's right next door to our house."

As they climbed in the car, Angela stared at the cabin, thinking. Then she nodded to herself. *It just might work.* Her thoughts trailed off.

"Have you?" Tulah's tone told her she had been daydreaming.

"Sorry, was just thinking about that cabin." Angela grimaced. "Have I what?"

"Ever had barbecue for Easter dinner?"

"Barbecue for Easter?" Crinkling her nose, Angela grinned. "Can't say that I have."

"Then you're in for a treat. Wait till you taste my daddy's brisket. It melts in your mouth." She smiled as they turned into the driveway. "Hope you're hungry."

Angela watched through the sunroof as they passed beneath the rows of ancient live oaks lining the drive. Their branches reached across, touching each other, creating a green canopy overhead. Tulah found a place to park in the crowded cul-de-sac in front of the house.

"Looks like the family's started arriving."

They walked up the flagstone steps to the cedar-and-limestone entry that was part of the wide, wraparound porch. People sat in small groups on rattan chairs, chatting, drinking iced tea or lemonade.

Brooke waved from the side lawn. Cupping her hands, she called to them. "We're finding Easter eggs. Want to help?"

They looked at each other. "No, that's okay," called Tulah. "We'll let you have all the fun." Then she whispered. "She loves this stuff."

Angela watched Brooke help some of the younger children find their eggs. "She certainly seems to love kids."

They made their way to the kitchen slowly, stopping every few feet for Tulah to introduce Angela.

"Oh, there you are," said Tulah's mother. "Can you two start carrying the food out to the table?"

"Sure." Angela inhaled the steaming platters' fragrance. "It all smells wonderful." She picked up one of the tureens. "What's this?"

"Fried black-eyed peas," said Tulah, "crunchy on the outside, and creamy in the center. 'Course Mom adds smoked paprika and brown sugar for a little zest."

"Sounds delicious." Suddenly, Angela realized she was famished.

They carried out baskets of freshly baked hot cross buns, tureens of fried black-eyed peas, smashed potatoes, fresh buttered peas with caramelized pearl onions, and platters of deviled eggs that looked like Easter chicks with olive-slice eyes. They brought out the plates, silverware, napkins, and several pitchers of iced tea and lemonade. At a second table, they set out several bottles of their label's merlot.

Angela did a head count. Not including the children, she saw twenty-four people. "How large is your family?"

"Oh, this is just Daddy's side." Tulah chuckled. "You should see when the whole family's here."

Tulah's father and uncle carried over deep pans of barbecued brisket. Then her father rang the triangle near the grill. "Come 'n' get it!" He waited for the group to gather, led them in a prayer, and said, "Dig in!"

Angela and Tulah brought their plates to the sunny side of the covered, wraparound porch. Comfortably shaded by the roof, they could look out at the irrigated vineyards.

"The vines look so healthy," said Angela, "yet we're in a drought."

"Like I said, half Texas's water goes for irrigation," said Tulah. "In this case, gray water, but without it, these vines would wither and die like the scrub grass you saw along the road."

Angela nodded thoughtfully as the talk again turned to water. "Maybe you can help me pick a topic for my internship paper."

"Sure, we were just talking about irrigation. What about the role water plays in agribusiness? Helping out at the winery would give you plenty of background material for your paper."

Angela's forehead creased as she thought it over. "That's true, but I can't stop thinking about that turtle and about something you said on the way home."

"What was that?"

"You mentioned over-allocation of surface water. You said the rivers could run dry in a drought, that practically no water's been set aside for wildlife." Angela looked at her. "What if I write a paper, not just about the water shortage in general, but specifically about the lack of water for wildlife?"

Tulah nodded. "Texas is blessed with all sorts of feathered, finned, and furry critters. It wouldn't hurt to increase public awareness."

"And something else." Angela studied her friend. "I can't stop thinking about that cabin. You said it's near here?"

Tulah pointed to the crushed granite path alongside the vineyard. "That's the same path you and I took to the stream. The cabin's just past that stand of live oaks."

Angela craned her neck and could just make out the hanging baskets on the front porch. "Instead of imposing on your family this summer, what if I stay in the cabin?"

"No, you're welcome to stay here. There's plenty of room."

"Appreciate that." She smiled. "But I don't want to be in the way. Staying in the cabin, I'd only be a stone's throw away, yet not underfoot."

"We wouldn't have invited you if we hadn't wanted you to stay."

Angela shook her head. "With Brooke pregnant and Kelby out of commission, your family has enough to deal with. You don't need a live-in guest, too."

Tulah nodded as she shrugged. "I can see your point, but that cabin's haun . . . might be haunted. Wouldn't you be afraid to stay there alone?"

Angela set down her fork and grinned. "Let's just say, the idea of ghosts doesn't scare me."

"You mentioned seeing the 'Guardian of the Rock.'" Tulah's eyes opened wide. "That wasn't mist or your imagination?"

Angela shook her head. "I've been given a gift." Then she smiled. "Look at it this way. With me staying in the cabin, I'll end any rumor that it's haunted, and your parents will be able to rent it out."

"They'd like that." Then she caught Angela's eye. "Like I said, it's a bed and breakfast. You're a two-minute walk away from all your meals."

"Which reminds me, you're right about your dad's brisket. This is wonderful." She took another bite. "Something tells me I'll need to watch my weight this summer."

Kelby stumped toward them on her crutches. Angela pulled out a chair for her as Tulah took her crutches and pulled up a second chair.

"Here, rest your leg on this."

"No need to baby me." Kelby made a sour face. "I'm going to have this cast on for the summer. Might as well get used to it."

"Kelby . . ." Angela rolled the word on her tongue. "I've never heard that name before. Does it have a meaning?"

Kelby shared a grin with her sister. "It's Gaelic for 'place by the fountain or spring.'"

"I like that." Angela nodded as she turned toward Tulah. "And your name's unique, too. What does Tulah mean?"

"It's short for Tallulah, as in Tallulah Bankhead." She blushed. "I guess with the name Bankhead, my parents just couldn't resist."

"Are you related?"

Tulah shrugged. "Who knows? Supposedly, a distant cousin of our grandfather was her father, but it may just be a family story."

"Does the name have a meaning?"

Tulah nodded. "It's Choctaw for 'leaping water.'"

Angela smiled as she glanced from Tulah to Kelby. "Leaping water, place by the fountain or spring, and your sister's name is Brooke. Does water play any role in your parents' lives?"

Cabin and Phantom

It is far more difficult to murder a phantom than a reality.
– *Virginia Woolf*

The following week, Tulah paused, the key in the door. "You're sure about this?"

"For the umpteenth time, yes." Angela chuckled at her friend as she brought in her suitcase and Frank's carrying cage. "It's six o'clock in the afternoon. The sun doesn't set for another two hours. To hear you talk, you'd think it was midnight in the church cemetery."

"All right." Tulah pursed her lips and unlocked the door. "Here it is, basically three rooms." She pointed out the cabin's features as she gave the tour. "This is the dinette/living area, two bar stools, two sitting chairs, and a desk. Just behind the bar is the kitchenette. It's got a mini-fridge, coffeemaker, and microwave." She turned on the faucet. "And running water."

Angela glanced at the limestone wall with its river-rock fireplace.

"Through this door is the bedroom/bath. Nothing fancy, but it's got a tub and shower."

"Are you kidding?" Angela looked around the interior. "This is perfect."

The bedroom walls were finished in knotty-pine car siding. The bed's headboard and footboard were made of hand-hewn, varnished logs. At its foot was a bench made of a halved log, smooth side up with a glassy finish. A matching armoire and nightstand completed the set.

Angela pushed open the door to the full bath. Deep plush towels hung on the rods, and fresh wildflowers were in a vase. Smiling, she picked them up, inhaling their scent.

"You and your mother have thought of everything."

"You're sure you won't be afraid to stay here alone?" Tulah raised her eyebrows skeptically.

"I love it here." She gave her friend a hug as she again glanced around the cabin. "I have all the comforts of home. Actually, more."

"There's a phone by the bedside if you change your mind." Tulah swung back the doors of the armoire. "And there's a TV for company."

"This is absolutely perfect." Angela opened her eyes wide, trying to convince her friend. "I'm going to be fine. Don't worry so much."

"Just call if you have second thoughts, or if you get sc—change your mind. We're two minutes away."

Putting her hands on Tulah's shoulders, Angela turned her toward the door. "I'm fine. Relax. I'll see you in the morning."

"Breakfast is at eight, but come over any time, and don't forget to call if you need anything or get sc—want some company."

Angela gently pushed her friend toward the door. "To hear you talk, you'd think I was a thousand miles from civilization."

Tulah grimaced. "As long as you're sure about staying here."

"I'm sure! Go, already. I'll be fine."

"Okay, then here's the key. I'll see you in the morning." With a sigh, Tulah handed it to her, started to close the door, but turned back and tried again. "I'd still feel better if—"

"Go!" Angela chuckled as she shoved her friend across the threshold. "I'll see you tomorrow. Good night." She closed the door and gave a deep sigh.

"I'm two minutes away if you need anything." Tulah's voice was muffled as she walked to the nearby window and spoke through the glass.

"I'm fine. See you in the morning. Bye!" Angela waved and then let down the shade with a bang. Leaning against the wall, she took a deep breath. *Finally.*

After she let Frank out of his cage, she called Kio to share her day, hear his voice, and give him the cabin's phone number. Then she hoisted her suitcase onto the bed, meaning to unpack. One glance at the cat curled up asleep on the fluffed pillows, and she realized he wasn't the only one exhausted.

Yesterday's all-nighter and today's exams are catching up with me. A nap sounds so appealing. She lay her head on the pillow and within moments was dreaming.

She woke with a start. *What was that?* Except for a glimmer of moonlight coming in through the window, it was dark. *Where am I?* Gazing around, she remembered. *The cabin.*

Then she heard it again. Laughter, deep, masculine laughter. What started as an evil chuckle became an eruption of laughter, an echoing explosion. It resonated through the cabin, bouncing off the hard surfaces of the stained cement floor and ricocheting off the walls.

Frank hissed and growled.

She reached for the lamp on the nightstand. It took a moment, but when she found the switch and turned on the light, the laughter stopped.

"Relax, Frank." Petting the cat, Angela got out of bed and began opening her suitcase. She heard the laughter a third time and paused, T-shirt in hand. Then she calmly went about the business of unpacking.

Again demonic laughter filled the cabin's space, so loud this time Angela winced and covered her ears as the cat hid under the bed.

"All right, that's it! There's no need to scare Frank."

Silence.

Angela listened a moment and then began hanging her clothes in the closet. "That's better." She took a deep breath. "My name's Angela Brannon. What's yours?"

Again silence. Then a whistling began in the chimney, growing in decibel level until it became a mournful, piercing shriek.

Angela hummed to herself as she went about unfolding and hanging her clothes. Frank peeked out from under the bed.

The sound died away. Moments later, the television came on, blasting at full volume.

Angela turned it off, and sat on the bench at the foot of her bed. Crossing her legs, she cupped her knee in her hands. "How old are you? Fourteen? For heaven's sake, show yourself."

The television turned on.

"Oh, come on, you've already tried that. It doesn't work." She sighed as she crossed her arms. "What else have you got?"

After several minutes, the television turned off. Then silence. She sighed again and crossed her legs in the other direction.

"I've got all night, and this is all I have scheduled on my social calendar." She jerked her chin, challenging him. "I know you're a 'he.' Don't be shy. Show yourself!"

"How would you know I'm a 'he'?"

She stifled a smile. "I saw you rocking on the porch swing the day we brought the turtle here."

"You saw me?"

"Don't sound so surprised." She chuckled. "Yes, I saw you."

A harsh laugh echoed through the cabin. "Then describe me!" The attitude was overbearing.

"Don't you use that tone with me, mister." She took a deep breath and tried again. "Can't we be civil, courteous?" When she didn't hear a response, she added, "Or aren't you 'man' enough to discuss, instead of shout, order, or wail?"

"Dang it, woman! You're infuriating!"

"And you're cowardly. Show yourself."

Suddenly, he materialized. Wearing a chambray shirt and faded jeans, he appeared literally out of thin air. A thick shock of dark hair surrounded his finely chiseled face, and he stared at her through hauntingly pale blue eyes.

"That's better."

"Better? *Better?* Everyone else has high-tailed it when I showed myself. Ain't you got the good sense to be frightened?"

Angela swallowed a smile. "No, do you?"

Like a cougar, he moved sinuously as he walked closer, all the while scrutinizing her. "You ain't afraid of me? Why?"

"I've been able to see ghosts since I was born." She shrugged. "It's a gift."

"What are you doing in this cabin?"

"My cat and I are going to live here weekends through May and then stay for the summer."

"That remains to be seen." Crossing his arms, he leaned against the wall. "But why are you here?"

"It's going to be my home while I work at the park and winery."

"This is *my* home." Standing at his full height, he crossed toward her, towering over her.

Angela jerked her chin as she peered up at him. "Actually, the Bankheads own this cabin, and I'll be staying here as their guest."

"I own this cabin." He stretched out his large hands, splaying his fingers. "I built it with these two hands. It's mine."

"You may have built it," she said calmly, "but the Bankheads bought and improved it. It's theirs now, and mine while they allow me to stay."

"While *I* allow you to stay. That is, *if* I allow you to stay."

She rolled her eyes. "There's no need to be so territorial." She took a deep breath and changed the subject. "Why are you here?"

"I told you. It's my cabin. I built it."

"Yes, but why are you *still* here?"

He scowled at her. "It's mine."

She stifled a sigh. "You're dead. Why haven't you moved on?"

His blue eyes became pensive, looking so pale, they seemed nearly translucent. At that moment, Angela felt she could see into the depths of his soul. Angela looked away, feeling like an intruder. *He's a sweet pers . . . soul.*

He began slowly. "During the days, I'm confined to this plane, this place. Nights, I'm compelled to return to the stream."

"For how long?"

Raising his shoulders, he shrugged. "For a spell."

Angela suddenly pitied him. She asked gently, "Why?"

He looked at her with luminous, nearly transparent eyes. "Because of the most precious substance on earth."

She squinted as she searched her mind. "Love?"

He shook his head. "The most precious *substance* on earth."

"Gold?"

His laughter was dry, mirthless. "Water. I was murdered because of water. I'm bound to this plane, this land, because of water."

Again she squinted, trying to understand. "Why?"

The blue of his eyes deepened as he gazed into the distance, and an unexpected calm came over him. "I homesteaded this property in 1847. Penateka Comanches still hunted here. Buffalo still roamed, but a cattle baron ruled this land."

"Then you were a rancher?"

His eyes homed in on hers as he shook his head. "I was a dirt farmer with only a hundred and twenty acres, but I owned the stream behind this cabin. That was priceless. Because it flowed year round, it was the only reliable water source for the Comanches and the wildlife. I didn't begrudge sharing it with them, but I didn't take kindly to the cattle herded through my property. They destroyed my crops, my land. To protect it, I put up barbed wire."

She sniffed. "Bet the cattle baron loved that."

"His drovers cut the wire and purposely stampeded the cattle through my fields. They destroyed the crops, the fences, and everything in their path. When I complained to the sheriff, the rancher hired a gunman."

Angela took a deep breath as she raised her eyebrows.

"They may have killed me, but I never left. I've stayed here, defending this water, even after death. When the ranchers brought their cattle to drink, I spooked the herds, sent them stampeding time and again."

Unsure if he realized the passing of time, she spoke gently. "There are no more cattle here to drink from the stream. The herds are long gone."

"Nowadays, it might not be cattle barons stealing it, but water translates to power. Where there's power, you'll find opportunists. I'm here for one reason: to protect the water, the most precious substance on earth."

Angela took a deep breath. "I didn't steal any water, yet you tried to run me off."

He focused his blue eyes on her. "That's true. You brought the turtle here, and your friends put in a cistern."

She smiled gently. "A rainwater-collection system."

He nodded. "Both weigh in your favor." His eyes narrowed as he crossed his arms, as if deliberating. Finally, he gave a stiff nod. "I reckon you can stay, but on one condition."

She eyed him skeptically. "What's that?"

"Help save the stream. In a way, I'll be handing over the reins to you."

Save the stream? Tilting her head back, she frowned. "I'm not sure how, but I'll do what I can." Then she peered at him, trying to read his eyes. "Will you be able to move on now?"

As his eyes twinkled, his face relaxed into a smile. His hands in his pockets, he hunched his broad shoulders. "My ride here's not over. I can't move on until I come to the end of this trail."

"You said you're destined to stay here."

"That's right."

"Where will you stay the nights I'm here?"

"In my cabin." His blue eyes opened wide.

Angela studied the attractive man, her eyes sweeping over him from toes to nose. Though spirit, he appeared as solid as flesh and blood.

What is it about him that makes me uncomfortable? Her nostrils flared as it occurred to her. *His maleness.*

Knitting her brow, she swallowed. She had never met a territorial ghost before. "You'll be here all night, every night?"

"Where else?" He peered at her. "Don't tell me you're prudish." He broke out laughing as she looked on. "A ghost doesn't frighten you, but the idea of a man does."

"It isn't that you frighten me." Squirming, she thought of her fiancé Kio. "It just doesn't seem . . . proper."

"Propriety's got nothing to do with it. I'm an idea, an illusion, mist, not man. I have no body."

She sighed. "That's true." She looked into his face. "Maybe if you told me your name."

"I'm William Hall, Ma'am."

His courtesy caught her off balance as she studied him. "Which do you prefer, William or Bill?"

He bowed his head for a moment and then gave her a shy smile, a dimple showing. "No one's called me by my Christian name in a long while. I'd be right pleased if you'd call me Billy, like my mother did."

"All right, Billy." Eyelashes fluttering, she blinked as she composed herself. *Why does he make me feel so unsettled? We're exchanging names, for heaven's sake, not wedding vows.* She grounded herself with a deep breath. "Call me Angela."

Silence.

"Billy?" She listened. "Billy?"

When she heard no response, she finished unpacking. Then she showered, and as Frank purred at her feet, she read in bed until she began dozing. As she turned off the lamp, a voice spoke in the dark.

"Ma'am, never let anyone criticize your physique."

Clutching the covers about her, she sat bolt upright in bed, her eyes wide open, looking left and right.

The next morning, she woke feeling refreshed. *Must have been the nap followed by a deep sleep.* Smiling to herself, she fed Frank, dressed, and went next door for breakfast. Before she knocked, the door opened.

"Well? How was it?" Tulah's eyes watched expectantly as Kelby and Brooke peered over her shoulder.

"It was fine," Angela smiled. "That mattress is a dream. I don't recall the last time I slept so soundly . . . like a baby."

The sisters looked at each other, blinking.

Tulah gathered her wits first. "Good, come on into the dining room. Mom's making waffles."

"Ever try agave nectar or prickly-pear syrup?" asked Kelby, shuffling along on her crutches.

Angela shook her head. "Neither, but with nectar and syrup in their names, I'm guessing they're sweet."

"They're delicious. You've never tasted waffles so good."

"Sit down. Tell us all about your first night in the cabin." Tulah patted the chair next to hers.

"Don't leave out a single, scary detail," said Kelby, sitting to her left.

"Did you hear anything odd?" asked Brook, sitting across from her. "See anything?"

"Did you see a ghost?" Kelby's eyes flashed with anticipation. "Tell us everything."

Angela had not been prepared for the cross-examination. She licked her lips as she debated how much to divulge.

"Girls, let Angela relax at breakfast." Mrs. Bankhead set a steaming platter of waffles on the table and lifted the lid off a chafing dish. "There are hot sausages in here, and help yourself to freshly brewed coffee."

They said grace, and then Kelby smiled mischievously. "You're with friends. You can tell us. What happened last night?"

Taking a deep breath, Angela decided on discretion. She shrugged. "Like I said, I don't recall the last time I slept so soundly."

Tulah gave Angela a quick tour of the winery before it opened its doors to visitors. "I thought I'd do Kelby's job today, with you riding along to watch. Think that'll work?"

"Whatever you think's best. I'm here to help." Angela grinned. "Okay, today I'm here to learn."

Visitors started arriving at ten o'clock. As Angela tagged along, Tulah showed the guests to the tram, gave them a tour of the vineyards, and then drove them to the winemaking complex for their barrel-tasting tour.

As they walked into the temperature-controlled cellar, Angela saw barrels stacked on racks from floor to ceiling. Each barrel was marked with a code, a timestamp, and an A or F.

"Ladies and gentlemen," said Tulah, "this is what we call our wine library. During your private tasting, you'll sample and compare wines aged in various oak barrels just as our vintner does."

"What do the F and A mean?" asked a visitor, pointing to the stacked barrels.

"French and American, all the barrels are hand-crafted white oak, but some are made from French oak and some from American Oak, usually from Wisconsin or Minnesota. The various oaks have distinctive grains and properties. Each ages and flavors the wine in a unique way."

"Do you use charred barrels?" asked one of the tourists.

Tulah nodded. "We do. Charring adds color, flavor, and even a certain amount of texture. Some barrels are lightly charred on the inside. Others are medium charred, and some are toasted or fully charred. Each imparts a different flavor to the wine as it ages. Flavor notes of wines aged in charred oak range from spicy cloves and cinnamon; to honey and caramel; to toffee, mocha, and smoke."

"Are the barrels ever reused?" asked another visitor.

"Good question. We use them for three seasons. Each year the barrel adds a different amount of oak tannin, so a different essence to the wine. After that, the barrel is 'neutral' since it doesn't add any more tannin. Vintners need to balance the charring, type of oak, aging, and grape varieties to blend award-winning wines."

Tulah led them to a wet bar with wine glasses stacked on shelves. As Angela watched, she handed each visitor a glass. "Now you'll experience wine as the vintner does." Tulah pointed to three oak barrels with spigots. "First you'll taste a merlot aged for a year in a medium charred American oak. The second tasting is a merlot aged for two years in a lightly charred French oak, and the final tasting is a merlot aged for three years in a toasted American oak."

After everyone had compared notes and selected their favorite merlot, she led them into a private wine bar. Bottles of aging wine lined the walls. High, wood-paneled ceilings with exposed rafters drew their eyes upward to crystal chandeliers. Then Tulah called their attention to the wine lists on the granite bar. "Select any six of these wines to taste."

Angela noted how she poured small samples of the chosen wines into each person's glass as she described the characteristics or foods they complimented.

"This blend of Syrah and Cabernet has overtones of blackberries with hints of tobacco. The Merlot and Cabernet blend expresses characteristics of blueberries and violets. It pairs well with Cheddar or Manchego cheese."

Tulah then wrapped the bottles the visitors had bought and drove the group back to the main winery. After seeing them off, she turned to Angela. "And that's really all there is to it."

Angela grinned. "That's all, huh? How long is it going to take to sound half as knowledgeable as you?"

She handed Angela a wine list. "Just study this. By tomorrow, you'll sound like an expert."

As they waited for the next tour's passengers to board the tram, Angela saw a red convertible speed up the driveway and screech to a halt in a cloud of dust. She nodded toward it.

"Isn't that our 'friend' who raced past us last week?"

Tulah turned to look. "It's the same cloud of dust." She swallowed a giggle. "Reminds me of Pig-Pen, the Charles Schulz character. You know, Charlie Brown's dusty friend."

They watched as two men stepped out of the sporty convertible. The driver was tall, lanky, seeming to stretch out endlessly from the low-slung car's confinement. He had dark-brown hair and dark moody eyes beneath bushy eyebrows. His lips seemed to curl in a perpetual sneer. The rider had cropped blond hair and walked with an air of authority. Both were dressed in sports jackets and trousers, their button-down shirts open at the neck.

Angela compared their clothes to Tulah's and hers: winery-logo T-shirts tucked into jeans. She felt underdressed, somehow inadequate.

Tulah whispered. "They sure don't dress like Pig-Pen."

They watched as the two men walked into the winery. Then just as Tulah started the tram's engine, the two hopped aboard.

Tulah spoke into the microphone as she introduced Angela and herself. "Welcome to the Water-to-Winery vineyards. We'll begin the excursion driving through the Cabernet vineyard, then the Merlot, and finally the Syrah."

When they arrived at the winemaking complex, Tulah whispered to Angela. "This part's easy. Try it. I'll be right here if you have any questions." Then she turned to the group. "Angela's going to tell you about the wine's aging process in these oak barrels as you sample three wines."

Angela swallowed hard and echoed all she recalled of Tulah's first tour. When she struggled with a visitor's question, Tulah fielded it.

As that segment ended, Angela led the group into the private tasting room. This time, she helped Tulah pour the samples. When asked about the wines, she referred to the list.

"Easy, peasy," she whispered to Tulah as they took the orders and wrapped the bottles.

Tulah grinned, and then bent her head to whisper. "What do you think of Astin?"

"Who?" Tulah nodded her chin toward the lanky driver, and Angela raised her eyebrow. "You mean Pig-Pen?"

"Yeah . . . no." Scowling, she whispered, "His name's Astin Starr."

"Where did you learn that?"

"He introduced himself."

Before she could say more, he approached with his surly smile. "Tulah, can you recommend something to serve with pinot noir?"

"Sure, since it's a light red wine with a distinctive body, it pairs well with turkey or gamey foods, such as venison. Its silky tannins give it versatility." Her eyes smiled at him. "It also works with beef tenderloin kebobs, roast pork loin, and grilled salmon steaks."

"You sound as if you speak from experience." Never taking his stone-cold eyes from her face, he chuckled. "Sold, I'll take a case."

"A case?" Tulah blinked and then gave Angela a sidelong glance. "Great, I'll ring it up for you."

A few minutes later, Tulah handed Angela the key and showed her how to start the tram. Angela drove the group back to the main winery, trying to parrot what Tulah had said in the first run as she thanked them for taking the tour. Tulah sat behind Angela in the second row of seats with Astin and his friend.

"You seem so knowledgeable about pairing foods with wines," said Astin, "maybe you could recommend a restaurant for Greg and me."

"Sure." Tulah named three establishments in town.

"Which is your favorite?" asked Astin.

"The Purple Onion," Tulah said, "especially if you like pulled-pork fajitas and bluegrass music."

Through the rearview mirror, Angela watched Astin share a surly smile with Greg.

"Maybe you and your friend would like to join us," said Astin, his voice louder as he directed it to the front seat for Angela's benefit. She rolled her eyes

"Thanks," she heard Tulah say, "but my . . . the winery owner doesn't allow the staff to socialize with guests."

Angela heaved a sigh of relief as she grabbed the microphone and loudly thanked everyone for joining the tour. "End of the line," she said, smiling brightly at Astin and Greg. "Goodbye."

"Be right back," Astin told Greg as he set the case of wine on the sidewalk.

A moment later, he returned, his red convertible screeching to a stop. As he kicked up a puff of caliche dust, Angela looked at Tulah, deadpanning.

"Always conserve energy," said Astin. "Drive when you can walk. Sit when you can stand. Lie when you can sit." He winked at Greg as he lifted the case of wine into the trunk. Then, two fingers to his temple, Astin gestured a tipped hat.

Tulah swallowed a smile.

As he drove off in his usual cloud of dust, Angela muttered under her breath. "Pig-Pen."

"What?" Tulah gave her a sharp look.

She grimaced. "A little too alpha for my taste."

Tulah shrugged. "It's moot since we won't see him again, anyway." She checked her watch. "Lunch break. Mom packed us fried chicken and potato salad. Hungry?"

"Starved."

"Let me show you where we take our breaks."

Kelby was in the office, sitting at the computer, her back to them.

"Have you eaten yet?" asked Tulah.

Kelby swung around in her chair. "Not yet." Her eyes were wide as she turned the computer screen toward them. "Have you seen this?"

"Seen what?"

"A Houston company, Agua Purificación, has drilled unregulated, commercial wells near here. It plans to sell *our* groundwater to a subdivision in Boerne," said Kelby.

Tulah moved closer to read from the screen. "The total amount of proposed pumping is over five million gallons per day, more than one-point-eight billion gallons a year."

Eyes wide, she turned toward her sister. "What? That would pump the Trinity Aquifer dry. This whole area would be a desert."

"I know," said Kelby, her face drawn. "The water level would drop, probably dry up all the nearby home, ranch, and business wells, including ours. Had you heard anything about it?"

Tulah shook her head. "This is the first I've heard *anything*. How did you find out?"

"Would you believe Facebook? A friend posted the link." Kelby sniffed. "There hasn't been a single public notice, hearing, or announcement. What're they trying to pull?"

"I don't know, but it isn't good." Tulah again leaned closer to read from the screen.

"Agua Purificación (AP) plans to pump from the Trinity Aquifer. It would cause a serious drop in the water level, negatively impacting wells and property values for the surrounding homes and businesses.

"Currently, no regulatory entity manages this area. It's just outside the eastern boundary and jurisdiction of the Barron Trinity Groundwater Conservation District (BTGCD). Although it is within the North Edwards Aquifer Authority (NEAA) boundaries, the NEAA has no jurisdiction because these wells are being drilled *through* and *below* the Edwards Aquifer into the underlying Trinity Aquifer.

"AP's found a legal loophole." Tulah grimaced.

Suddenly Billy's words came to mind. *Help save the stream.*

"Where's this Agua Purificación drilling wells?" asked Angela.

"Not sure." Tulah ran her finger over the screen until she found the spot. "It says 'in the area of State Highway 53, near the old Hall Road.' That's the back road we took to the cabin where you're staying, the old Hall homestead."

Angela inhaled sharply. "What would happen to the creek behind it?"

"Probably dry up."

Angela thought of the turtle. "Without that creek, where would the wildlife get water?"

"They wouldn't." Kelby sighed. "That's the only reliable water source for miles in every direction."

Angela stiffened at hearing Billy's words paraphrased. Exhaling, she shook her head. "This is unconscionable. What can we do?"

"I saw something. Just a sec." Tulah ran her finger over the screen until she found the information, then read it aloud.

"Contact your elected officials. Ask them to manage the proposed AP pumping. Urge them to protect your water supply, and attend local meetings as a visible show of solidarity."

Tulah again traced her finger over the message while she silently skimmed the rest of the article. "Hey, there's a hearing at the court house tonight." She turned to Angela. "Want to go?"

Angela and Tulah arrived early, finding front-row seats in the cramped meeting room. "I'll bet the whole county will turn out—standing room only." Tulah winked as they sat on a wooden bench.

Angela looked left and right at the benches, feeling the varnished surface. "If I didn't know better, I'd say these were—"

"Pews." Smiling, Tulah nodded emphatically. "Yup, they got these from a church."

Angela watched the people arrive. As Tulah had predicted, the seats filled fast. With standing room only, people lined the walls, three deep.

Suddenly she felt a nudge. Angela turned toward her friend. "What?"

"Don't look now, but look who just showed up." In unison, the two turned their heads toward the door. There stood Astin.

"Pig-Pen," Angela muttered, shaking her head. Then she turned toward Tulah, whispering. "He looks like a senator or governor . . . slumming with the locals."

She grinned. "He does, at that."

"Uh-oh . . ."

Tulah whispered, "What?"

"What a coincidence seeing you here." Astin stood in front of them, smiling. "You have no idea how good it feels seeing faces you recognize." Then gracing the people beside her with his charismatic smile, he asked, "Mind if I squeeze in?"

Angela rolled her eyes, but the people moved aside as he crowded into the front row. Tulah looked on, smiling.

The chairman called the meeting to order. "Because of the interest in item 3A, I move that the agenda items be rearranged to begin with the planned well field, and the other items be tabled until next time."

The board members mumbled "Aye" amid murmurs from the attendees.

"Does anyone wish to address the assembly?"

"I do," said a man, hurrying down the main aisle. "I'm Joseph Conroy, a concerned Barron County resident and property owner near Hall Road."

Tulah bent her head toward Angela, whispering, "He lives about a half mile from your cabin."

Angela nodded.

"My family's lived on this property for three generations," said Conroy, "ranching and growing peaches."

Tulah whispered, "They have a pick-your-own-peaches business just down the road from you."

"If Agua Purificación pumps even a fraction of its proposed water from the aquifer," he said, "it spells the end for my family's business. The water table will drop, and the well will run dry. Without irrigation, we'll be selling fuzzy pits instead of juicy Fredericksley peaches. When the peaches dry up, so does business." He gave a curt nod, began to step away, and then momentarily turned back to the board members. "Thank you for listening."

As he walked to the back of the room, Angela heard a smattering of polite applause. She looked around the assembly. *T-shirts and jeans. This is middle-class America trying to protect its basic right. Survival, spelled W-A-T-E-R, something you take for granted until it's taken away.*

A woman strode to the front of the room. In a loud voice, she introduced herself as Mia Hadd, addressed the board members, and then turned to face the crowd of gathered citizens.

"We're here tonight because we're concerned that a well field built near Fredericksley could drain the area's already stressed groundwater resources." Hadd stared down the crowd. "The antiquated Rule of Capture is the crux of the issue. However, what concerns me *equally* is the series of political connections and potential conflicts of interest associated with the project."

Murmurs raced through the crowd.

"The connections show the hand-in-glove nature of politics and development in Barron County." Hadd spoke in a strident voice, talking over the chatter. "It's still a community of small towns and familiar faces despite being so close to the Austin-San Antonio corridor, the country's fastest-growing area. Companies involved in building the water infrastructure for Houston-based Agua Purificación's well field include those with ties to a former county judge and state legislator."

Whispers ran rampant through the group. "TEX-AM, the firm that was hired to do an 'independent analysis' of the threat to nearby wells was also working on the same project for AP. This, my friends, is a blatant conflict of interest. Additionally, that firm's Blanco office is managed by a former Barron County judge with strong political connections and insider information.

"Bayou Bay, a small community near Galveston, cut a deal with AP in 2012 to manage its municipal waterworks. As a result, water rates there rose nearly twenty-eight percent. Though city residents were promised a four-year rate freeze, it never materialized. When the town's people complained to their officials, that judge ruled against them in favor of AP. A recent survey of residents' financial distress indicated people were falling so far behind on their bills, the city had increased its liens against their homes, which has led to a marked rise of Bayou Bay foreclosures."

As the courtroom erupted in chatter, the board president banged the gavel. "Order," she called. "Order!"

When the assembly quieted, the woman continued.

"In these private equity water deals, higher rates help the firms earn higher returns." She sneered. "In this case, to the tune of eight to eighteen percent, substantially more than what regular for-profit water companies expect. To further accelerate their returns, AP's applied a common strategy from the private equity playbook. Parlaying Bayou Bay yields, they're flipping their investment to this venture, pumping from the Trinity Aquifer.

"Earlier this month, Hank Porter, a Houston-area legislator with ties to AP asked the attorney general for an opinion on the Barron County groundwater district's jurisdiction." Mia Hadd's face went cold. "The attorney general's decision cleared the way for AP to build the well field near old Hall Road."

Angela caught Tulah's eye.

"AP Manager Steve Whitman stated there were no conflicts of interest in the project, that all the firms involved were reputable. He said AP will not pump if it's proved there's not enough water in the ground.

"However, local residents question this because AP's wells are being built in an *unregulated* area near the intersection of two groundwater districts. It exposes a loophole in Texas's water conservation laws. All groundwater usage must be regulated, but no groundwater district controls this particular parcel of land. As I've already pointed out, the company hired to do the 'independent analysis' of the threat to nearby wells is none other than TEX-AM, which coincidentally works for AP."

The courtroom exploded. The board president banged the gavel repeatedly. "Come to order! Come to order!"

Speaking above the hubbub, Hadd continued. "The Rule of Capture can't be the only statute that applies to commercial distribution of water resources. Just because a corporation is the first in line to draw water from the ground, it doesn't excuse them from their responsibilities to the community. Corporations must be held accountable. We need to protect landowners' water rights. More importantly, we can't allow excessive pumping to destroy the already declining Trinity Aquifer.

"The well field is in the territory of the North Edwards Aquifer Authority. But AP is drilling *through* the Edwards rock to capture water from an underlying layer of the Trinity Aquifer. As a result, neither the Conservation District, nor the Aquifer Authority has jurisdiction because the wells are beyond their borders. No group has the authority to regulate that area. And without regulation, AP can take as much water from the aquifers as it wants, no matter what its PR reps tell us."

The courtroom flew into a rage, everyone chattering, some shouting. The board president banged the gavel repeatedly. When the decibel level did not subside, she said, "Come to order, or I will have this room cleared!"

The uproar slowly waned, and the speaker continued.

"Spokespersons have discussed plans for the well field to be annexed into either the Conservation District or the Aquifer Authority." The woman paused as her eyes traveled around the room, seeming to emphasize the importance of what she was about to say.

"However, *two days* before he retired from the state legislature, Hank Porter sent a letter to the attorney general's office, asking for an opinion about an area outside his jurisdiction. Keep in mind, Fredericksley is nearly two hundred miles away from the Houston-area voters that elected him."

Again, she paused. "Porter asked for a decision as to whether *any* groundwater district had the power to regulate that area. Why would he concern himself with something two hundred miles away?" Hadd peered at them. "*Why?* Porter's from Houston. AP's from Houston, again *two hundred miles away.*"

When the assembly began chattering, the woman held up her hands for quiet. "It came to light in an interview with Houston attorney Peter Smythe, that his former clients include TEX-AM, the environmental company founded by Hank Porter; the law firm of Greg Porter, one of the state representative's two sons; and TXA Engineering, which is owned by George Porter, the other of Porter's sons. With the environmental company, law firm, and engineering company working in cahoots, keeping it 'in the family,' it's sheer nepotism.

"Hank Porter owns TEX-AM, the same company that made the environmental study for AP. This sounds innocent enough until you realize AP made substantial campaign contributions to Legislator Hank Porter while he was in office. Hank Porter's son George owns TXA Engineering, which is involved with AP's water-drilling deal. And Hank Porter's other son, Greg, is head of the law firm that represents AP in its bid to drill these wells. One hand has been washing the other . . . using our water."

The speaker slowly turned, looking each person in the eye. "Why would Houston attorneys and firms concern themselves with local water policy in Barron County . . . two hundred miles away? Because they found a legal loophole, and unless we stop them, they're going to steal our groundwater out from underneath us."

She nodded to the group and then returned to the back of the room amidst heavy applause and chatter.

"Scary." Angela caught Tulah's eye. "How can tiny Barron County defend itself against these Houston shysters?"

Tulah grimaced. "How can it afford it?" Then as Astin spoke to her, she turned away from Angela, toward him.

Astin asked, "What're you doing here?"

Angela thought his smile was a patronizing sneer.

Tulah's amused sniff passed for a chuckle. "You mean, what's a nice girl like me doing in a place like this?"

His lip lifted in a sarcastic smile. "Something like that."

"My family lives a mile from the proposed well fields. If AP takes that much water, our well would go dry. We'd lose our home, our business, even our land."

Angela couldn't help overhearing. "Why would you lose your land?"

The board president banged the gavel. "Come to order. Is there anyone else who would like to address this hearing?"

Several other speakers followed, rephrasing the issues in their words.

Then the president thanked everyone for attending the informational hearing. "On behalf of the board, I want to assure you, your concerns will be directed to the Governor, Lieutenant Governor, and Speaker of the Texas House." She banged the gavel and dismissed the group.

Angela turned toward Tulah. "Why would you lose your land if AP starts drawing water?"

"If they draw five million gallons a day, as they say, our well would dry up. Who'd buy property without water?" Shrugging, she lifted her hands, palm up. "No water. No sale." Then she turned toward Astin. "Now, it's my turn to ask. What're you doing here?"

"You mean, what's a nice boy like me doing in a place like this?" He all but sneered. "I just moved here, and I like to know what's happening." He shrugged. "It's my business to be informed."

"What is your business?" Tulah lifted her eyes to his.

A half smile twisted his lips. "I'm an attorney."

Angela narrowed her eyes, scrutinizing him. "Just moved here . . . your business wouldn't be connected to Agua Purificación, would it?" She caught his eye before he glanced away.

"Isn't everyone connected in one way or another?" he asked.

"What was the name of that state representative?" Angela turned toward Tulah, "the one who sent a letter to the attorney general two days before retiring?"

She tried to recall. "Port, Porta . . ."

"Hank Porter, that's it." Angela leaned forward to better see Astin. "You wouldn't by any chance work for his son, Greg Porter's law firm, would you?"

"How intuitive." He nodded his head in a mock bow. "Have you ever thought of going into law?"

"Nope." Angela smiled sweetly. "But you haven't answered my question. Do you work for the Porter law firm?"

"Guilty as charged." He shrugged his shoulder. "I'm just one of many associates."

"Really?" Angela stared him down. "What does an associate do?"

Again he shrugged. "Nothing very interesting."

"Oh, but I'm very interested." She held his gaze as she gave him a tight-lipped smile.

"I simply gather facts, so my client can make informed decisions."

"Your client? You mean Agua Purificación?"

"I said clients."

Angela shook her head. "You said client, singular."

He pursed his lips momentarily and then put on a dazzling smile as he stood. "Singular, plural, enough talk of grammar. I see you're off work, so can I buy you ladies a cup of coffee?"

Angela shook her head. "Thanks, but—"

"That'd be nice, wouldn't it?" Tulah turned toward Angela, so only she saw her raised eyebrow.

Angela took a deep breath and then remembered. *You've got the car keys.* "Sure."

It was a balmy evening, so they walked to an outdoor cafe three blocks away. The street lights cast a warm glow as the moon rose over the storefronts' nineteenth-century facades. They found a table and sat facing the stage, where a singer accompanied himself on a guitar.

When the waitress approached, Astin checked his watch. "Actually, I feel more like a glass of wine than a cup of coffee." He turned to Tulah and Angela. "What would you like?"

"I'll be up all night if I drink coffee at this hour." The corner of Tulah's lips lifted in a smile. "I think I'll join you."

Angela did not want coffee, wine, or anything else. She wanted to go home. She was tired and something else. *Wish I could talk over this water issue with Billy.* She slowly nodded to herself as the conscious thought registered.

"Angela, what'll you have? Angela?"

She looked at Tulah, embarrassed at being caught daydreaming. "I'll have whatever you're having."

Astin nodded to the waitress. "Instead of three glasses, better make that a bottle, and do you have Water-to-Winery pinot noir?" A twinkle in his eye, he glanced at Tulah. "I hear that label is the perfect digestif."

Minutes later the waitress returned with salsa, chips, the pinot noir, and three glasses.

"Have you lived here all your lives?" Astin asked as he poured.

"I have," said Tulah. "Angela's from the Austin area, but we've both been staying in San Antonio."

"What do you do when you're in San Antonio?" His eyes on Tulah, he directed his question to her.

She glanced at Angela and shared a smile. "We're roommates at UTSA."

"So how often are you in Fredericksley?"

"Weekends for now, but starting in a few weeks we'll be spending the summer here." Tulah watched him as she sipped the wine. "You said you just moved here. Did you buy, or are you renting?"

"I'm leasing a furnished apartment."

"Long term?" Angela watched his reaction.

"Until my business is finished here." He met her eyes with a cool glance and then looked away.

"You mean when Agua Purificación starts drawing water?"

"I'm part of an ongoing study," said Astin. "AP did an environmental-site assessment prior to acquiring the property. Now it's doing an environmental-impact assessment to determine how it would affect this area, as well as creating computer models to recommend options."

Angela pantomimed applause. "Sounds impressive, but what was the name of the environmental company Agua Purificación had hired?" She caught his eye. "Wasn't it TEX-AM? Didn't the speaker say it was founded by Hank Porter, the same state legislator who sent a letter to the attorney general's office, asking whether the Barron Springs/Edwards District could regulate groundwater?" She gave him a close-lipped smile, bordering on a sneer.

Astin set down his glass. "You don't like me, do you?" He grinned. "Don't deny it. You don't."

Arms crossed, Angela took a deep breath. "I don't like what you represent . . . literally."

"Okay, you two, time out." Tulah raised her glass. "Here's to you both. You may not be as wise as owls, but you're always a hoot."

Angela chuckled as she clinked glasses and sipped. "Now, my turn." She raised her glass. "To your very good health. May you live to be as old as your jokes."

Astin sneered. "Though I'm but a mere thorn between two roses—"

Angela and Tulah groaned.

Astin looked from one to the other as he raised his glass. "Let me continue. May your coffee and slanders against you be ever alike—without grounds."

"Spoken like a true lawyer." This time, Angela smiled.

Dropping his smirk, Astin grinned back.

Angela did a double take. *It's the first time he's dropped his guard.*

"At the risk of creating further dissention, I have to say . . ." He paused before staring openly into their eyes. "I agree with you. I'm also conflicted about the well field, but Texas is one of the country's fastest growing states, and the Austin-San Antonio Corridor is one of the state's fastest growing regions. With a population that doubles every twenty years, that area needs water supplies to keep up with the demand. Barron County's a less populated region with good water reserves. Doesn't it make sense to share some of that water with the more populous regions?"

"But we're in a drought." Angela watched his eyes, trying to read his thoughts. "Water's already in short supply here."

"And what water we have is needed for agribusiness," said Tulah. "The Hill Country produces most of the state's wine and peaches." She held up her glass. "Without water, there's no wine."

Astin drew in a deep breath. "There's no easy answer. At this stage, we're dependent upon computer models to recommend options, solutions. Current findings suggest the best option's a distribution of water reserves."

"Distribution of water reserves," repeated Tulah, her stare distant, as if recalling a memory. "I wish we could share some of the white water of the Deschutes River."

His jaw lax, blinking, Astin looked at her. "Have you rafted the Deschutes?"

She nodded. "Yeah, why?"

"So have I." Their eyes met.

Her voice warming, she asked, "Really?"

He nodded. "I'd like to hear about your trip," he glanced at Angela, "some time."

"I *love* white water rafting!" Tulah blinked. "I'd enjoy comparing notes."

He laughed to himself, his shoulders shaking. "I'll have to tell you about the time we sprang a leak in the raft, had to patch it on shore, and were three hours late getting back."

Tulah's eyes flashed. "I'd definitely like to hear about that."

Again he glanced at Angela. "Tell you what." Reaching into his pocket, he brought out two business cards, handing one to Angela and one to Tulah. His eyes homed in on Tulah's. "My cell number's on there. Why don't you call me? Maybe we can set up a time to swap stories?"

Looking like the cat that caught the canary, Tulah accepted the card.

Angela rolled her eyes. Then she made a show of checking her watch. "Hate to be a party pooper, but tomorrow comes early."

Tulah and Astin shared a private smile. Then Tulah checked her watch. "Yikes. It is late." Holding up her glass, she said, "Happy trails."

Astin clinked his glass against hers and smiled. "Until we meet again."

Oh, brother. Angela held up her glass without clinking, said, "Cheers," downed her wine, and stood up. "Ready?"

Again Tulah and Astin shared a private smile. This time Tulah stood up. "Ready." Her eyes never straying from his, she said, "Thanks for a great evening."

He smiled at her. "It really was my pleasure."

Angela watched him closely but detected no hint of sarcasm. *He's good.* She sniffed. *But I still think he's playing her.*

On the drive back, Angela thought about Tulah's childhood sweetheart. "Have you seen Clay recently?"

Tulah turned her head sharply, momentarily taking her eyes from the road. "No, not since Christmas vacation. Why?"

Shrugging, Angela backpedaled. "Just wondering."

"You weren't 'just wondering' because Astin's coming on so strong, were you?"

Angela chuckled. "Was I that obvious?"

Tulah took her eyes from the road long enough to look down her nose at her. "Ya think?"

Angela shrugged. "I can't help it."

"Can't help what?"

"The feeling that he's trying to use you," Angela took a deep breath, "that Pig-Pen's trying to pull you into whatever angle he's working."

"I already have a mother, thank you. One's enough." Tulah pursed her lips.

They rode silently until Tulah dropped Angela off at her door.

"Thanks for the ride." Angela grimaced. "I didn't mean to—"

"I know." Tulah took in a deep breath and blew it out. "I didn't mean to snap at you, either." She smiled. "I'll keep the headlights on the front door. Wave when you get inside safely. See you at breakfast."

Water of Life

The earth has a vegetative spirit in that its flesh is the soil, its bones are the . . . interlinked rocks of which mountains are composed . . . and its blood is the water in the veins

– Leonardo da Vinci

She turned on the lights.

"Have you seen the time?" Billy paced as he talked. "Where have you been?"

"Excuse me?" Angela raised her eyebrow.

"In my day, young ladies didn't come home at all hours of the night." Chin high, wearing a sour expression, Billy scrutinized her.

Angela took a deep breath and looked him in the eye. "Things are different today. 'Young ladies' come home when they're good and ready."

He lowered his eyes. "I reckon times have changed."

"You reckon right." She gave a firm nod. Then her shoulders slumped. "There's something I want to discuss with you."

"What?"

Angela told him about Agua Purificación. "It's drilled several unregulated wells near here and wants to sell our groundwater to Boerne."

His pale blue eyes narrowed. "How much water are they talking?"

"More than five million gallons per day, roughly one-point-eight billion gallons a year."

He whistled. "That sounds like a lot of water being pumped."

"Especially during a drought." She watched his eyes, mesmerized by their pale blue color.

He slowly shook his head. "If the water table fell, the creek could dry up."

She thought of the ancient cypress trees and the dusty turtle they had taken there. "That'd be a shame."

"You remember our bargain?"

She nodded. "At the time, I couldn't imagine how to help save the stream, but then it occurred to me. I'll write an internship paper, not just about the water shortage in general, but about the absence of water for wildlife, specifically the impact AP's unregulated drilling would have on the area's ecology."

"I knew you'd help from the first moment I saw you."

"When you were swinging on the porch swing?"

He nodded as his eyes lit up with an inner glow. "Come with me. I want to show you something."

She glanced around the cabin. "Where?"

"By the creek."

She looked at her watch. "It's nearly midnight."

"It's something I think you'll like." His slow smile was reassuring.

"Okay." Angela shrugged and met him outside the front door.

The moon was full. After a minute, as her eyes adjusted to the light level, she had no trouble following him along the path. Once they reached the riverbed, the limestone rocks and placid water reflected the moonlight, making it seem like twilight, not midnight.

Angela looked around the now-familiar stream, but she saw it in a new light. The stars above twinkled, adding a silvery glow to the tops of the cypress trees and the tips of their feathery branches. Lightning bugs flickered and blinked.

"This is lovely, a fairyland." She smiled as she took in its nocturnal beauty. "I'd felt a special connection with it before, but this is a world I didn't know existed." She breathed in deeply, inhaling the fragrance of the mountain laurel wafting on the night's breeze.

"It's a special location, but I want you to see something." They walked beneath one of the ancient cypress trees. There, curled within its woody knees, they found a white-spotted yearling buck, its wet, black nose tucked against its hind legs.

Angela caught her breath. Then trying not to frighten it, she whispered, "What a cutie."

The deer rose to its feet and approached Angela, gently head-butting her with his nubby antlers that were just beginning to show.

She chuckled, putting up her hands, first to hold him at bay, and then to gently finger his forehead. "What a sweet, little guy." She turned toward Billy. "Is he the reason you brought me here?"

He nodded.

"Why's he so friendly?"

"My guess is he's a bottle baby."

She turned toward him, thinking she had misunderstood. "A what?"

"A bottle baby, I think someone's bottle-fed an orphan and now tried to release him, but bottle babies rarely make it in the wild. I've been keeping an eye on him. The local herds won't let him join."

She smiled. "A Rudolph complex?"

"Rudolph?" He shook his head. "I don't understand."

"You know, from Johnny Marks's song, 'Rudolph the Red-Nosed Reindeer.'" Again Billy shook his head, so she sang the lyrics.

His eyes narrowed skeptically. "I don't know that tune."

Angela pressed her lips together. "Of course, you don't. It came out in the thirties or forties . . ." She sighed. "Sorry, I wasn't thinking. Why can't he join the deer herds?"

"He competes with them for food, so they drive him away. Bottle babies usually die of stress before they die of starvation. He's imprinted on humans. They're his herd. He smells like them."

Wonder if whoever fed him did it from kindness, not realizing the ultimate hardship on him?

"Then why did you bring me to see him?"

Billy turned toward her. "You can help him adapt. Wean him off humans while he learns how to be wild again." He paused. "But try not to touch him."

"Aww . . ." She knelt down until she was eye-level with the young buck. "Hey, little guy, we're going to be friends . . . for a while, anyway, until you learn how to be a deer. I've got some carrots back at the cabin."

"They'll be good to draw him to you, but don't hand feed him. Put the food down, and walk away. Let him eat alone, and buy him some feed. Carrots are nothing but candy for him."

Single file, Billy led Angela back to the cabin, the yearling following behind. As they left the shoreline, she glanced over her shoulder. The water mirrored the moon, while the limestone softly reflected the moonlight. The yearling dogging her footsteps seemed to trust her intuitively.

Then it occurred to her. *Billy's made me responsible for the water and now this bottle baby.* She looked at the yearling's big, dark eyes and smiled.

The next morning, she rose early. After cutting carrots into bite-sized pieces, she put them in a sandwich bag and went out to look for the yearling.

How do I find him?

"Hey, little guy," she called.

He was nowhere to be seen. She whistled. She clapped her hands. She shook the bag of carrots and tossed one or two on the ground, hoping he would smell them. For the first five minutes, nothing. Then she spotted his face peeking through the trees.

"Hey, little guy," she called, tossing a carrot near him.

He tentatively approached the carrot, nibbled at it, and then began eating it. Angela threw another carrot piece closer. Never taking his big eyes from her, he came closer, inspected the carrot, and ate it. Angela set down all the pieces but one, tossing it between the yearling and the carrot pile. Then she went inside the cabin.

He doesn't need to imprint on me. She peeked through the window, watching as the yearling finished his breakfast and disappeared back into the trees. Only then did she walk next door for breakfast and her ride.

Tulah drove them to the earliest mass and then on to work. Hands on the wheel, she turned to Angela.

"So what do you think of Astin?"

"You heard me tell him. I don't like what he represents."

"Yeah, but what do you think about *him*?"

Raising her eyebrow, Angela turned toward her. "The truth?"

Tulah nodded.

"I don't trust him."

"What makes you say that?" Frowning, Tulah glanced at her.

"Call it a hunch, a woman's intuition." Angela met her eyes. "I have a gut feeling he's up to something." *Up to no good.*

"Name one concrete reason."

"The way he drives. Think of the first time we saw him. He was flying down the road in a cloud of dust. If we hadn't happened along when we did, that turtle would have been dust, too. Pig-Pen doesn't care about wildlife."

Her forehead wrinkling, Tulah turned toward her. "You don't know that."

"I know he doesn't care for people's safety. He flew past us like a bat out of . . . well, you remember."

"Oh, Astin's just exuberant." Tulah smiled. "After all, he lives in the fast lane."

"You can say that again," Angela mumbled.

"What?"

Angela sighed. "He's only concerned about himself, not anyone, not anything else." Crossing her arms, Angela sat back. "I don't trust him."

Tulah shrugged. "That's your opinion. I see Astin as a fast-paced, highflier who's going places." She smiled to herself.

Angela looked at her. "What?"

"Oh," she breathed deeply. "I wouldn't mind going along with him for the ride."

Angela did a double-take. "Why would you want to connect with someone so self-centered? Besides, you don't have anything in common with him."

"Shows how much you know." Tulah glanced at her. "We both like white water rafting."

Angela rolled her eyes. "That's certainly a basis for a relationship."

"It's a start." Tulah spoke sharply. "I'm sure once we talk, we'll find lots more in common."

"I can't help comparing him to Clay."

"That's strange." Tulah deadpanned. "There's no comparison. Clay's the salt of the earth, and Astin's the brightest star in the heavens." Then she grinned as she glanced at Angela. "Do you know what the name Astin means?"

Angela shook her head.

"It's French for starlike, so his name's actually Starlike Starr." Her eyes glowing, Tulah asked, "Isn't that a great name?"

"Yeah," Angela said dryly.

"Tulah Starr, Mrs. Astin Starr, has a ring to it, doesn't it?"

Angela took a deep breath. "Whatever happened to you and Clay?"

Tulah turned up her nose. "I don't know what I ever saw in him."

"Hasn't he been your boyfriend since you were both six?"

"Five."

"But . . ."

Grimacing, she sighed. "He's such a child, such a . . . a goody two-shoes."

"Goody two-shoes?" Angela chuckled. "Haven't heard that in a while."

"It's what I called him all through junior high." She glanced at Angela. "Teasing, of course."

"Of course."

"He's just so straight-laced, so self-righteous."

"I thought you two had a pact, some kind of agreement?"

Tulah rolled her eyes. "In eighth grade, we promised we'd marry each other when we graduated from college." She made a face. "It was a dumb idea. He was my childhood sweetheart, but now he's so . . ."

Angela grinned. "Straight-laced and self-righteous?"

"Exactly!" Tulah's eyes twinkled. "Which reminds me. After work, do you mind dropping me off in town and driving yourself home?"

"Why?"

"Astin and I are meeting for dinner." Tulah squealed. "Isn't that great?"

Angela cocked her head. "Wouldn't it be sa . . . better if you have your own transportation home, just in case?"

"In case of what?"

"In case this shyster isn't the prince charming you think he is."

Tulah clicked her teeth. "This is my chance to get out of this town." Her eyes held Angela's. "I don't want to be stuck here the rest of my life."

"What's wrong with this place? It's charming."

"It's boring, like Clay." Her eyes took on a faraway glow. "I want to go places, not be stuck here the rest of my life. Like Clay." She glanced at Angela, her eyes pleading. "Can you drop me off tonight and drive yourself home?"

Angela grimaced. "If it means that much to you, I guess so."

As Tulah parked at the winery, she turned toward her. "Thanks, you're a real friend."

After work, Tulah drove them to town, parking just as Astin's convertible pulled alongside.

"Hi, ladies." He turned toward Angela, his eyes like flint. "Will you be joining us?"

"Oh, no." Embarrassed to be thought tagging along, she rushed to explain. "We're just switching places. I'm driving Tulah's car back home."

His eyes softened. "In that case, have a drink with us."

Angela started backing towards the driver's seat. "Thanks, but I'd better get back." She opened the car door.

"One quick drink and then you can be on your way."

Tulah looked at Astin. Taking his lead, she chimed in, "Sure, join us."

Angela looked at Tulah for confirmation and then closed the door. "Maybe an iced tea before I leave."

They found a table beneath an ancient live oak. Astin ordered a bottle of pinot noir.

"Iced tea, please," Angela told the waitress. "I'm driving."

They chatted about the weather as a duo sang in the background. The woman played a mandolin, while the man accompanied them on a guitar.

Then the man began singing *Ghost Riders*. Everyone in the restaurant's courtyard stopped speaking to listen.

As the hairs on Angela's arms and neck bristled, she thought of Billy. *Can't wait till it's dark to see him again.*

When the music ended, the audience applauded, and then the chatter resumed.

"That song always reminds me of wild mustangs and the old west." Tulah's eyes were wistful.

Astin nodded. "I think everyone has a soft spot for mustangs. They symbolize the American spirit."

Her eyes wide, Tulah turned toward him. "You like mustangs?"

"Sure, doesn't everyone? They're iconic. They represent freedom and independence."

Tulah cocked her head as she considered his face. "You're an attorney."

"Yeah." His eyes narrowed. "Why?"

"Do you ever do legal work for non-profit groups *gratis*?"

He nodded slowly. "Occasionally, I perform *pro bono* public service." His eyes watched hers. "Again, why?"

"My family and the neighboring ranch have Texas Mustangs, a 501(c)3 non-profit group that rescues wild horses." Tulah's eyes lit up. "Think you might be able to help?"

Angela's ears perked. "Isn't that—"

"It's a 501(c)3, you say?" Astin pursed his lips, seeming to consider it. "Tax exempt?"

Tulah nodded. "Yup."

Angela tried again. "Is that—"

"I currently volunteer with a foundation, but if it's a charity that appeals to me, I could use another tax deduction." He smiled.

"Really?" Eyes flashing, Tulah's enthusiasm bubbled over.

"As long as it's tax exempt, I'd be happy to learn more about it." Raising his eyebrow, his eyes sparkled as they peered at Tulah. "Especially, if it's you, who does the briefing . . ."

Angela decided the mood was quickly getting personal. *Now or never*. "Isn't that the non-profit your family and Clay's started?"

Tulah's head snapped toward her. Her eyes dark and unblinking, she scowled at Angela. "Yes." Then she turned back to Astin. "I'd love to show you the rescued horses."

Okay, time to go. Angela downed her iced tea and held up the empty glass. "Thanks for the tea." She peered at Tulah. "See you in the morning."

Tulah pressed her lips together and glanced at Astin. "Be right back, just want to walk Angela to the car." As soon as they were out of hearing distance, Tulah shook her head. "Sorry, didn't mean to be short with you. When you mentioned Clay's name, something snapped. Really sorry about that." She hugged Angela.

"No harm done." Then Angela peered into face. "Are you sure you'll be all right getting home tonight?"

"Positive. Don't be a mother hen." Smiling, Tulah gently took Angela by the shoulders and turned her toward the car. "I'll be just fine. See you in the morning."

"Don't forget." Angela turned back to watch Tulah's expression. "We have to leave early to drive back to San Antonio. I've got a nine o'clock class."

Wearing a strained smile, Tulah rolled her eyes. "Yes, Mother, I'll see you in the morning."

Angela remembered to buy a bag of deer feed on the way home. Then she dropped off the car at Tulah's house and briefly explained her whereabouts to her parents over dinner. *How much detail should I go into?* After helping with the dishes, she carried the feed to the cabin and found the yearling waiting for her, prancing back and forth near the tree line.

"Hey, little guy, are you hungry?" Opening the sack, she dumped a small mound on the grass. Then recalling Billy's words, she left while he ate, carrying the bag inside the cabin.

He didn't say anything about watching from a distance. She slowly pulled aside the curtains and peeked while the deer nibbled his feed.

After the yearling left, she decided to walk to the stream. Halfway along the trail, he caught up with her, following in her tracks.

"Hey, you, I'm not supposed to encourage any bonding."

The deer tentatively approached, and then began bunting his nubby head against her thigh.

"Little man, we're not supposed to socialize." She laughed. "No bunting."

Turning, she continued toward the stream with the yearling bunting her thighs from behind.

"Hey, stop it." She turned and scolded him, tapping his head lightly with her fingertip.

He walked a foot away and began sniffing a patch of Blackfoot daisies. As he nosed about, a Swallowtail butterfly landed on his snout, rhythmically spreading and folding its lacy, yellow-black wings.

She chuckled. "If I hadn't seen it with my own eyes, I'd swear this only happens in Walt Disney cartoons."

She watched until the butterfly flew away. Then she turned, continuing toward the stream. Again the yearling followed her.

At the stream, she breathed in deeply, enjoying the quiet solitude, the sanctity of the towering cypresses, and the clear, running stream. She sat on a boulder, looking at God's beauty. The yearling curled up beside her on the mossy bank.

Without warning, Angela found herself sobbing. The sheer beauty of the scene, the trust of the yearling, overwhelmed her. She thought of the woman who had adopted her and raised her, and she cried for the first time in months.

With her mother gone, she felt alone. Lonely. Looking at her engagement ring, she thought of Kio, a five-hour drive away. *I didn't think a long-distance relationship would be so lonesome.*

Then the tears stopped as she looked at the yearling, calm, relaxed, his sharp hooves gently touching her shoes. Inches away, she saw two squirrels merrily chattering, chasing each other's tails, apparently oblivious of her.

Angela blinked. *This has never happened before.* "Am I suddenly invisible?" she asked the deer. "Or are you a magical stag that makes nature accept me when I'm with you?"

Never looking up, he contentedly chewed his cud, his mouth rhythmically moving left to right.

"You need a name." Deep in thought, she looked up at the sky and noticed it was a deep blue. The moon was rising. *How long have I been here?* She checked her watch.

"Kitz," said a voice.

Angela turned at the sound and saw Billy appear from the leaves. "Glad you could join us." Squinting, she asked, "What does Kitz mean?"

"It's German for fawn." He smiled. "Since the little buck's adopted you, you might as well name him."

"How do you know German?"

He chuckled. "With the name Hall, in German *Halle*, how couldn't I know a few words, at least?"

"German? So Fredericksley really was settled by Germans." Angela nodded to herself.

"Why do you think cowboys yodeled?"

She shrugged. "I don't know."

"Their German heritage, woman." Billy spread his hands in obvious frustration.

She swallowed a smile. "Makes sense." Then she looked up at him. "Can you yodel?"

He blinked. "I used to." Grimacing, he added, "It's been so long since I last tried."

"Go for it."

There, in the stillness of the evening, Billy began singing *The Yellow Rose of Texas*, yodeling between verses. Tentatively, at first, he gained confidence until the night rang with his song.

Enjoying the experience, Angela listened in wonder to his strong voice. Then she looked about. The yearling and squirrels also seemed to be listening, as if charmed by his music. When he finished, Angela applauded.

"You're really talented." She looked up at him in the moonlight, and their eyes met. She gasped as it occurred to her. *Am I attracted to him?* Ruffled, she looked away, her eyes resting on the yearling. "Kitz, I like the name."

"It fits him."

Angela peeked up at Billy through her eyelashes, watching his strong face relax into a smile. Then she recalled the mid-term week left. "I'd better be getting back. Have to leave early in the morning."

His smile drooped as he took a step toward her. "You're going away?"

To quiet her pulse, she tried to take a deep breath, but she felt constricted. Breathing shallowly, she felt breathless. "Just until Wednesday night, Tulah and I are driving back after classes."

She stood up, finding herself inches from him. Unsettled by his nearness, again she tried to draw in her breath. She looked up at him, suddenly faint as she weaved slightly closer.

She watched him take another step toward her, freeze as he clenched and unclenched his jaw, and then turn away.

His back to her, he mumbled. "I'll walk you to the cabin."

As quickly as the tension had surfaced, it receded. The atmosphere lightened as the tightness eased in her chest, and Angela took a deep breath.

While they drove along Interstate 10 the next morning, Angela studied Tulah. Sleep still in her bloodshot eyes, she yawned.

"How much rest did you get last night?"

Tulah glanced at her with a mischievous smile. "Not much."

"I gathered that," Angela said dryly. "Got any mid-terms today?"

Tulah nodded as she yawned again. "One," she said, halfway through the yawn.

"Are you going to be all right?"

"Oh, sure." Tulah gave her a sleepy smile as she picked up her cup. "That's what coffee's for."

"Now that you've gotten to know him, what do you think of Pig-Pen?"

Tulah scowled at her. "Wish you'd stop calling him that! Astin told me all about his plans, his goals last night."

Angela snickered. "Did you get a word in edgewise about your plans or goals?"

"Why do you say things like that?"

"Because I think he's a self-centered, egotistical shyster." Opening her eyes wide, Angela gave a conclusive nod.

"For your information, he's donating his legal services to our non-profit organization." Tulah arched her eyebrow as she glanced at Angela. "Do you call that the sign of a selfish person?"

"Isn't it a write-off for him?"

"Yeah, but that's not why he's doing it . . . at least, not the only reason."

Angela gave her a smug grin. "Keep telling yourself that."

"Wednesday, he's coming over to see the facility, meet the horses—"

"Meet the volunteers?" Angela raised her eyebrow. "Will Clay be there?"

Tulah shrugged her shoulder. "So what if he is?"

"Could be uncomfortable . . ."

"Speaking of which—"

"Not that you're changing the topic or anything."

Tulah chuckled. "You haven't said a word about the cabin since that first morning. Any ghosts? Anything out of the ordinary?"

Angela paused, debating how much to divulge.

"Yes . . .?"

"Did you know there's a bottle baby on the property?"

Tulah glanced at her. "A what?"

"A bottle baby, a yearling buck that someone's bottle-raised and then released."

Tulah shook her head. "Nope."

"He's a cutie." Angela chuckled, thinking of him.

"Have you named him?"

"Yup, Kitz." Angela smiled, recalling how he had followed her and sat at her feet. "It's German for fawn."

Tulah took her eyes from the road. "I didn't know you spoke German."

"I don't."

"How did you come up with that name?"

Angela stiffened briefly and then shrugged. "Must have heard it somewhere."

Wednesday, Tulah drove Angela to the non-profit facility after classes ended.

"Astin should be here any minute." Tulah checked her watch. "In the meantime, want a tour of the place?"

"Sure." Angela followed her into the pasture.

Tulah put two fingers to her lips and gave a shrill whistle. Within a minute, four mustangs galloped toward them, tails and manes flying in the wind. She laughed as they stopped just inches away.

Angela stood behind her, unsure how to approach them.

"Here," said Tulah, dropping four bite-sized treats in her hand. "Hold your fingers together like this, your palm flat, so they can't nibble your fingers by mistake. Give each horse a treat, and you'll be friends for life."

Angela put one treat on her palm and placed the others in her pocket. Then she tentatively held out her hand to a speckled white horse. She felt the velvet of its muzzle and its soft breath on her hand. When she saw its big teeth, she squeezed her fingers together tightly and let him take the treat with his lips.

Once she realized it was not only painless, but fun, she chuckled, and tried to pet the horse's nose.

"Get over to the side of him, so he can see you. See how his eyes are set? He can't see you when you're right in front of him. He sees everything on the right and everything on the left. Stand over here, where he can see you. Then pet his neck."

Angela repositioned herself and gently stroked his neck and coarse mane.

"See how his ears are up?" Tulah smiled at her. "He likes you."

Angela tried the same tactics with each of the other horses, and within ten minutes had learned their names, found a brush, and was learning how to groom them.

"These horses are gorgeous, but they each look so different. Are they all mustangs?"

"Yup, they're a mixture of breeds, but most say they're descended from Spanish horses, like the Andalusian."

"That's right, they escaped from the conquistadors." Using long, sweeping motions, Angela brushed the dust off the horse's back.

Tulah grinned. "That's the traditional story, but recently a new theory's come up."

Still grooming the mustang, Angela glanced at her. "What's that?"

"Now some scientists are saying horses originated in North America."

"Really?"

Tulah nodded. "From North America's western Plains, they traveled over the Bering land bridge into Eurasia."

Angela nodded. "Makes sense."

"Even within this theory, opinions differ," said Tulah. "Most researchers believe horses died out in North America after they migrated about twelve thousand years ago, but some think pockets of the native horses survived on the Plains, that they didn't become extinct here. Then, when the Spanish horses escaped, they interbred."

"How can they tell?"

"From horses' DNA."

Angela surveyed the four mustangs, comparing them. "Is that why they all look so different?"

"There's been so much interbreeding over the past five hundred years, mustangs are a conglomeration of all breeds."

Angela stroked the horse's neck. "What basic breed is this speckled white one I'm grooming?"

"Appaloosa, and it's interesting you ask about this breed."

"Why?" Angela turned toward her.

"The Nez Perce people bred these. See how different the coat is from the other horses'? Some scientists point to Appaloosas as proof the native horses didn't become extinct in North America."

"What kind is that one?" Angela pointed to a black horse with a long, flowing tail and a mane that hung down to its legs.

"There's definitely some Friesian in that gelding."

"But it's still a mustang, right?"

"Right." Tulah nodded. "They're all mustangs, just interbred with one breed's traits more dominant than the others."

"What about this brown one with the big feet?"

"That mare has some draft horse in her. See how big she is? She's a work horse, bred for plowing and pulling heavy wagons."

"And that sleek horse over there?" Angela pointed to one that was pawing.

"From her temperament and conformation, that mare has some Thoroughbred in her. They were bred for racing, so she's a little higher strung than that docile draft horse."

Angela glanced from one horse to the other. "I had no idea mustangs were this diverse."

"They're amazing creatures." Tulah looked at her watch and sighed. "Where's Astin?"

"What time was he supposed to meet us here?"

Tulah grimaced. "Twenty minutes ago."

They heard a car on the caliche driveway and looked up. Instead of a red convertible, Angela saw a silver pickup. "Who's that?"

"Three guesses," said Tulah, "and the first two don't count."

"Clay?"

The truck parked, and out stepped a tan, muscular man in jeans and a T-shirt. His eyes swept Tulah from head to toe and then homed in on her eyes. Never glancing left or right, he walked up to her.

"Good to see you." His eyes smiled at hers.

Tulah gestured to Angela. "You remember my roommate, don't you?"

He turned toward her and smiled. "Sure do, Angela. What brings you to Fredericksley?"

"Just helping out at the winery until Kelby's leg heals."

His smile dimmed. "What happened to her?"

"We were climbing Enchanted Rock," said Angela. "It sprinkled just enough to make the granite slippery. Long story short, she slipped and broke her leg."

"Sorry to hear that." Clay turned back to Tulah. "Please say 'hi' to her for me."

"Will do." Tulah nodded. Then she pursed her lips and stared past him at the gate.

"Expecting someone?" He scrutinized her.

"Yup." Her eyes lit up as the red convertible flashed into view.

Leaving a cloud of dust in his wake, Astin sped up to the pasture fence, caliche crunching beneath his tires. He removed his sunglasses and stepped out of the car as if he were in a fashion shoot.

"Who's this dude?" Clay mumbled, his lip curling.

Tulah ignored the comment, walking into Astin's open arms. When he bent his head to kiss her, she discreetly avoided him, turning toward them with a shy smile. "Angela, you know Astin. Clay, this is Astin Starr. He's an attorney, who's going to help Texas Mustangs with legal work."

Astin held out his hand. "Pleased to meet you."

Clay brought a smile to his face, nodded, and shook hands. "Astin, is it?"

"Yup."

"What kind of paperwork were you planning to help us with?"

Astin glanced at Tulah. "I hear Texas Mustangs needs bylaws and a copyright. I can help with those."

"Just so you know, we have a tight budget." Clay shook his head. "We don't have—"

"*Pro bono*, my friend, *gratis*." Astin gave him a quick smile.

"Your payment will be a write-off." Angela watched him closely. "Isn't that right?"

Astin cocked an eyebrow as he glanced at her. "*Quid pro quo*, a fair exchange."

"Nothing for nothing." Angela all but sneered.

Astin responded by turning toward Tulah. "I wonder if you could you give me a tour of the facilities."

"My pleasure." Her eyes sparkled in the sunlight.

Taking Tulah's hand, Astin glanced at Clay. "Nice meeting you." Then he gave a parting nod to Angela as he followed Tulah toward the barn.

Clay joined Angela as they watched Astin put his arm around Tulah's waist. He crossed his arms. "When did this start?"

"About two weeks ago."

Clay took a deep breath. "I don't trust him."

Angela snorted. "That makes two of us." She told him about Astin's involvement with Agua Purificación.

Clay shook his head. "The Houston company that's trying to steal Barron County's water?"

She nodded.

"And this guy works for them?"

"Yup."

"What a shyster."

Angela burst out laughing. "That's what I call him."

Uncrossing his arms, Clay turned toward the horses.

Angela followed his gaze. "What?"

"Sally's lying down." He took off at a run, Angela following.

The Thoroughbred mare was rolling on the ground, kicking and biting at her flanks.

"What's wrong with her?"

"Looks like she's colicking."

Angela peered at him. "What's that?"

"It's abdominal pain that can be very serious. Watch out for her legs! I don't want you to get kicked. A horse in pain forgets any training." Then holding his finger to his lips for quiet, he stooped, listening to the horse's stomach. After a minute, he straightened up.

"What were you listening for?"

"Gut sounds, and she doesn't have any." His eyebrows meeting in a deep V, he speed-dialed a number on his cell. "Got a colicky horse. Anyone available for an emergency ranch call? Lamar, if his schedule's open." He listened for a moment and nodded. "Thanks."

"What's happening?" asked Angela. "What can I do?"

He grabbed a halter off the fence post. "She's colicking. The vet's on a ranch call nearby, but if we don't act fast, she could die."

"Ohmigosh! How can I help?"

"Once we get her to her feet, I want you to keep her walking. Don't let her lie down. Keep her moving. Got that?"

Angela nodded as he buckled a halter on the horse and hooked on a lead rope.

"Come on, girl, get up. Get up!" Clay wheedled and bullied the mare until she finally rose to her feet. Then he handed the lead rope to Angela. "Keep her walking. I've got to get some meds from the barn."

Angela nodded as she kept a taut rope and gently pulled Sally. "Come on, girl, let's keep you moving."

Clay raced toward the barn and returned a minute later with castor oil. He unscrewed the top and poured its contents down Sally's throat. Then he turned to Angela and reached for the lead rope. "Thanks, I've got her."

"What can I do?"

He shook his head. "Pray."

Ten minutes later, the vet's pickup pulled up. "Clay," he said, "what have we got?"

Clay brought him up to speed, and the vet checked the color of her gums. Then he listened to her heart rate, respiratory rate, and gastrointestinal sounds. He pulled on rubber gloves and did a rectal exam.

"Looking for any abnormalities," he said. Then he pushed a tube through the horse's nostril. "Checking her stomach for reflux."

Angela looked to Clay for an explanation.

"He's looking for any fluid backed up in her stomach, which could mean surgery."

The vet pulled out the tube and turned toward them. "It's not good. I'm not sure at this point, but I think she's got a twisted intestine."

Clay crossed his arms and inhaled sharply.

"I'll give her something for the pain, but only time will tell if she can work it out or . . ."

Clay finished for him. "If she needs to be put down."

Tulah ran up to them, panting. "What's wrong with Sally?" She looked from Clay to the vet.

"She's colicking." Clay's mouth was grim.

"What's the fastest route?" asked Astin.

The vet shrugged. "Put her down."

"Then put her out of her misery." Astin reached into his back pocket. "I can make a donation."

"Hold on just a minute." Clay's eyes narrowed. "We haven't determined whether or not she can recover."

"What are the options?" Ignoring Clay, Astin turned toward the veterinarian.

"After I give her an injection for the pain," said the vet, "there are two: put her down or wait and see."

"I say, save her the suffering. Put her down." Astin pulled out a credit card. "Do you take plastic?"

Clay took a step toward him. "Who the hell do you think you are coming in here and ordering Lamar to put down our horse?"

The vet stepped between them as he looked from Clay to Tulah. "Sally's got a fifty-fifty chance. I can give her banamine for the pain, and you can keep her walking until she recovers, if she recovers, or I can administer a lethal injection." Again he looked from Clay to Tulah. "Your call."

"I'd hate her to suffer if the end result's the same." Tulah wore a pained expression. "If we choose the first option, how long before we'd know if it was the right choice?"

"As long as it takes." Lamar shrugged. "Could be all night. Could take an hour or two. Either way, you'd have to keep her walking the whole time."

Tulah looked at Clay, her mouth tight and grim. "We could take shifts."

He nodded. "I agree." Clay turned toward the vet. "Give her the banamine, and we'll do all we can to help her through this."

Angela watched Astin grimace as he put away his wallet.

"I'll hold Sally while you give her the injection." Tulah got a tighter grip on the lead rope with one hand, and held her halter with the other.

Two minutes later, the vet shook their hands. "Call me if she takes a turn for the worse. I'll be here as soon as I can."

After he left, Astin turned toward Tulah. "Bet you could use a bite to eat." He checked his watch. "It's dinnertime."

She looked from him to Clay. "I don't think I'd better leave Sally . . ."

"Go ahead." Clay's voice was gruff. "I'll take the first shift. See you in what? Two hours?"

Tulah looked at Sally. "No, it'd be better if we were both here the first shift. We can take turns walking her while the other feeds and grooms the rest of the horses." She turned toward Astin. "Sorry this came up. Maybe we can continue our conversation tomorrow?"

Astin gave her a grudging smile. "Rain check, I'll call you tomorrow." As he kissed her cheek, Clay stifled a sigh.

Tulah grabbed Astin's hand as she held his gaze. "Thanks, see you tomorrow." She waved as Astin walked back to his car and drove away in a cloud of dust.

Then she turned to Angela. "No need for you to stay. Why don't you take the car and come back for me in two hours?"

"You're sure?" Angela searched her brain for a way to help. Then she got an idea. "How 'bout I bring back dinner for Clay when I pick you up?" She looked from one face to the other. "Don't worry about your bags, Tulah. I'll drop them off at your house."

Angela drove to her cabin, anxious to see Kitz. *I wasn't here to feed him yesterday.* She put a scoop of feed on the grass and whistled.

Within a minute, he appeared, his head low as he nosed through the wild persimmon bushes.

Remembering Billy's words, she left him to eat and began walking toward the stream. Halfway there, Kitz caught up with her and began walking alongside her.

She took a deep breath, feeling content. *No, more than that. Privileged.* Angela looked in awe at the wild creature that had adopted her.

At the stream, she sat on her favorite rock, and Kitz curled up beside her. She watched the clear water, gently flowing beneath the ancient cypresses. She heard its gurgling as it rippled around the boulders. She breathed in the grape aroma of the mountain laurel, their purple flower clusters hanging like lilacs. She felt at one with nature, an integral part of it, not a bystander, not a trespasser. She sensed no contention, no man-versus-nature conflict, just harmony, oneness.

A lizard approached, and then another. They scampered about her feet oblivious of any danger. This time, Angela was not startled by their acceptance. "I'm beginning to believe you are a magical stag," she told Kitz.

He took it in stride, chewing contentedly.

Her mind drifted to the drama playing out with the mustang. Silently, she prayed. *Please let Sally survive.*

She thought of Tulah and Clay . . . and Tulah's car. *Living out here, I can't be so reliant on her.* Suddenly an idea came as plainly as if someone had spoken. *Be free.* She glanced at Kitz and squinted. "Is it my imagination, or do you even make my thoughts clearer?"

As if in answer, he began licking her forearm.

Angela watched, mesmerized, as she shook her head. "This is weird." She chuckled as his velvety tongue lapped the body salts off her arm. "It tickles."

Then she glanced at her watch, remembering she had to drop off Tulah's bags, eat dinner, help with the dishes, pick up Clay's dinner, and deliver it all in less than an hour. She wanted to stay, prolong the moment. She sighed. "Sorry, little guy, I have to leave."

She could not resist running her hand over his head, feeling his little nubs of downy antlers just barely poking through. *Love you.*

Angela drove through Texas Mustangs' gate wondering what scene would unfold. She saw Tulah walking Sally in the distance. Clay was grooming the draft horse.

She held up a small cooler as she got out of the car. "Tulah's mother made you dinner: pulled-pork sandwiches, potato salad, and peach cobbler."

"Be right there. Just need to pick her feet."

Angela watched him clean the mare's hooves and then turn her out to pasture.

"Thanks," he said, joining her. As he unpacked the dinner, he inhaled. "Mm . . . smells wonderful."

"Tastes wonderful." Angela grinned. "Tulah's mom is a terrific cook." Then she glanced toward Tulah and the Thoroughbred. "How's Sally?"

"She's still standing, still holding her own, but we won't know until she poops."

Angela thought she had misunderstood. "What?"

"When Sally colicked, her colon folded back on itself, and peristalsis stopped. The only way we'll know if her intestines are functioning right is if she poops."

"I didn't know that." Angela scratched her ear. "This is the first time I've been around horses."

As Tulah approached the fence, leading Sally Clay surveyed her. "Why don't you go home? You look like you could use some rest."

Tulah shook her head. "I don't want you to have to deal with this alone."

"We said two hours on and two hours off." He raised his eyebrow. "Go on, I'll see you in a couple hours."

"If you hadn't had to worry about me, you'd have had your car here when you wanted it." Angela bit her lip. "I've got to get a car."

Clay's ear perked. "New or used?"

Angela shrugged her shoulder. "Just something to get me around, so I'm not dependent on Tulah."

"My dad's got a car he wants to sell. Nothing fancy, but it's got a lot of miles left in it."

Tulah nodded. "If Clay's father owned it, you can bet it's in good shape."

"Perfect, when can I see it?"

"I hear you're working at the winery. Will you be there tomorrow?"

Angela nodded.

"I'll bring it by then." Clay smiled. "If you like it, you can buy it."

"That's easy enough." Angela thought of how the idea of buying a car had come to her when she was with Kitz. *Be free*. She smiled to herself.

Tulah turned toward her. "Okay, give me a minute with Sally, and I'll be ready to go." Then wearing a grudging smile, she looked at Clay. "I really appreciate your staying with her. I'll be back in two hours."

With his lips pressed together, he nodded.

On the drive home, Angela said, "Clay seems like a level-headed guy."

Tulah nodded. "He's solid as a rock."

Angela turned her head quickly to watch her expression. "Then why did you break up with him?"

"He's so . . . predictable." Her mouth twisted in a wry smile. "I want excitement, surprises."

"So does Astin surprise you?" Angela's eyes narrowed. "He doesn't surprise me."

"What do you mean?" Tulah took her eyes from the road to glance at her.

"Let's just say he's consistent."

"Meaning?"

"From the way he drives, he doesn't seem concerned about wildlife, and today he showed how much compassion he had for Sally. His first thought was to whip out his credit card and pay the vet to put her down."

"Just the opposite." Tulah's eyes flashed. "He proved he cares by trying to save her from suffering."

Angela stifled a sigh. "I don't know what kind of rose-tinted glasses you're viewing him through, but you don't see him for what he is."

"And what is he?" Tulah's face was taut, white.

"He's self-centered. Astin's only concern is Astin." Angela tried another approach. "What do you see in him?"

"I see a determined man, who goes after what he wants and gets it." Tulah scowled at her, her eyes narrowed. "I like cacti, not pretty posies. I like mustangs, not pretty ponies. Even if they're prickly, I always go for the strong-willed." Her glance was withering. "Not the 'solid.'"

Angela did not want to argue. "I just don't want to see you get hurt."

"You're not my mother, and it's none of your business."

They rode in silence until Tulah dropped her off at the cabin.

"See you in the morning."

Before Angela could answer, Tulah drove off.

Self-imposed Limitations

We never know the worth of water till the well is dry.
– *Thomas Fuller, Gnomologia*

Angela stared after her until the dust settled. *Great, I've offended her. Maybe I should just learn to shut up.* Grunting, she bit her lip.

Then she heard: *Be a friend.*

She glanced around to see who had said it but saw only Kitz approaching from the underbrush. "That's the second time I've 'heard' someone, yet no one's been near me but you. Okay, I'm hearing with my inner ear. I get that, but . . ." She shook her head, laughing at herself. "This is beyond ridiculous, but are you trying to tell me something, give me some kind of message?"

In response, he nibbled the red Turk's Caps buds.

Angela chuckled. "Good answer." Seeing the yearling reminded her of the stream, of how she had hated leaving its calm refuge earlier. "Come on, let's watch the moon rise."

Dragonflies and fireflies flitted about them on the wooded path. Angela rested her hand on the back of the yearling's neck, and the two walked side by side.

At the stream, she perched on what was now 'her' rock, her arms hugging her knees, while Kitz sat at her feet. Thinking of Sally, she said a silent prayer. Tulah, Clay, and Astin entered her mind and popped out. She sighed as memories of her mother made welcome guest appearances and then disappeared. She thought of Kio and sighed. *If I had a car, it would be so much easier to meet him.*

When she looked up, the moon had risen and was clearing the treetops.

"Penny for your thoughts."

She glanced at Kitz, but he seemed to be sleeping. Suddenly alert as her body stiffened, her eyes searched the riverbank for an intruder. Then she spotted Billy.

She gave a sigh of relief. "It's you."

"Who were you expecting?"

"Twice today, I've 'heard' voices, but no one was there."

"No one?" He arched his eyebrow.

"Kitz was, but no *one*, no person."

"Hmm." He nodded thoughtfully but said nothing.

Her eyes adjusting to the night's light level, she peered at him in the moonlight. "I've been meaning to ask you."

"About what?"

She studied his profile before answering. "I've seen spirits all my life, but you're the first that hasn't followed the laws of physics."

He turned to face her. "What do you mean?"

"Other spirits come and go at will. They're not controlled by time or space."

He cocked his head.

"They're not limited to day or night, yet you are. Why?"

His blue eyes became so pale, they seemed like opals reflecting the moonlight. She sensed his vulnerability and felt she was trespassing.

He remained silent, apparently lost in thought, so she tried again. "You said during the days, you're confined to the cabin, and nights you're compelled to return here." Letting go her knees, she leaned toward him. "Why can't you come and go, day or night?"

He sighed. "It's difficult to describe. It's not so much a place as a plane." He gestured to the surrounding area. "I'm here, but . . ."

"Why haven't I seen you in the daytime?"

He blinked, apparently at a loss for words. Then he turned his pale eyes toward her. "Except for you, nobody's been able to see me at all, unless I allowed it. Maybe . . ." His words trailed off. "I don't know."

She wracked her brain to find a reason. "What about when you were killed, what happened? Think back. Was there anything specific about the time?"

"After he shot me, the gunman laughed. I heard him tell the ranchers, 'He'll never see the light of day again.' His words echoed over and over in my mind." Billy looked to her for an answer. "Could the darkness be of my own choosing?"

She shrugged. "Maybe, I've never heard of such a thing, but the mind is a powerful tool. If the gunman's words imprinted themselves on you at the moment of death, maybe they influenced your choices. Maybe they caused some kind of self-imposed limitations." She peered up at him. "Have you ever tried to show yourself in the daylight?"

He shook his head. "Now that you mention it, I haven't."

"Let's try it in the morning."

When Angela woke the next day, she drew back the curtains to let in the sunlight. Dust shimmered in its bright light. Humming to herself, she crossed into the kitchen and came to a dead stop.

There stood Billy, visible but nearly imperceptible. She could see the walls, the furniture right through him. Only the dimmest traces of his outline were apparent.

"Well?"

"I see you, but barely." She could hardly make out his facial expressions.

"What do you mean?"

"I nearly walked into you. You're there, but the light seems to bend around you." She studied him. "That, or you're giving off a faint light that's lost in the sunshine." Pursing her lips, she grunted. "I've never seen anything like it."

"But the point is, you see me!"

Angela could hear the glee in his voice, but she could only guess he was smiling. She grinned. "That's true, but all your features are washed out in the daylight. I can't make out your eyes or mouth, only a rough outline of your head."

"Can you see me move?" He crossed to the other side of the kitchen.

"I wouldn't call it 'see you move' as much as seeing the air shimmer around you as you're moving."

Walking behind the breakfast bar, he stood in a windowless corner of the kitchen.

She grinned. "Yes! I see more of you now. The darker it is, the more detail I see."

He grinned back. "You've helped me overcome a limitation—"

"A *self-imposed* limitation."

"That's true. I'm not confined to the night as I'd thought." He turned his head, looking off into space. "I wonder if that means I'm not confined to this area?"

"You said you're here for a reason: to protect the water."

"Yes." He nodded. "That's my purpose, but I wonder if I've limited myself in another way."

"How so?"

"If I was restricting the hours, the time I could be here, maybe I was also limiting the space."

Angela opened her eyes wide as an idea took form. "Do you think I could see you anywhere, *everywhere*, not just here?"

"That's exactly what I'm wondering." He took a step toward her. "If it's true, I don't have to stay here. My universe is expanding, and it's all because of you." He took another step, leaning toward her as if to hug her. "Angela, I . . ."

As she looked up at him, a strong attraction gripped the pit of her stomach. She leaned across the breakfast bar, suddenly wondering what his arms would feel like around her.

They leaned closer until their bodies were inches away. Physically drawn to him, Angela arched her back, lifting her lips to his. She drew in her breath and closed her eyes, waiting. Waiting.

As if a switch had been thrown, she felt the tension vanish. On. Off. After a moment, she opened her eyes to see what had happened.

He was stiffly leaning away. His eyes a darker, more intense blue than she had seen before, he straightened his spine and stepped back.

Blinking, wondering at the swift change, she swallowed. The mood was broken. She felt misled. Deprived of his touch, she felt cheated. Humiliated. Guilty.

Dumb! Really dumb! She glanced at her ring. *I'm engaged.* Then she shook her head to clear it. *He's not even a man. He's a ghost. What was I thinking?*

Clearing her throat, she turned and called over her shoulder. "If you'll excuse me, I have to get ready for work."

Two minutes later, she was knocking at Tulah's door.

Kelby's face lit up when she answered. "Just in time for breakfast."

Angela glanced at her miniature tricycle and smiled. "Looks like you're getting along just fine with that knee scooter."

"Can't let a broken leg slow me down." She scooted toward the table and patted the chair beside her.

"Morning, Angela." Brooke sat down across from them.

"Good morning." Angela noted the increasingly rounded belly. "Your baby certainly 'looks' healthy."

Brooke smiled and rested her hands on her stomach. "I think he or she's anxious to get out of this cramped space and see the world."

Angela thought of Billy and grimaced.

"What's wrong?" A frown overshadowed Brooke's features.

Angela looked up. "Nothing, why?"

"For a moment, you looked like you'd lost your best friend."

She shrugged. "Just thought of something."

Kelby pointed out each bowl's contents. "Help yourself to granola, Greek yogurt, and dried fruit." She grinned. "Made breakfast today by myself."

Angela spooned yogurt into her bowl. "Where's your mom?"

"She and Dad had some business in San Antonio." As Kelby spotted Tulah, she added, "They left before dawn, just after you got in last night." She winked. "Getting back with Clay?"

Tulah rolled her bloodshot eyes. Then she yawned. "We took turns walking Sally last night."

Angela looked up. "How's she doing?"

Tulah gave her a grudging smile. "She's holding her own. Still don't know. Clay said he'll update us if she improves or . . ."

"At least, it's not bad news." Angela smiled hopefully, and Tulah returned the smile.

"Thanks."

"Have you heard the latest about Agua Purificación?" Kelby's eyes lit up.

"No, we've been studying for exams the past few days. What's happening?" Angela helped herself to granola.

Kelby unfolded a printed email and summarized as she read. "The North Edwards Aquifer Authority filed a suit in Barron County District Court Friday to stop AP from pumping until they get groundwater-use permits."

Her eyes narrowing, Kelby looked up. "The suit says the Rule of Capture violates groundwater property rights."

She skipped over several paragraphs, running her finger down the page. Then Kelby looked up, grinning. "The NEAA's also asking the Texas Supreme Court to overturn the Rule of Capture as it applies to groundwater. *Yes!*"

Angela looked up from her yogurt and granola. "What's the Rule of Capture?"

"Landowners are entitled to take all the water they want from beneath their property."

"No matter what happens to neighboring wells? Even if it causes other wells to go dry?"

Kelby nodded. "Listen to this op-ed piece." She ran her finger down the paper until she found it. "It's an outdated law, it says, 'from a 1904 decision that referred to groundwater as secret and occult. Science has a better understanding of groundwater today. The time's ripe to challenge that antiquated law.'"

"They want a temporary injunction to stop AP." Kelby sneered. "It couldn't happen to a nicer company."

Angela glanced at Tulah over Kelby's head. *Wonder if Tulah's told her family about Astin's connection with AP.*

As Angela got in the car with Tulah, she glanced sideways at her.

Tulah was watching her from the corner of her eye and gave her a shy smile. "Sorry I got so huffy yesterday about Astin."

Angela returned a wry smile. "And I'm sorry I stuck my nose in your business. I'll try not to act like a mother hen."

They hugged across the console.

As Tulah drove them to the winery, Angela took a deep breath. "At the risk of stirring up a wasp's nest, have you told your family about Astin's link to AP?"

Tulah raised her eyebrow as she glanced at her. "Why do you ask?"

"Kelby seems awfully upset about AP taking the water. How do you think she'll react when she finds out he's their lawyer?"

Tulah sighed. "I'll worry about that when the time comes." She sniffed.

When they arrived, Clay was standing beside a Ford Fiesta wearing a wide smile.

Tulah jumped out from behind the wheel. "How's Sally?"

Clay pushed back his cowboy hat and grinned. "She pooped."

"Yes!" Tulah leaped into his arms and hugged him. "You did it!"

"We did it," he said, twirling her around. As they came to a stop, he became serious.

Tulah stiffened, let go of his shoulders, and took a step back. "I'm really glad she made it."

Their eyes locking, they stared at each other as the silence lingered.

To break the tension, Angela asked, "So poop is proof everything's . . . moving?"

Tulah nodded as if in a daze.

"Thank God," said Angela. "That's great news."

Clay broke his stare and turned toward her. "Yes, it is." He glanced at Tulah as he spoke. "I had my doubts she'd come 'round, but she did." Then he turned back to Angela. "Mustang mares can be headstrong, but they're tough."

Angela smiled and then glanced at the car. "Is this your dad's car?"

"Yup," he grinned sheepishly. "It's what you might call a 'classic,' but like I said, it's got a lot of miles left in it."

Tulah nodded, seconding it. "Clay's father babies every vehicle he's ever owned. He changes the oil more often than I stop for gas." Chuckling, she glanced at Clay. "Remember his old one-fifty?"

"Do I! That's the one we . . ." He broke off as he dropped his smile and then cleared his throat.

Tulah sighed uncomfortably as she turned toward Angela. "That's the one we took to the Senior Prom, got a flat on the way home, and ended up hitchhiking back in the rain." She groaned. "You should have seen my prom dress."

Angela gave a polite smile but kept her thoughts to herself.

"I'm, uh," Tulah pointed toward the winery. "I'm going to open up while you two talk business." With a wave, she turned and walked into the building. "Bye, Clay," she called over her shoulder.

"Bye, Tulah." His eyes followed her until the door closed behind her.

Angela watched. When he turned back to her, she said, "You two seem to have a history together."

He gave a wry laugh. "We were two peas in a pod from kindergarten until this semester." His eyes clouded.

"What happened?"

He took off his hat and ran his fingers through his hair. "You tell me."

Angela shrugged. "I don't know."

"What's with this Astin character?"

She took a deep breath. "Look, this is something between you and Tulah. I've already been caught in her crosshairs once. Let's just say, I'm gun shy."

"Fair enough." He readjusted his hat, put on a smile, and gestured to the car. "What do you think?"

"Could I test drive it?"

"Sure." He tossed her the keys. "Hop in."

She drove around the parking lot with the windows open, listening to the engine, trying out the windshield wipers, turning on the radio and air conditioner. Then she turned toward him. "What's wrong with it?"

He snickered. "Nothing. My dad just doesn't have any more use for this car. Trust me, it's in good running condition."

"It sounds like it, looks like it." She peered up at him. "How much is he asking?"

"Make an offer."

Angela mentally tallied what she would earn from her summer job at the park and named a low price.

"Sold."

"Just like that?" She blinked. "Don't you need to check my references or driver's license or checking account or something?"

"You're a friend of Tulah's." He gave her an easy smile. "That's good enough for us."

Suddenly, she realized how Billy had felt. *Free, not tied to someone else's schedule, not stuck in one place, but free.* She drew a deep breath.

As Angela drove the tram through the vineyard, she overheard two visitors.

"Oh, look, there's a deer," said one, pointing, "and another."

"I've never seen so many deer, except in Nara Park," said a Japanese lady.

"Where's that?" Angela glanced through the rearview mirror as she drove.

"Near Osaka, it's one of Japan's Shinto shrines." She gave a tiny bow and then gestured with her hand. "It's where the mountains separate heaven from earth and create a home for the gods. For many Japanese, it's sacred ground."

"It sounds lovely, and you say it has deer?"

"Yes, over a thousand *Sika* deer make Nara their home."

"Really? Are they a nuisance?"

"A what? Sorry, my English is not that good."

"Are the deer a problem?"

"Oh, no, deer are spiritual beings that speak with the gods." She smiled gently. "They're messengers of the Shinto gods. Until the nineteen-forties, they were still called divine."

"Why?"

"Ever since the shrine's god arrived, riding a white deer in seven hundred and sixty-eight, deer have been sacred in Nara."

"Are they considered beasts of burden?"

"Sorry?"

"Are they like horses that people ride or pack animals that carry loads on their backs?"

The Japanese woman shook her head. "No, they're messengers of the gods."

Messengers of the gods. Nodding, Angela smiled to herself. *Yes, I do believe Kitz is a messenger from God, but what's his message?*

When Angela arrived home in her new-to-her car, Kitz was watching for her in the bushes. The moment she stepped out of the car, he appeared from behind a mountain laurel.

"Hey you." Angela scratched behind his ears. "That car didn't fool you for a moment, did it? You knew it was me."

She got a scoop of feed from the house, set it down for him, and began walking toward the stream. Five minutes later, Kitz caught up with her.

Glancing at him, she recalled how clear her thoughts became in his company. "When I was worried about transportation, I 'heard' someone say, *Be free.*" Squinting, she studied him. "Are you 'talking' to me?"

In answer, he fluttered his ears, brushing away gnats.

Angela laughed. "Right."

Ignoring her, Kitz browsed on wildflowers.

Then Angela remembered the night before, when she had worried about Tulah being annoyed. "I 'heard' someone say, *Be a friend.* Was that you?"

Kitz looked up at her and blinked with his ultra-long eyelashes.

She chuckled to herself. "Okay, bat your eyelashes once for yes, and twice for no."

In answer, he began nibbling a honeysuckle vine.

"Haven't you figured it out?"

She turned at the sound of the familiar voice. *Billy.* Though still daylight, she could easily make out his features. "Haven't I figured what out?"

"You're relaxed. You're letting nature fill your senses. Nature connects the body, mind, spirit, and soul. How couldn't your thoughts become so clear that you can 'hear' them?"

She stared at him, surprised to view him in anything but moonlight or incandescent light. "But Kitz seems to be the reason. When I'm with him, nature accepts me. Lizards and squirrels actually come up and play at my feet. They're not afraid of me, or I'm somehow invisible to them."

He gestured toward the stream, trees, wildflowers, and yearling. "Though Kitz may be the stimulus, what you're sensing is a harmony with life. You're meditating, communing with nature. With less mental scatter, you're attracting ideas," he grinned, "even lizards."

She nodded, but pursing her lips, she sighed. "I don't disagree with any of that, but I sense Kitz is more than just the stimulus."

"How so?"

Shrugging, she turned up her palms. "I can't help feeling he's a messenger, that I have some spiritual lesson to learn from him."

"Maybe. My grandmother was part Lipan-Apache. She said deer have keen eyesight, insights."

Angela looked at Kitz's big, brown eyes.

"She said they can see between the shadows, hear what's left unsaid." Billy glanced at her. "When you're out here, communing, what thoughts enter your mind?"

Again she shrugged. "Different ones, but twice now I've 'heard' a little voice in my mind, advising me. 'Be free. Be a friend.'"

"Maybe that voice is your conscience."

"Could be. I just can't help feeling Kitz has something to do with it."

"My grandmother always said if a deer crosses your path, trust your instincts to guide you."

Glancing up, she gave him a half smile. "I thought I always did trust my instincts."

"Maybe you're treading in deeper water, wading from instincts into intuition."

"What's the difference?"

His brow creasing, he stared into space, as if collecting his thoughts. Then his eyes rested on the deer nibbling red Turk's Caps.

"Kitz acts on instinct. It's a physical response to his environment, an impulsive reaction. If he sees tender wildflowers, instinct tells him to eat them. Instinct's a kind of genetic memory."

"And intuition?"

Billy gave her a wry grin as he gestured toward a patch of poison ivy. "Intuition is a psychological response. It comes from experience. If you touch a shiny, three-leafed plant and break out in a rash, you'd think twice before touching it again. If such-and-such occurred in the past, you'd expect such to happen in the future. You'd either embrace it or avoid it depending on your experience, your *intuition*. It's a learned response to your environment."

She nodded. "Makes sense. So you're saying I'm delving deeper into my intuition, and Kitz is my guide?"

"Maybe." He lifted a shoulder. Then he glanced at the deer. "Or, instead of guide, maybe he's your inspiration, your muse."

Angela looked at Kitz and laughed. "He's browsing. He isn't paying the slightest bit of attention to us or our conversation."

"That doesn't mean he isn't operating on several planes."

Tilting her head, she frowned. "I'm not following."

"Just because he looks and acts like a deer doesn't mean he's not the conveyer of some inspiration, some idea, some—"

"Message." She caught his eye and chuckled. "Isn't this where we came in?"

"Maybe so." He grinned as he sat down on a rocky ledge.

"You said your grandmother was Apache?"

He nodded. "Her people had camped in this area from the early 1700s."

Angela thought of the spirit she had seen on Enchanted Rock. "Did she ever mention anything about Enchanted Rock?"

"She called it a sacred place. She said the Giver of Life had sent mountain spirits there to guide, protect, and teach the Apaches how to live and cure illness."

"Did they have a name?"

"She called them the Ga'an and said they inhabit Enchanted Rock's caves."

Angela raised her eyebrow. "Really. Have you ever seen them?"

He shook his head. "Have you?"

Angela told him about Kelby's fall and Tulah's legend about the 'Guardian of the Rock,' the shaman named Wind Spirit.

Working his jaw, he nodded thoughtfully. "Maybe Grandmother's stories were true."

Angela swallowed a smile.

"What?"

She grinned. "Don't you think it's a little odd that you're skeptical of spirits?"

"Oh." He chuckled. "I guess you're right."

"And another thing. It's bright sunlight, yet I can see you as clear as day. What happened?"

"You did. You've helped me shed a self-imposed limitation."

As their eyes met, conversation ceased. Unconsciously leaning toward him, Angela again felt drawn, attracted to him.

Then, as if a bucket of cold water had been thrown on her, she sat bolt upright. Shuddering, she remembered the morning's near kiss that had ended in frustration. *Intuition. If I've learned one thing, it's not to confuse spirit with flesh and sinew. No matter how solid-looking.*

As she watched his smile droop, she stifled a sigh, wondering how much was her doing. She forced a smile. "Shed a self-imposed limitation, huh? What do you say we test that theory?"

A glow flickered in his eyes. "What do you mean?"

"This morning you said you had self-imposed limitations on time and space. You've sloughed off the time limitation, now what about the space?"

He shook his head. "I'm still not following."

Standing up, she grinned. "How would you like to go for a ride?"

"You mean in that horseless wagon you drove home?"

"Yup, let's see if you're not only visible at other *times*, but in other *places* besides here."

Ten minutes later, they were sitting in her car. Angela checked that Kitz wasn't behind her, then slowly backed up, turned around, and drove down the caliche driveway. Going twenty-five miles an hour, she turned to see Billy's expression.

"This is exciting!" Grinning from ear to ear, he laughed. "It's like galloping on horseback. Just more comfortable."

At the end of the drive, she waited until a car whizzed by before pulling out. She glanced at Billy and chuckled.

"Your eyes are as big as saucers."

He looked from the retreating car to her. "How fast was that wagon going?"

She shrugged. "Fifty, fifty-five."

"Miles per hour?" His eyes opened even wider.

Nodding, she accelerated. "Hold on to your horses."

As she pulled into traffic, she increased speed gradually, trying to lessen the shock. A quick glance showed Billy pressed against the passenger seat, bracing himself. His jaw slack, he wore an expression of sheer terror.

She swallowed a smile. "Billy, you're dead. Nothing can harm you."

A silly grin tugged at the corners of his mouth. "You're right. What am I worried about?"

Laughing out loud, she stepped on the gas. "Do you recognize any of this land?"

He looked left and right at the many driveways leading off from the road, the fences, the houses in the distance, the billboards and signs. "Barely."

As they rounded a curve, she glanced at him. "How about now?"

When Enchanted Rock came into view, his eyes lit up. "This, I remember."

She gave him a wry smile. "How different this must all seem to you."

"I was shot in 1847."

"A lot's changed since then."

Pursing his lips, he nodded.

Then it occurred to her. "I can see you—here—off the property and in broad daylight. All your limitations must have been self-imposed. Nothing's keeping you from moving on."

He blinked, seeming to absorb the idea.

Angela pulled into a roadside overlook, turned off the engine, and stepped out of the car. When Billy joined her, she smiled.

"I could see you in the car, but you'd gotten in the car while still at the cabin. Just wanted to make sure I could see you *here*."

Nodding, he smiled shyly. "Thank you."

"For what?"

"Proving I have no limitations, other than what I'd placed on myself."

She inhaled. "That could be said for a lot of us."

He glanced at Enchanted Rock. "My grandmother taught me about this place. She said the Apaches considered it sacred because of the Ga'an, the mountain spirits. Dancers could summon them for protection from illness or war."

"Dancers?" Angela studied him.

He nodded. "Four Ga'an dancers wore elaborate crowns or headdresses and painted themselves black and white to represent the four sacred directions. A fifth dancer, painted gray, was a prankster who acted as a messenger, communicating with the spirit people. The ceremony took four days to complete."

"Four dancers, the four directions, four days, what's significant about the number four?" Angela searched his face.

"Grandmother said it was a sacred number to the Apache. According to their creation story, the world was created in four days, so all rituals used the number four. Even their day was divided into four parts."

"No minutes or hours?" She glanced at the sunset's vibrant peach, coral, and golden tones. "Couldn't they have used the sun to tell time?"

"They used the morning star."

"Venus," Angela nodded, "which can also be the evening star."

"When it reached its highest point in the sky, it marked the beginning of the new day."

"Like our midnight."

"Grandmother also told me about the vision quests on Enchanted Rock."

"Vision quests." Angela's eyes opened wide. Then she glanced at the rock reflecting lilac-pink in the sunset's fiery glow. "Here?"

He nodded. "They believed if you prayed for a vision before spending the night on Enchanted Rock, your dreams would advise you."

"Really." She looked at the rock, trying to imagine how many people through the ages had gone there, looking for insights, messages. Again Kitz came to mind.

Her cell phone rang and buzzed simultaneously, giving Angela a start.

Billy flinched at the sound. "What's that?"

"Just my phone." She shrugged as she lifted it from its holster. Then it occurred to her how foreign it must be to him. "It's a way to communicate—"

The ringing interrupted her explanation.

"I'll tell you later." Unlocking the phone, she answered.

"Hey there," said Kio's voice.

Angela felt a warmth tiptoe into her body and penetrate her soul. "Hey, yourself." Smiling, she stepped away from Billy and turned her back. "How's the new job going?"

"It's finally making enough sense that I can come up for air now and then." He chuckled. Then his tone softened. "Sorry I haven't called in a couple days. Adjusting to the midnight shift's been harder than I thought."

"No worries." She glanced over her shoulder at Billy. *Was that the attraction? I was just lonesome?* She took a deep breath, letting the thought sink in. "Glad we're connecting now."

"What've you been up to?"

Angela told him about Agua Purificación. Then she mentioned Kitz and Billy. She hesitated about confessing the kiss that never occurred. *I* was *attracted, tempted, but nothing happened.* "Sorry. What?" Penitent about daydreaming, she listened as Kio repeated his question.

"How would you like some company next weekend?"

"Yes!" Surprised at her enthusiasm, she chuckled self-consciously. "Kio, I miss you. I can't wait to see you."

"Me, either." The warmth in his voice came over the phone. "I flexed my time and got Friday off, so I'll see you mid-morning."

"Perfect, I'll talk to Tulah's family. They rent cabins, B&Bs. I'll bet they'll have something."

"Sounds great."

Wincing, she hesitated. "Darn. I'll have to work a few hours Saturday and Sunday afternoons." Her voice brightened as an idea occurred. "Maybe you'd like to take the winery tour? It'd be a way to spend time together while I work."

"It's sounding better and better, but I've gotta go. Talk with you in the morning. Love you."

"You, too." Hunching her shoulders, she hugged herself as she put away the phone.

A moment later, Billy's voice broke through her thoughts. "What was that?"

"That was Kio, my . . . my fiancé."

He shook his head. "*What* was that?"

"This?" She touched her cell on her belt. "Haven't you seen me use this before?"

As he shook his head, it occurred to her. *With his reverse schedule, Kio and I usually call after I leave for work or school.* "It's a way to talk over distance."

Billy squinted. "How?"

She took a deep breath. *How do I explain telecommunication?* "I don't know the science behind it, but voices carry through the air. Phones pick up their sound waves."

"You mean like you heard voices when you were with Kitz?"

She grinned. "No, nothing like that." *How could he relate to telephones?* Then she remembered history. "It's like the telegraph, but we use our voices, not Morse code."

Nodding, he seemed to accept it. Then he peered into her eyes. "So you're engaged?"

She held up her left hand, letting the sun's last glimmer reflect off her ring. "Yup."

Again Billy nodded, this time more slowly. "I thought that ring was just today's fashion."

She gave him a sympathetic half smile. "It's more than that."

"So you're spoken for, promised to another man."

Lips pursed, she nodded as she appraised him. *Another man? Is that how he feels?*

He glanced at the sky. "It's nearly dark. I s'pose it's time to head back."

The following Wednesday, after the last class, Angela packed a bag, coaxed Frank into his carrying cage, and drove to Fredericksley. Kio called her just as she pulled into the cabin's driveway.

"Can't wait to see you Friday." His smile came through his voice.

Like steaming coffee on a frosty morning, his warmth instantly recharged her. "Me, either." Then she remembered. "The Bankheads' B&Bs were completely booked for this weekend. In fact, all the hotels, motels, and B&B are full thanks to the bluebonnets in bloom . . . but I've got an idea." Her voice rose on the last phrase, lilting.

He laughed softly. "I'm liking the sound of this already."

"How 'bout I save the details for when you get here?"

This time he teased. "Keeping me in suspense, huh?"

"Yup!" She laughed, happy with life, in love with Kio, relieved her classes were over for the week, and very glad to be back at the cabin's tranquility. She glanced at the welcoming green setting and sighed. "Love you."

"You, too."

Before she had unlocked the front door, she saw Kitz peeking out from behind the persimmon bushes.

"Hello, little man. Did you miss me?"

In answer, he paced back and forth, his sign meaning he either was hungry, wanted to say hello, or both.

Chuckling, she let herself in as she called over her shoulder. "Let me get Frank's water bowl and litter box set up. Then I'll be right out with your feed."

A half hour later, she walked next door to the Bankheads' house. Brooke opened the door with a smile and a hug.

"Glad you're back." She opened the door wider. "How 'bout a glass of iced tea?"

Feeling she had come home, Angela eagerly stepped inside and looked around the cozy home. "It's good to be back." Her half smile twisted, she laughed at herself. "Sometimes, I feel Fredericksley is more 'home' than San Antonio." *Especially since I don't have Mom's house to go home to, anymore.*

"A lot's happened since you left."

"Really? What?"

Brooke set two glasses of iced tea on the kitchen table. "For one thing, the drought situation's worse, which impacts the next. Without water, wine production's off, which cuts into the winery's income. To make ends meet, Mom and Dad are thinking of putting the old Hall property on the market."

Angela's eyes opened wide. "The cabin?" At Brooke's nod, she thought about Kitz, the turtle, and all the wildlife the stream supported. She thought of Billy and the promise she had made him about protecting that stream. "I had no idea things had reached this point."

Brooke bit her bottom lip. "My parents don't like to spread gloom. They waited as long as they could, but they said now they don't have a choice. They're meeting with the realtor this morning."

Angela felt her spirits droop. Suddenly the sunny, spring day seemed to have clouded over. She sighed, thinking out loud. "What can we do?"

Brooke shrugged her shoulders. "We've all been asking ourselves the same question, but everything comes down to money."

"Anyone home?" Kelby and Tulah called as they came in the front door.

"In here," Brooke called.

"Hey, you're back." Tulah gave Angela a quick hug. "What time did you get in?"

Angela checked her watch. "About an hour ago. I thought you were working at the winery today."

"Business was so slow, Mom said to bring Kelby home. No sense in stressing her knee." She rolled her eyes. "Wednesdays are never busy, but today the winery was dead."

"I just told Angela the news about selling the old Hall property." Brooke made a sour face.

"Isn't there any way around it? Anything we could do?" Angela looked from one face to the next.

Tulah shrugged, but her grim expression spoke volumes.

Eyes blazing, Kelby rolled over on her knee scooter. "There is something we can do. We can fight to keep it."

Admiration growing for her, Angela watched Kelby's enthusiasm bubble over. "How? What do you suggest?"

"We know that cabin's old. Maybe we could get it listed on the National Register of Historic Places. How old is that place, anyway?"

"Billy was shot in 1847—"

"Billy?" Kelby studied her. "Who's Billy?"

Angela avoided Tulah's suspicious grin. "William Hall died on this land in 1847. Penateka Comanches still hunted here. Buffalo roamed, and cattle barons ruled this land then."

"How do you know so much about it?" Kelby's skeptical eyes challenged her.

"I . . . uh, I did a little research."

"I thought so." Wearing an ah-ha grin, Tulah turned toward her sisters. "Angela has a gift. She can see spirits—"

"What?" Brooke's eyes widened.

"Are you serious?" Kelby rolled closer.

"So tell me," Tulah continued, "have you seen a ghost at the cabin, or haven't you?"

Sighing, Angela saw no way out of answering directly. She nodded.

"I knew it. *I knew it!*" Wearing a gleeful smile, Tulah slapped her hands together. "So the cabin's haunted, after all?"

Again, Angela nodded.

"His name's Billy?" Kelby's eyebrows shot up.

"William's his Christian name, but . . ." Angela grimaced, guessing at Billy's aggravation if others bothered him. She sighed uneasily. "Let's just say he values his privacy. *A lot.*"

"So, when can we meet him?"

"Seriously, if we want his help, I wouldn't tweak his nose." Angela appealed with a half smile. "Let me approach him alone. I think he'll be more cooperative." She tried to change the subject. "I'm curious. Why do you think listing the cabin on the National Register of Historic Places would help?"

When the conversation's focus changed, Kelby's face became animated. "I did a little research myself. First of all, if it's listed, it'll allow a tax break, and second, it may be eligible for federal grants, especially if it's designated as a landmark."

"What happens to the property's water rights once it gets listed as a historic place?" Angela began wondering if she could work this into her term paper on water rights.

"It's got to be a minimum of fifty years old."

Angela sniffed. "It's over a hundred and seventy years old. What else?"

"It has to look pretty much as it had—at least from the outside."

Angela raised her eyebrows. "The inside's been redone, but the outside looks rustic." She made a mental note to ask Billy about any inconsistencies. "What else?"

"Most importantly, is the property significant? Was it associated with anything or anyone historically? Could it hold clues to the past through archeological investigation?"

Angela hemmed. "That's harder to prove. We'd need documentation—evidence of some sort—but the idea's worth exploring." She turned to the others. "Any other ideas?"

They silently looked at each other, shaking their heads.

Angela took a deep breath. "In that case, let's all research this property, see if we can't find some historical link." With a firm nod, she added, "I know where I'm starting."

Kelby's eyes lit up. "With Billy? Can I come?"

Angela shook her head. "He doesn't like company, and if we want to learn from him, we can't pressure him. Let me find out if he knows anything that will help."

"I hope he can." Kelby frowned. "Agua Purificación's at it again."

Angela's ears perked. "What are they doing now?"

"Besides setting up offices near Hall Road and drilling twenty unregulated commercial wells, AP's just announced it's entered a fifty-year contract to supply five million gallons of water *per day* to Boerne and to the Pecos Water District." Kelby sniffed. "Fifty years? At that rate, I doubt the aquifer will last fifteen."

Angela shook her head. "Is there any good news?"

“The Barron County Commissioners Court did pass a resolution. They’re creating legislation to oversee the groundwater conservation districts, both the Barron and North Edwards areas. And it gave the Barron District default jurisdiction.” With her puckered brow, her smile looked closer to a grimace. “It’s a start.”

When Angela returned to the cabin, she saw Kitz waiting behind the persimmon bushes. “Hey, you.” She did a double take and then took a closer look at his head. “Your antlers are sprouting.” Grinning, she lightly ran her hand over the bony protrusions.

In response, he playfully bunted her hand, seeming to want more.

She laughed as she rubbed his head. “Oh, you like that, do you?”

Feigning a scowl, Billy appeared in the greenery’s shadows. “You’re supposed wean him off humans,” he paused, “not touch him.”

“I know, but he’s so affectionate. It’s hard to keep my hands off him.” She sighed. “You’re right. It’s more important that he’s reintroduced to the wild. I’ll try not to touch him again.” Then remembering the task at hand, she grimaced.

“What’s wrong?” He took a step closer.

“I have some news you’re not going to like.”

His face hardened. “What?”

“Long story short, the Bankheads put this property up for sale.”

“What?!” His eyes narrowed to slits. “They can’t do that.”

“They had to—”

“It’s not theirs.”

She gave him a sympathetic smile. “Legally, it is.”

“Why are they selling?”

“So they can pay their bills.” Speaking softly, she added, “This drought is costing them their business, and they have a family to support.” She thought of Brooke. “Several.”

"It doesn't matter. They can't. I homesteaded—"

"Maybe there's a way around it."

"I'm listening." He crossed his arms over his chest.

She swallowed a smile at his body language. Then she told him about Kelby's idea. "Do you know of any historical event that happened here?"

"The Apache and Comanche tribes used this stream as a campground."

"Is there any proof?"

He shrugged. "I s'pose we could find a couple arrowheads."

She rubbed her chin. "Can you think of anything that's documented or could have enough archeological significance to support this being designated a national landmark?"

He thought for a moment. "There is one place I discovered that you might find interesting."

"Can you take me there?"

He nodded. "It's dark there. Do you have a torch?"

"A torch?" Angela squinted, trying to guess what he meant. "A flashlight? Yes, there's one in the drawer."

Billy led her toward the stream as Kitz followed, bringing up the rear.

Angela studied the familiar scene and frowned. "There's a cave here? Where?"

He chuckled. "Near here. Keep following along the streambed."

Another ten-minute walk, scrambling over stony hills and piled river rocks, led them to an indentation beneath a rocky outcropping.

Angela looked at the small depression. "I thought you said it was a cave. This is just a tiny dip in the ground." She made a face. "I would've walked right past it."

"Most people have." Swallowing a smile, he looked for a gap between the rocks. "Shine your light down there."

As the beam connected with the cave floor several feet below, she caught her breath. Reflecting the light, piles of white bones and what looked like a tusk came into view.

She glanced up at him. “Billy, what is this?”

“My grandmother told me it’s a burial ground.”

“A cemetery?” She recoiled.

He shook his head. “No, an ancient animal graveyard. A friend lowered me in there on a rope once when I was a boy. It holds bones and teeth I’d never seen before or since.”

“Do you mind if I share the location of this place?”

“If it’ll help save the stream, with my blessing.”

Hide and Horn

Other states are carved or born; Texas grew from hide and horn.

– *Bertha Hart Nance, 1932*

Over dinner, the Bankheads announced they had placed the old Hall property on the market that morning.

Conversation ceased until Tulah voiced their thoughts. "It's one thing to talk about it happening in the future, but another when it happens."

Kelby shared her idea about getting the land placed on the National Register of Historic Places.

"That's a fine idea," her mother glanced at her father, "but that takes time. Not sure how long this property will take to sell, but I doubt there's time for all the paperwork to go through."

The phone rang, and Mr. Bankhead took the call.

Angela thought the lull would be an opportune time to bring up the cave. "Actually, something happened today—"

"You're not going to believe this," said Mr. Bankhead, returning to the table. "Someone's already made an offer on the property, sight unseen."

"What?!" Kelby paled.

"Who?" Mrs. Bankhead looked at her husband. "Anyone we know?"

His forehead creased as he shook his head. "I don't recognize the name, Starr."

Her lips white, barely moving, Tulah asked, "Astin Starr?"

"Yes, that's it." Her father turned toward her. "Do you know him?"

Tulah caught Angela's eye, then looked away. "He toured the winery."

"Huh." He looked thoughtful. "Is he from around here?"

Again, Tulah glanced at Angela. "He just moved here."

"Where from?" Kelby watched her.

"Houston."

"What's he do?" Kelby's eyes narrowed.

Tulah lifted a hand loosely, palm up, as if indifferent. "I don't know. He's an attorney or something."

"You seem to know a lot about him." Kelby eyed her suspiciously.

Tulah shrugged.

Kelby's expression changed as she began putting the pieces together. "Just moved here from Houston, he's an attorney . . ." Her eyes flashing, she challenged Tulah. "He wouldn't work for Agua Purificación, would he?"

Tulah shook her head. "He works for the Porter law firm—"

"From what I've read online, it's the same thing." Kelby's eyes were dark, accusing. "How come you know so much about him?"

Again, Tulah shrugged.

"If there's anything you know about this prospective buyer, don't you think you should share it?" Raising his eyebrow, Mr. Bankhead spoke softly, appealing to his daughter's sense of fairness.

Tulah slumped in her chair. She sighed. "I've gone out with him a couple times." Then brightening, she ventured a half smile. "In fact, he's agreed to help Texas Mustangs *pro bono*. I think he's—"

"After the water rights," snapped Kelby.

Tulah inhaled. "I was about to say, he's a fine addition to the community."

Her tone antagonistic, Kelby faced her. "And I think—"

"Girls!" Mrs. Bankhead looked from one to the other. "First Corinthians 16:14: Do all your work in love."

Kelby took a deep breath. Her eyes dark, she glanced at her mother. "I can't help it. This guy is AP's hired gun. He's just after the water rights, and we're the stooges." She turned to Tulah. "And you." She gave a disgusted sigh. "You're fraternizing with the enemy."

Tulah raised her voice. "He's *not* the enemy!"

"Girls!" Mr. Bankhead glanced at the faces around the table. "We've put the property up for sale. If Mr. Starr or anyone else wants to purchase it, it's his choice." He turned toward Kelby. "He's the buyer, not the enemy."

Kelby mumbled, "One and the same." Then she met his eyes. "But if there was a way to come up with the money, so you didn't have to sell, would you take it off the market?"

Her parents exchanged a look. "Sure," said Mrs. Bankhead, "if we could come up with two million dollars."

Kelby's eyes widened. In a whisper, she asked, "Did I hear you right? Two million?"

Her mother nodded. "That land's been in our family for four," she looked at Brooke's swollen belly, "nearly five generations. Though we inherited it, and it probably didn't cost a fraction of that all those years ago, its value's increased over the years."

Her eyes wide with wonder, Tulah glanced at Kelby. "To us, it was just our swimming hole, a place to explore, climb trees, and learn how to ride horses." Grimacing, she turned toward her parents. "It has a lot of sentimental value, but I had no idea it was worth anywhere near that much money."

"While you girls were growing up, your father and I thought it important you have a safe place to play, but now . . ." She looked at her daughters. "Brooke's married, with her first child on the way. You're going into your last year at UTSA, and Kelby will go off to college next year." She glanced at her husband. "It's time to sell that parcel."

Mr. Bankhead gave them a wry grin. "Besides, with the drought, we don't have a choice. It's either sell the property, or lose the winery. This is the land's value today. If the drought continues, that could change."

His wife glanced at him. "It was a good thing Bob contacted us when he did."

Kelby sat up straight. "Bob?"

"Bob Anderson from Anderson Realty," said her mother.

"You're telling me this wasn't your idea, that a realtor contacted you about selling it?" Kelby's eyes narrowed.

"That's right." Mrs. Bankhead nodded. "Your father and I had been thinking of it, but when Bob contacted us, telling us the market value, we realized the income would more than pay off the winery's debt."

"So this wasn't your idea." Squinting, Kelby worked her jaw. "The realtor contacted you, and the day you put the land up for sale, he calls you with a buyer?"

Mrs. Bankhead glanced at her husband and back. "Not six hours after we signed the contract."

Taking a deep breath, Kelby looked at the faces around the table. "We've been set up."

Angela raised her eyebrows, silently agreeing, but she kept her thoughts to herself.

"Kelby's right," said Brooke. "This is happening way too fast to be a coincidence. This realtor and shyster are in cahoots."

"If you're referring to Astin Starr, he's no shyster." Tulah's face was pale, her lips were white, and her chest heaved. "If Astin wants to move next door, I say more power to him."

Kelby's eyebrows shot up. "Astin?"

Before Tulah had time to answer, Angela spoke up. "Hadn't you said, if we could raise the money through grants," she glanced at Kelby, "we might be able to save the land, save the water?"

Kelby nodded. "If the property's significant in some way, associated with something historical, or if it has archeological value, maybe we could get it listed on the National Register of Historic Places."

"Having it listed wouldn't guarantee grants or funding, and even if the property qualifies, all that takes time." Mrs. Bankhead glanced from her husband to her daughters. "Sorry, girls, but it sounds like we have a ready buyer. I say strike while the iron's hot. Ephesians 5:16-18, Make the best of the present time, for it is a wicked age."

Angela debated whether to enter the argument. *I don't have the luxury of time to be a timid spectator*. Smiling, she brightened her tone to suggest she was changing the topic. "I came upon something interesting this afternoon."

Mrs. Bankhead politely responded. "What was that?"

"I found what looks like a cave. When I pointed my flashlight down a tiny shaft beneath boulders, a crawlspace, I saw what appeared to be bones . . . even possibly a tusk."

"What?" Kelby's face broke out in a grin. "This may be exactly what we need." She turned to Tulah. "Isn't Clay a caver?"

Tulah grimaced. "He likes to explore caves." She rolled her eyes. "And he's a geology major with a minor in archaeology."

"That's perfect." Kelby turned toward Angela. "Can you show us this cave?"

"Sure." She gave Kelby a sympathetic smile. "Unfortunately, it's over rocky ground. Your knee scooter wouldn't be able to handle the terrain."

Kelby grimaced. "Kinda figured that." She turned toward Tulah. "Can you invite Clay to go along?"

Tulah hesitated but nodded. "I'll text him."

"My fiancé, Kio, will be here this weekend, and he likes caves. Maybe he can join us." Wearing a grin, Angela glanced at the family. "Which reminds me, could we borrow some camping gear?"

Kio pulled in the driveway at ten Friday morning. The first to spot him, Frank let Angela know by mewing and rubbing against the screen door.

"Anyone home?" Kio called from the porch.

"Come on in." Angela opened the door and held out her arms. "Oh, it's good to see you." She closed her eyes as he wrapped her in his arms and kissed her. "Good to feel you," she murmured, holding him, gripping his shoulders and back.

Billy crossed her mind, but Kio's flesh-and-blood presence instantly reconnected her to the moment.

When they broke apart, Kio held her at arm's length, looking at her. "It's good to see *you*. I've missed you, you know. West Texas can get lonely."

Again, Billy came to mind as a sheepish grin spread across her face. "The Hill Country can get lonely, too." Then, she glanced at the clock. "You're early."

"I started early and left straight from work." As he ran his hand across his chin, Angela heard the stubble. "Mind if I shower and shave to wake up—and clean up?"

Grinning, she pointed the way. "Extra towels are in the closet."

"Got your text and came right over." Clay beside her, Tulah spoke through the screen door.

"Come on in." Angela gestured toward the breakfast bar as she opened the door. "Kio's been up all night. Thought it might be a good idea to have some coffee and kolaches before we get started."

"Caffeine and sugar always work for me." Clay grinned. Then as they waited for Kio, he looked around the cabin, checking the kitchenette and the limestone wall with its river-rock fireplace. He peeked into the bedroom, glancing at knotty-pine car siding and the varnished, hand-hewn furniture.

"Your family did a nice job updating this old cabin." As if thinking aloud, he muttered, "Wouldn't mind living here myself."

Tulah did a double take but said nothing.

His hair still wet from the shower, Kio joined them. "Morning, Tulah, Clay."

Angela again gestured toward the bar stools. "Have a seat, everybody."

The moment Kio sat down, the cat jumped on his lap. "Hey, buddy, how're you doing?" In answer, Frank rubbed against him, purring.

Angela laughed. "Looks like I'm not the only one who missed you."

Nibbling at a kolache, Tulah raised her eyebrows. "These are delicious. Did you make them?"

Angela grinned. "Get real." Kio caught her eye, and they began laughing.

"Angela does a lot of things well," he winced, "but baking—"

"Or cooking—" She winked at Tulah and Clay, including them in the friendly banter.

"Let's just say those aren't skills she's developed." Kio's eyes twinkled.

Over coffee and pastries, they updated Kio about the water and property situations.

Then Clay turned to Angela. "What I'm wondering is how you found this cave."

She glanced at Tulah. "You didn't tell him?"

Like a "monkey in the middle", Clay looked from one to other. "Tell me what?"

Tulah took a deep breath. "Angela can speak to the resident ghost."

"You're serious?" Clearly skeptical, Clay scrutinized her.

"Dead serious." Angela's mouth grim, she nodded.

"Then it's not a tale? This place really is haunted?" Clay looked from her to Tulah.

"Yup."

"Huh." Sitting back, Clay thumped his hand against his forehead. "So you think this cave might be important archaeologically?"

"Important, yes." Angela thought it through. "But important enough to get funding in time to keep the property from being sold?" She took a deep breath. "That's asking a lot."

"There's only one way to find out." Clay brought out four headlamps and four pairs of work gloves from his backpack. "We'll need these if we're going underground." Then he gestured to the porch. "I left a pick ax, a couple shovels, and a rope outside. We may need those, too."

Angela nodded. "As I recall, several large rocks blocked the entrance to what looked like an oversized rabbit hole. We'll need to move those aside to access it." Then she glanced at them. "Everyone ready?"

"Now's as good a time as any." Clay handed out the gloves and headlamps. Outside, he and Kio picked up the tools and rope. Then he glanced at Angela. "Lead on."

With a nod, she started toward the stream. Kitz peeked out from behind persimmon bushes but scampered away at their approach. When Kio saw the stream, he set down the tools and stared at the scene. Dappled with sunlight, the sparkling water reflected the regal cypress trees above, creating a magical landscape where anything seemed plausible, possible.

"This creek's a hidden jewel." He turned toward Tulah. "How long has it been in your family?"

"Almost five generations if you count my sister Brooke's unborn baby."

"It must be tough selling a piece of family history." Kio shook his head.

Tulah glanced from him to Clay and nodded. "My sisters and I grew up splashing in this stream." She pointed to a sturdy branch overhanging the water. "A knotted rope used to hang there. We'd climb that tree, swing out over the water, and then shrieking at the tops of our lungs, let go and jump in." Smiling at the memory, she caught Clay's eye.

"I remember that rope." Grinning and wincing simultaneously, he set down his load. "One time, I got my leg tangled and ended up getting a rope burn on the back of my knee."

Tulah broke out laughing at the memory.

Trying to keep a straight face, he assumed an indignant expression. "That hurt."

"I remember." Tulah came down with a case of the giggles. "You walked funny for a week."

"Nice." Clay appealed to Angela and Kio. "You see what I've had to put up with. No wonder my childhood was warped." His eyes twinkling, he turned toward Tulah. "But as I recall . . ." Wearing a mischievous grin, he walked around the tree. "It's still here!"

"What is?" Tulah followed him, Angela and Kio on her heels.

Clay pointed to a heart carved into the tree, the initials barely visible. "This was where we pledged to marry each other after we graduated from college."

Tulah's smile faded. "That was in eighth grade." She grimaced as she nodded toward the stream. "A lot of water's flowed over these rocks since then . . ."

Inhaling, Clay's expression turned stony.

"Maybe we'd better keep moving." Angela checked her watch. "Kio's been up all night, working—"

"Yeah, let's move on. No sense dwelling on the past . . ." Her face expressionless, Tulah pushed past Clay.

Angela caught Kio's eye. He shrugged. Then he noticed something on the ground. He picked up a rock, peered at it, dipped it in the stream, and looked at it again. "Anyone know what kind of stone this is?"

Clay peeked and then turned it over in his hand. “Could be wrong, but I’d say you’ve found a Texas blue topaz.”

“The state gem.” Angela smiled wistfully.

Kio watched her. “How would you know that?”

“My father—that is, my adopted father gave my mother a set of Lone Star cut blue topaz earrings.” She blinked. “She left them to me.”

Kio gave her a warm smile. “If this turns out to be a blue topaz, it might be your ‘something blue’ at our wedding.”

Angela grinned. “What a great idea.”

Winking, Kio dropped the stone in his pocket, picked up his tools, and then gestured with his chin. “After you.”

She led them along the streambed, retracing Billy’s steps. Ten minutes later, she found the rocky indentation.

Tulah looked around. “Where’s the cave?”

With a grin, Angela pointed to the depression beneath a rocky outcropping. “Down there.” Kneeling, she pointed her flashlight through a gap in the stone heap. Again, the beam reflected off the piled, white bones.

“Whoa!” Clay took off his Stetson. “Would you look at that?” Pulling on his cowhide work gloves, he began moving the rocks aside. “Let me get a better idea of the width of this crawlspace.”

The four of them began hauling off the smaller rocks and rolling the boulders aside.

Clay put on his headlamp and leaned into the hole. As if diving, his hands and arms leading the way, he went in head first, contorting his shoulders, wiggling through the tiny crevice until he disappeared.

A startled look on her face, Tulah scrambled to the edge and shouted down the hole. “Are you all right? Clay? Clay?” When she got no response, she glanced up at Angela, her face white. “I’m going in after him.”

She put on her headlamp. Then, her hands and arms leading the way, Tulah slithered halfway through the hole. Only her hips, legs, and feet showed above ground. With a shriek, her other half slid in.

"Tulah?" Angela leaned over the hole and called in. "Are you all right?" She glanced at Kio. "Tulah?"

A grin on his face, Clay poked his grimy head out of the hole. "We're fine. I was just funning you." Angela heard a whap as Clay flinched. "Ow! Cut that out." His head disappeared.

"What's going on?" Angela again glanced at Kio, not sure what to think.

This time, Tulah's smudged face showed above ground. "That's what I get for worrying about him. While I was wriggling into the cave, he kissed me. Thought the whole thing of scaring us was one big joke."

Angela studied her. "Then you're both all right?"

"Yup." Tulah nodded. Then she gave them a mischievous grin. "Come on down. The weather's fine."

"Just to be on the safe side," said Kio, adjusting a device, "I'm getting our GPS coordinates. If anything should go wrong underground, I want someone to know where we are."

"Good idea." Tulah dipped back in the cave and reappeared moments later, her phone in her hand. Tell me what they are, and I'll text them to my sister."

Kio then tied one end of the rope to a tree and handed Tulah the other end. "It's always good to have a safety line."

Angela looked at him with new respect. "Where'd you learn all this stuff? I though you spent all your time in outer space, working at the observatory."

His face relaxed into an easy grin. "I like inner space, too. Caves have always fascinated me." He winked. "Now that a few precautions are in place, how would you like to see the cave?"

The thought momentarily terrified Angela. The whole idea had seemed exciting until she looked at the tiny hole, realizing she was going headfirst down into the ground. *What if . . .? What if what? I never come out? I can't breathe?* She took a deep breath. *This is ridiculous.*

"Anything the matter?" Kio watched her closely.

"No." She took another deep breath. Then another.

"Keep doing that, and you're going to hyperventilate." He studied her. "You sure you're okay?"

"Yeah. Fine." Angela rolled her eyes. *I don't even convince myself.* She took another deep breath.

"Okay, what's wrong?"

"I don't know. The thought of diving into that hole suddenly scares me."

Kio started laughing. "Ghosts, spirits don't bother you, but the dark does? Don't tell me you're afraid of the dark." He touched the light strapped to his forehead. "That's what these headlamps are for."

Angela shook her head. "Not the dark, it's the close space."

"You're claustrophobic?" His eyes opened wide. "Really?"

Shrugging, she turned up her palms. "Maybe." She swallowed. "I've just never gone into the earth before."

"Sure you have. You've gone into caves with me several times."

"*Walked* into caves with you, not gone in headfirst, wondering what we'd find."

"Look, this is the reason I'm going in last." Kio gave her an encouraging smile. "Try it. If you get in there and feel uncomfortable, I'll be right here to help you out."

Angela sighed. "As long as you put it that way, let me give it a shot." She smiled her thanks.

"Hey, think how I feel. I just took a shower, and now I'm going to get covered in dirt."

Managing a rueful smile, Angela put her arms together the way Tulah and Clay had, and began slithering through the hole. Halfway inside, she used her hands to guide the rest of the way. Two or three feet below the surface, she pulled and crawled her way onto a ledge. Then she looked down. Another two or three feet below was a rocky path leading to the cave's floor.

"You all right down there?" called Kio.

Grinning at Tulah and Clay in the dim light, she turned around and stuck her head up through the hole. "Yup, just had to get past that scared point. I'm fine now. Come on in." She slipped back onto the ledge and called, "Join us down under."

Small pebbles and dust preceded Kio's hands, arms, and head. Then he wriggled as his shoulders twisted through the small opening, his torso and legs following.

"Let's give our eyes a few minutes to adjust to the light level," said Clay's voice.

In the gloom, Angela could see the bright points of light that were their headlamps, but she had trouble making out faces or expressions. Visibility in the cave was no more than a few feet.

Gradually, Angela could see what looked like a path of river rock, leading down between two walls of stone, roughly four feet apart. Then she saw the white bones reflecting their dim light from the cave floor below. "There must be hundreds of bones down there."

"More like thousands." Clay's face came into focus as her eyes adjusted. "Can everyone see well enough to venture in?"

As each nodded, Angela could see their bobbing headlamps.

"You probably already know this," said Clay, "but try to touch as little as possible. Judging from what I've seen at this distance, Angela's found an archaeological treasure trove. Let's try not to contaminate it."

"You think this might be important enough to," Tulah hesitated, "to get grants to preserve it? Keep things the way they are?"

"I know a professor, who might be interested in these artifacts." Clay's smile came through his voice. "Come on. Let's take a closer look."

They carefully made their way down the steep slope, single file. Clay took the lead, Tulah and Angela followed, and Kio brought up the rear. Because of the loose river rocks, footing was shaky. Angela slipped once, but as she reached out to balance herself, Kio caught her.

"Take your time, slow and steady." Kio gave her an encouraging hug.

A few minutes later, they arrived at the floor. Half covered with soil, large caches of bones were strewn everywhere. Skulls with teeth, spinal columns with vertebrae were jumbled with rib cages and femurs.

"What happened here?" Angela looked to Clay for the answer.

"My guess is the opening was much larger eons ago. These animals ventured in, couldn't get out, and then died here."

"But why are their bones so heaped and shuffled together?"

"Again I'm guessing this area's been flooded." He pointed to the position of the bones. "See how they're all facing in roughly the same direction, as if water flow carried and then partially buried them?"

Angela nodded. "Can you identify any of them?"

Clay gave a thoughtful sigh. "I'm no authority, but this one looks like Equus."

"Horse?"

He shrugged. "Horse, burro, *but if my hunch is right*, an ancient relative of the modern horse."

She pointed to a rounded object. "Is that what I think it is? A tusk?"

Clay took a deep breath. "That sure looks like a mammoth tusk to me." He brought out his phone and began taking pictures. "I'm going to send these to my old professor. Before I say too much, I'd like to get Doctor West's opinion." Then he noticed an unusual spine. "If I'm right, that's a camel."

"What?" Angela squinted.

"A kind of extinct camel that used to roam around Texas."

"There were camels in Texas?" Tulah looked at him.

"Yeah, about sixty-five, seventy thousand years ago." Clay grinned. "I saw the skeleton of one in Waco last semester."

"Guys, I don't mean to be a party-pooper, but I'm fading fast." Kio stifled a yawn. "If I don't take a nap soon, you're going to have to carry me out of here."

Angela rubbed his shoulders. "Poor guy, how long have you been up?"

"Roughly thirty-six hours. I don't mean to be a wet blanket, but that's all I want to do." He gave her a sleepy grin. "Curl up with a blanket."

Angela turned to Clay. "Think you have enough snapshots to document this place?"

He grinned. "More than enough to stir his curiosity."

Angela saw Billy out of the corner of her eye, nodding. She did a double take, but he was gone.

Clay glanced at Kio. "There isn't really room to switch places without disturbing the bones. Want to lead us out?"

"He who is last shall be first." Grinning, Kio did an about-face. "Onward and upward."

Climbing the loose rocks proved harder than descending. Angela gripped the rope, but at times she practically crawled, using all fours to steady herself. When they finally made it to the ledge, Kio climbed out first, offering a helping hand as the others hoisted themselves up.

"That rope was a good idea." Angela gave him a grateful smile.

"Yeah," said Tulah. "It gave us some leverage."

"Glad it helped," said Kio, "but for now I think we'd better remove it and cover the opening. We wouldn't want any kids or critters falling in."

"Or trespassers snooping." Clay grimaced. "Other than telling Professor West and Tulah's family, I think we should keep this to ourselves."

"Agreed." Angela nodded.

A fifteen-minute walk brought them back to the cabin.

"Guys, it was nice seeing you again, but I've got to take a nap." Kio hid a yawn behind his hand. "Seriously, I can't keep my eyes open."

"No worries." Tulah hugged him and Angela. "I can't wait to tell my family the good news."

"Let's not get our hopes up too much, just yet." Clay gave Tulah a lopsided smile. "Let's wait at least till we hear back from Professor West."

"Hurry up and send those pictures." Tulah playfully punched his arm.

Waving, grinning, Clay called from the path. "Maybe we can all do something together tomorrow?"

Again, Tulah did a double take but said nothing. With a wave, she and Clay walked off.

Kio turned toward Angela with a sarcastic grin. "A lot of good that shower did this morning, other than wake me up." He glanced at his arms, his clothes. "Mind if I take another?"

"Be my guest. *Please.*" She glanced down at her own clothes. "When you're done, I'd better take one myself."

While he showered, she decided to leave Kitz's feed by the persimmon bushes.

Billy appeared. "Who's in my cabin?"

Raising her eyebrow, Angela took a deep breath. "We've been through this before. It's not your cabin. It belongs—"

"Who's buck naked in my cabin?" He glared at her.

"My friend's showering in the Bankheads' cabin."

"I'll see about that—"

"Billy, you'll do no such thing. Kio's my guest, as I'm the Bankheads' guest. He has every right to be here." Angela gazed at him steadily. "He does, and you don't."

"It's my cabin."

She crossed her arms. "Not anymore." Then remembering his reason for being attached to the land, she smiled. "Besides, Kio's helping us find some way to protect the water. If anything, you should consider him a friend."

He spoke slowly. "A friend wouldn't kiss you."

Her eyebrow shot up. "He's my fiancé. We're going to be—"

"Next," shouted Kio from the doorway.

"Be right there," she called back. She looked for Billy, but he was gone.

When Angela finished her shower, she found Kio fast asleep in the armchair, Frank curled up on his lap. She quietly closed the screen door behind her and drove next door.

Even before she knocked, she could hear the Bankheads' discussion.

Kelby opened the door. "So you found a way to save the water."

"Well—"

"Let Angela in before you start bombarding her with questions." Mrs. Bankhead smiled at her.

Angela grinned back. "Clay seems to think the pile of bones we found is an archaeological treasure trove. I hope his professor friend shares his opinion."

"Then you haven't heard the latest," said Tulah as she and Clay came around the corner.

"Doctor West wants to see it," said Clay. "He'll be here tomorrow."

"Really?" Angela glanced from their smiling faces to the strained expressions Tulah's parents wore. "Then what's the problem?"

Tulah took a deep breath. "Astin's already made an offer—"

"At a thousand dollars above the asking price," said her father. "No haggling, no negotiating, he's paying the full price, plus the extra thousand."

"He's put down earnest money." Tula's mother exchanged a look with her husband.

"And cash, no dealing with mortgage companies," said her father. "He'll bring a cashier's check to the closing."

Angela looked at them, comparing the worried expressions of Clay and the sisters to the relaxed smiles of the parents. She took a deep breath. *What about my promise to Billy?* "Have you accepted the offer?"

"Not yet." Tulah spoke for her parents.

"Can you stall?" Angela looked at the Bankheads. "How long can you wait before accepting?"

"Typically, three days." Mrs. Bankhead exchanged another look with her husband.

Angela wracked her mind for ideas. "Do you have any options?"

"They can accept, reject, or counter their offer with specific terms," said Tulah.

"Realistically, we have one option." Mr. Bankhead's expression was grim. "Without this cash flow, the winery goes out of business."

"That's not our only concern," said Tula's mother. "We have to think of you girls. Tula's still in school and Kelby starts next year." She attempted a smile. "Money doesn't grow on grape vines."

"But don't you see?" Kelby glanced at Angela for support. "If you sell this land to Astin Starr, you're actually selling it to AP. If saving the business is your reason for selling, you'll still lose it because there'll be no water. No water, no vineyard, no grapes, no wine, no winery." She shook her head. "You can't sell our land."

"If the land devalues, it would be wise to take the money now," said Mr. Bankhead. "We could set aside half of it for the family, education, and use the rest for the winery. That way, we can safeguard ourselves no matter what happens."

"In that case, you can't sell our land to that con artist. He'll just turn around and sell it to AP."

"You're jumping to conclusions," said her mother. "You have no evidence, no reason to suspect Mr. Starr of reselling the property to Agua Purificación."

"Where does a lawyer get two million dollars in cash? His law firm works for AP, so he's already on their payroll. I bet he's found some legal loophole to buy it in his name, using their money, with them owning the rights to it."

"Your mother's right. This is speculation, assumption. It would be reckless to reject his offer." Mr. Bankhead took a deep breath. "But we have three days to consider it. If you can come up with a better offer or a darned good reason to reject Mr. Starr's offer, we'll listen. But if not, your mother and I have only one option: accept."

With each person lost in their own thoughts, conversation lagged.

"Not sure if this is a good time to ask," said Angela, "but could I borrow your camping equip—"

"Oh, sure," said Tulah. "Meant to bring it over this morning, but I forgot. It's in the garage. Come on. Clay and I'll give you a hand."

Angela said goodbye to the family as she followed Clay and Tulah. "So what did the professor have to say, besides wanting to see the cave? Did he seem enthusiastic?"

Clay turned toward her, his eyes lighting up. "Doctor West's excited by the find. Actually, he's bringing a small team with him tomorrow morning."

"Tell her the best part." Tulah grinned at them.

Clay chuckled softly. "Apparently, he has some grant money left that he needs 'to burn this fiscal year.'"

"Are you saying what I think you are?" A smile playing at her lips, Angela looked from Tulah to Clay.

"Funding's available," he said, "which is good since there's no time to write, let alone apply for grants."

"How much? Enough to buy the land?"

Clay's smile drooped. "Probably nowhere near enough money to buy it, but maybe enough to lease the land awhile—"

"Maybe enough to cover operating costs at the winery . . . enough to postpone selling the land?" Tulah attempted an optimistic grin, but her bunched, worried eyes cancelled the effect.

Angela gave her shoulder a reassuring rub. "I hope so."

As Tulah's face relaxed into a smile, she turned toward Clay. "Come on. Let's give Angela a hand with the camping gear."

When Angela got back to the cabin, Kio was sitting on the porch swing. "Where were you?"

She grinned as she joined him. "Next door. You looked so peaceful sleeping. I didn't want to wake you." Snuggling, she kissed him. "Think that nap will be enough?"

His eyes twinkled. "I don't know. What do you have in mind?"

"First a wildflower tour." At his sour expression, she exhaled. "The bluebonnets are beautiful this year, and the pink primroses are just coming out." She sighed. "Okay, after that, gentleman's choice: hiking or rock climbing."

His eyes lit up. "It all sounds great, and I brought along my telescope. Think we could get a little stargazing in tonight?"

She nuzzled against him. "I know just the spot." Then she sat up straight. "I have a surprise for you. You knew the Bankheads' B&Bs were rented out, and hotel rooms in town were sold out."

He nodded. "So—"

"So you and I, my friend," smiling, she rubbed noses with him, "are going to sleep beneath the stars on Enchanted Rock."

Kio's eyes lit up, but he cocked his head. "You make it sound like fun, but, other than 'beneath the stars' and 'with you,' I don't like the sound of sleeping on a rock, enchanted or otherwise."

She chuckled. "I borrowed Tulah's tent, sleeping bags, all the gear we'll need, and I reserved a campsite this morning. We'll sleep in comfort, plus under a canopy of stars."

"Under a canopy of stars with you and without light scatter," he grinned, "what more could I ask for?"

"Thought you might enjoy the big sky experience. Plus . . ." She glanced up at his eyes. "I'd like to test a theory."

"What about?"

"Something Billy said."

He raised his eyebrow. "Who?"

"The spirit that's here, Billy, told me the Comanches held vision quests on Enchanted Rock."

Kio's shoulders sagged as he searched her eyes. "You're not planning to sleep on top of the rock, are you?"

"Our campsite's close enough, thank you." Grinning, she shook her head. "The Comanches believed if you prayed for spiritual guidance and spent the night there, your dreams would show you the path, the answer."

"Can't hurt." He shrugged. "Besides, how could your dreams be anything but magical in a place called Enchanted Rock?"

"Good point." Chuckling as she got up, she tugged at his hand. "Come on. Let's throw our things in my car and get going."

Twenty minutes later, they had fed Frank, left feed for Kitz, and were driving along one of the Bluebonnet Trail's wildflower loops, taking the scenic route to Enchanted Rock. As they came over a rise, Angela thought she saw a pond out of the corner of her eye. So blue, it looked like rippling water reflecting the sky. On closer inspection, she saw it was a field of bluebonnets, so dense their colors saturated the pasture.

Opening the windows, she smiled at Kio. "Take a deep breath." She inhaled, filling her lungs, her senses with the fragrance. "One blossom's scent is too subtle to detect, but a whole field of bluebonnets has a heady aroma."

Some pastures showed pink primroses competing with the bluebonnets, larger patches of pink than blue, while other areas presented nothing but royal blue, sky blue, and white petals combining into an indigo watercolor landscape.

Semiarid areas showed prickly pear cactus cropping up like thorny green ridges in a sea of bluebonnets. In sunny areas, a few early blooming Texas paintbrush and Indian blanket had cropped up, revealing crimson and scarlet reds among the blues. One sunny meadow showed a medley of bright, buttery yellow.

Kio glanced at her. "What kind of wildflowers are those?"

"Those are DYF." She swallowed a smile.

His forehead crinkled. "What are DYF?"

"Danged Yellow Flowers." She chuckled. "There are so many kinds of pretty, yellow flowers in the Hill Country, I can't tell one from another. Sometimes, I'm told, they even cross-pollinate, so they're both, neither one nor the other, but an endless, morphing continuity of yellow."

Kio shook his head, chuckling under his breath. "One of my colleagues just got back from a whirlwind European vacation. From the way he described it, back-to-back countries displaying their national colors, I get the feeling that's what we're doing. Driving along this trail, each field's a new experience of color. Each pasture, each 'country' is so close and yet so different, so unique."

"I love the analogy." She looked at the wildflowers, seeing them through new eyes, seeing them as flags of foreign countries. She glanced back at Kio, and she fell more deeply in love.

They took a left at Llano and continued the wildflower loop, following it into Fredericksley. Along this route, the Texas paintbrush and Indian blanket had taken over. Bluebonnets still flourished along the sides of the highway, but the fields of orange, red, and yellow overpowered the blue. The pastures billowed in red-yellow shades of bittersweet and ochre. One sun-drenched hillside showed a patchwork of ochre and gold.

Following the flowered trail to Enchanted Rock, Angela parked as close as she could to their campsite. She grimaced. "Sorry, but we'll have to haul our gear the rest of the way."

"Not a problem." Kio grabbed the heavier, bulkier items.

Angela slung on her backpack and carried what she could. "We'll need to make a second trip."

"No worries. We've got the necessities."

"I could've chosen a site closer to the parking lot," she said over her shoulder, as she led him along a footpath, "but I thought you'd like this spot."

When they arrived, she spread her arms wide, gesturing toward the landscape. From this close perspective, the rock loomed like a small mountain, filling the entire vista.

The campsite was open to the sky, no tree cover. He looked up, watching a single cloud float by in a sea of blue. "What a view—perfect for stargazing."

Watching him, Angela smiled. "Thought you'd like it."

"I do." Setting down his gear, he took her in his arms. "This is what I've thought about these past lonely months. Being with you. Holding you."

Kissing him, she tilted back her head, her senses reeling. *What'll it be like when we're married?* When they broke apart, a corner of her mouth lifted in a shy smile. "I love you, Kio." *If I ever had doubts, I sure don't now.*

"And I love you. Holding you feels right. Is right." Still embracing her, he looked into her eyes. "With this internship, you've shaved off a semester. You're done."

She nodded, blinking, thinking.

"Why don't we get married right after the semester ends?"

She took a deep breath. "It's not that I don't want to, but I thought we'd already decided we'd wait until the winter."

He shrugged. "Yeah, but that was before you squeezed in this summer session."

Part of her wanted to say *Yes*, and the sooner, the better. Part of her cried *No. This is my last chance to experience life on my own. Take the six months.*

She tried again. "Technically, I won't 'graduate' until after commencement in December. Why can't we get married in February, after graduation, like we'd planned?"

An easy grin came to his lips. "Because school ends in August."

Her arms fell from his shoulders as she shrugged. "Let's give it some thought, okay? It's only April. We've got plenty of time." She noticed his quizzical expression as his grip loosened and then let go. Stifling a sigh, she forced a smile. "Hey, if we want to climb the rock *and* hike around it before dark, we'd better get moving, but first we'd better set up camp."

An hour later, they were halfway up the hill. Stopping to enjoy the changing scene every so often, they watched the countryside open up as their vistas broadened.

By the time they reached the top, Angela was out of breath. "Exhilarating," she gasped, grinning.

From their bird's-eye perch, they looked across the miles. "It's like watching the world through a telescope, outside of time," said Kio. "Up here seems so removed from everyday life."

She nodded as she drank in the intoxicating views. Despite the drought, a patchwork of blue, red, orange, and yellow spread out before them. Amid the wildflowers, a few green oases sprang up in the reddish-brown soil. One looked like a green snake undulating through the dry land.

"The green dots must be springs," she said, thinking aloud. "The green arc must be the creek behind the cabin."

She thought of Kitz, the dusty turtle they had taken there, and all the wildlife that depended on the creek. In her mind's eye, she saw the ancient cypress trees, wildflowers, and grasses that flourished along its banks. Not just water, the creek provided food. It was life itself.

The Bankheads came to mind, along with the generations of families that had carved an existence out of this land, yet had been good stewards, conserving the water for future generations. *So many depend on the fragile water supply.* Recalling what Billy had said about the vision quest, as well as her promise, she said a silent prayer. *When I dream tonight, please tell me how I can help, what I can do.*

On the climb down, they saw a small pool of water reflecting the blue sky. On closer inspection, Kio said, "I thought you said it hasn't rained here in a while."

"Not since the day Kelby broke her leg." Then it dawned on her. "This must be one of those vernal pools I've read about."

Eyebrow raised, Kio gave her a puzzled look.

"Vernal pools are microhabitats of plants and animals found only in this area. When it *does* rain, the water collects in these little pits. Fairy shrimp that have been dry and dormant for months suddenly burst to life. They reproduce before the birds eat them, and their microscopic eggs lay dormant until the next time it rains."

"Life is so fragile, yet so determined to survive. Amazing." Shaking his head, Kio sniffed. "With these micro-miracles happening all around us, how can anyone question God's existence?"

"Beats me." Angela lay on her belly, staring into the puddle. "If you look really close, you can see them. They're about the size of mosquito larvae."

Kio crouched down to see better. "Yes, I see them now, but they have tiny gills that make them look like miniature tadpoles."

They got up carefully to avoid disturbing the pool and then backtracked to the base. After finding the Loop trailhead, they began walking the perimeter of Enchanted Rock. Crushed granite beneath their feet, they hiked what looked like an old trail, following the Sandy Creek flood plain as it headed west.

"These rocks look like mushrooms with their narrow stalks and wide caps." Angela ran her fingertips over the pink granite's smooth surface. Then wearing a grin, she scooped up a handful of the gritty particles below, crumbling them between her fingers. "Look! I can crush granite with my bare hands."

"Wonder Woman." Kio grinned as he pretended to test her bicep.

As they walked, they flushed out robins, mockingbirds, doves, even a woodpecker. Then they saw something glittering in the sun's last rays.

"What's that?" Kio squinted, trying to make it out.

"Broken glass?" Angela looked from him to the litter on the trail.

As they approached, they found crystals peppering the nearby hillside, spilling onto their path. Angela pointed to an exposed quartz vein. Gleaming in the last rays of the setting sun, glassy chunks of all sizes appeared to have burst free.

"The vein must have eroded, releasing its buried treasure." Angela picked up a shard, holding it against the sunset's fiery glow. "Beautiful. No wonder the early settlers told stories about veins of diamonds." She looked at the low angle of the sun. "We'd better keep moving. It'll be dark soon." Dropping the crystal where she had found it, she brushed her hands, and they pressed on.

They followed the trail to the parking area, picked up the rest of their gear, and headed back to their campsite.

As Kio looked at the deepening twilight, a relaxed smile spread across his face. "Good idea to camp here tonight, but I'm glad we set up camp while it was still light."

"Me, too." Angela brought out a thin loaf of French bread. "Now, if we can get a fire started, there are chicken breasts and veggie kabobs for grilling."

"And I've got a bottle of wine."

"It's a feast." She met his smile with a warm one of her own, glad they were spending time together.

They sat beside each other, watching Enchanted Rock glow an intense pink in the last vestiges of the golden sunset and then turn rosy lavender as the dusk deepened.

They watched birds ride the thermals above the rock and then land on the granite outcrops as the sun went down.

"Are those vultures?" asked Kio

Angela nodded. "Hence the name. Buzzard's Roost."

Nodding, he turned the chicken and kabobs on the grill. Then as he refilled her plastic cup, the bottle midair, he froze, listening. "Did you hear that?"

"That hollow, creaking sound?" At his nod, she added, "Yup."

"Did it come from the rock?"

"I think so," Angela whispered. They held their breath, listening.

Again, the rock creaked. Catching his eye, Angela smiled and nodded knowingly.

"I've heard several legends and ghost stories to explain it: a sacrificed Indian princess; a different Indian princess that jumped to her death; a band of warriors that fought to their death; and even a kidnapped pioneer woman. But I read it's the rock's outer surface that makes those groaning noises as it cools and contracts."

"Eerie." Kio shuddered. "I can understand why the Native Americans named this Enchanted Rock."

The moon rose while they ate dinner, casting a cool light over the rock's surface. All at once, a faint, bluish light hovered several feet above the rock, making it seem to glow in the moonlight.

"Do you see that?" Angela glanced at Kio.

"You mean that . . . that halo?" His adam's apple bobbed up and down quickly. "Sure do. What is it?"

Shrugging, she shook her head. "Tulah told me about this, but I thought it was just an urban legend. She said the granite acts like a big battery that absorbs the sun's heat during the day. Then at night, when it cools, the rock changes the solar energy to light as it releases it."

He glanced from the peculiar glow to her. "Did she say why?"

"She said the granite's mildly radioactive."

When they looked back, the glow was gone.

"What the—" He snickered. "We *did* see it, didn't we?"

"See what? I didn't see anything." Angela deadpanned before she broke out laughing.

"You little minx." His eyes flashing, he leaned over to kiss her just as a light drizzle began.

Angela yelped as they scurried inside the tent. "Where'd that come from?" She took a deep breath, recalling the surprise shower when Kelby had fallen. "That's the second time rain's appeared out of nowhere. At least, it guarantees the fairy shrimp another week or two of life."

Sitting in the tent, peeking out through the flaps, they watched the shower stop as suddenly as it had started. Angela opened the flaps wider and stuck her hand out. "I don't feel anything. Think it's safe to sit outside again?"

Kio shrugged. "We can try it."

They ventured outside cautiously. Angela wiped down their chairs as Kio stoked the fire. "Good as new. Ready for dessert?"

"What did you have in mind?"

She watched his eyes light up in the fire's reflection. "S'mores." Grinning, she pulled graham crackers, chocolate bars, and marshmallows from the cooler. Then she pulled two sharpened sticks out from under her chair and handed him one. "I don't know about you, but I worked up an appetite on that hike."

Sticks in hand, they sat browning their marshmallows over the flames. "Now, what's going on?"

Following the direction of his eyes, Angela looked at the rock and caught her breath. Its surface seemed to glitter.

"What is that?" Kio glanced from the rock to her and back.

Taking a deep breath, she shook her head. "I've read about that, too, but I've never seen it before. The going theory is the moon reflects off either wet feldspar or water trapped in tiny hollows in the rock's surface, so it appears to sparkle."

"Said it before, and I'll say it again." Kio broke a graham cracker in two, added a chocolate square, and then making a 'sandwich' with the other cracker half, slid the gooey marshmallow inside and off the stick. "No wonder the Native Americans named this place Enchanted Rock."

She grinned mischievously as she finished toasting her marshmallow. Then she offered her skewered marshmallow in exchange for his assembled s'more.

With a good-natured smile, Kio made the trade. As he began making another for himself, she held her s'more eye level, watching its crispy, gooey marshmallow meld together with the chocolate.

Then she glanced at the rock. "Just think how all the sights and sounds of the rock must've psyched the Comanches for their vision quests."

Her grin fading, she remembered her promise to Billy. *When I dream tonight*, she silently prayed, *please tell me how I can help, what I can do.*

"What are you thinking?"

She glanced up and caught him staring at her. Shy about expressing her thoughts, she shrugged. "I'm praying for a vision. I know it sounds silly, but—"

"What harm can it do?"

She gestured toward the rock. "This place does have a mysterious air about it. Maybe God will answer my prayer here, show me what I'm supposed to do to protect the stream."

Kio held up his s'more in a toast. "To visions and answered prayers."

"Cheers." As if they held wine glasses, she touched her s'more to his. Then she bit into the melted delight. "Oh, this is wonderful." Grinning like a little girl, she said, "I'd forgotten how delicious."

Kio gently wiped the chocolate smudge from her lip and licked it from his finger. Then leaning toward her, he kissed her.

She kissed him back, tasting his chocolaty breath, feeling his soft lips pressed against hers while his five o'clock shadow gently grazed her cheek. When he nibbled at her neck, his breath tickled, sending tingling chills down her spine. It felt good. *Too good.*

Sitting up straight in her folding chair, she leaned away, catching her breath. As she composed herself, she glanced up at the sky. *Stars!* "The clouds are gone. That must have been a passing shower. The stars are out." She glanced at him, wondering if he'd take her lead.

His brow furrowed, Kio watched her through guarded eyes. Then blinking, he took a deep breath and glanced at the sky. "There's no light scatter. It's nearly as dark and clear here as at Fort Davis."

"Did you want to set up your telescope, do some stargazing?"

Again, he studied her by the firelight, swallowed, and nodded toward the burning logs. "We'd have to douse the campfire, remove that source of light. And heat. The night air might get chilly—"

"That's okay," she answered a beat too quickly. She gave him a half smile.

"I'll start setting it up, should just take a few minutes. Then we can smother the fire."

She cleaned up the camp site, tossing their paper plates in the red embers. For an instant, the flames flared up, and she thought she saw Billy standing in the shadows. As quickly, the blaze flickered and died out, leaving only the hot coals.

Kio finished tightening the last joint of the telescope. Then he glanced from the campfire to her. “Okay, time to smother the flames. You’re good at that.”

She did a double take. *Is he implying . . .?*

He caught her eye, then as quickly glanced away, grimacing. “Never mind, I’ll do it.” Before she could reach for the jug of water, he picked it up and poured it over the red-hot embers.

The cinders hissed angrily, their steam rising in the chilly air.

Angela stifled a sigh. “Kio—”

“Let’s just try to enjoy the evening before anything else puts a damper on it, clouds, cold showers . . .” His eyes narrowing, he grimaced.

“I just don’t want to start anything we—”

“I get it!” As he took a deep breath, his scowl relaxed into a half smile. “All right?”

Biting her lip, she gave a curt nod.

He stepped toward the telescope and looked through the eyepiece. “The Lyrid meteor shower’s expected to peak at the end of April, but a full moon will make it difficult to see. Though we’re a few weeks early, the moon’s a waxing crescent tonight, hardly a sliver in the night.” Wearing an apologetic smile, he glanced at her. “Maybe we’ll get lucky and see a shooting star or two. Want to take a peek?”

A smile began at the corner of her mouth. “Yeah, I’d like that.”

An hour later, both were yawning. Kio glanced at her and chuckled. “Why don’t we call it a night?”

"Good idea." Nodding, she stifled another yawn. "I can hardly keep my eyes open."

"I'll put away the telescope."

"And I'll unroll the sleeping bags." She snickered.

A smile playing at his lips, he looked at her. "What?"

"We sound like an old married couple."

The smile faded as he stepped closer and put his arms around her. "I'd like to make that a reality. And as soon as possible. What do you say to an August wedding?"

"Right after the summer semester ends?" Her arms around him, she looked up into his eyes.

"The same day, as far as I'm concerned." He raised his eyebrow. "What do you say?"

Looking at him, she felt another pleasing shiver run down her spine. *In some ways, tonight's not too soon.* "It's tempting." She took a deep breath. "Could I sleep on it?"

His hold on her loosened. "This isn't part of your vision quest research, is it?"

Smiling, she shook her head. "No . . . at least, it hadn't been, but that's a good idea. Right before I go to sleep, I'll pray about it and hope to have an answer in the morning." She looked into his eyes. "Deal?"

He hugged her to him, murmuring before he kissed her, "Deal."

In their respective sleeping bags, Kio reached for her hand before he turned off the lamp. "Sleep tight."

She laughed softly in the dark. "Don't let the bedbugs bite . . . or any other bugs. You did zipper and snap the tent flaps, didn't you?"

"Yes, dear." Kio's smile came through his voice. "Sweet dreams."

Angela closed her eyes and silently prayed. *Please tell me what to do about our wedding. Should we marry in August or wait till*

February like we'd planned? If You could tell me in a dream, I'd appreciate it.

She sighed. *And if it wouldn't be too much to ask, please tell me how I can help protect the water, what I can do to help preserve Billy's stream for the wildlife.*

Within minutes, she fell asleep, slipping into a lush, green paradise. She saw Kitz and followed him to the stream. She saw him drinking, lapping up the fresh water. He raised his head and looked at her, water droplets glistening in his whiskers as the sun backlit him. Then the turtle paddled through the water, creating gentle waves as he crawled onto a log and began sunbathing. Birds chattered in the regal cypresses and then swooped down to drink or bathe.

Suddenly, the scene sped up as if someone had fast-forwarded a tape. Birds flew in and out in the blink of an eye. The stream became sluggish, shrank to a trickle, and then stopped flowing. The once sparkling water became muddied, polluted with green algae. Then the stream shriveled into cesspools of murky bilge water.

Minnows still swam in its ever-shrinking puddles, but like fishing in a barrel, birds picked them off and flew away. The bones of rotted fish and the empty shells of turtles lay beside flattened water bottles and crushed cans on the now-dusty arroyo. Only a clump of thick clay remained. Kitz licked at it, trying to drink the last of its moisture. His mouth open, panting, he turned away.

As clearly as if Kio had spoken, Angela heard a voice. Startled, she half woke. "As a deer yearns for running streams, so I yearn for you, my God." *Psalm forty-two, my favorite.*

Lulled by the verse, she fell back asleep. This time, she saw herself sitting at a desk in the middle of the stream, typing. Papers surrounded her, each containing a single word or phrase. One by one, she picked up each page, read it, and the wind blew it from her hands.

Troubled waters. Won't hold water. A fish out of water. In hot water. Keep your head above water. Water under the bridge. Up the river without a paddle. Sold down the river. Streaming video. Stream of light. Stream of thought. Stream of consciousness. Mainstream. Carpool. Office pool. Dirty pool. Baby shower. Bridal shower. Cold shower. Send to the showers. Rain check. Rained out. Rain on parade. Raining cats and dogs. Spring a leak. Spring to mind. Spring up. Spring back. Spring into action. Hope springs eternal.

Again, she heard the voice. "As a deer yearns for running streams, so I yearn for you, my God."

She sat up, wide awake. *That's it! Water is an archetype. It's so essential, so integral to life, it's made its way into our speech, our idioms, even the Bible.* She thought of Noah and the flood. The parting of the Red Sea. Moses getting water from a rock. Jesus as the living water. Baptismal water. Holy water. *Water imagery fills our language, as well as our religion.* Nodding to herself in the dark, she smiled. *Thank You, God, for the vision, for showing me how to protect the stream.* She smiled as she began drifting to sleep. *Now, if You could just show me what to tell Kio in the morning . . .*

Instantly, she saw herself sitting at a desk in the middle of the stream, typing on a laptop. Her inbox chimed, and she checked her email.

"Got it," she mumbled in her sleep.

Night Vision

A dreamer is one who can only find his way by moonlight, and his punishment is that he sees the dawn before the rest of the world.

– Oscar Wilde

The next morning, Angela woke, feeling fresh, rested. Stretching, she looked across the tent, but Kio's sleeping bag was rolled up. Then she sniffed the air. "Is that coffee I smell?"

"You called?" Kio ducked through the tent's opening, a cup of steaming coffee in hand.

"I never realized you were a mind reader." Sitting up, she grinned as he handed her the cup.

"Careful. It's hot."

Suddenly bashful, she flushed. "I'm not used to being waited on."

His grin widened. "You'd better get used to it when we're married."

Like a familiar scent, a gong sounding, his words brought the dream to mind. *This is going to be harder than I thought.* Pressing her lips together, she grimaced.

"Uh-oh." He inhaled. "I know that look. What's wrong?"

"About that—"

"About what? Getting married?" At her nod, he raised his eyebrow. "Yes . . ."

She forced a smile, trying to lighten the mood. "I have good news and bad. Which do you want to hear first?"

He crossed his arms, silently staring at her.

Angela took a deep breath. "The good news is, whether you call it a vision, a dream, or the answers to prayers, God showed me what I need to do." She grimaced. "The bad news is, the dream showed me being offered a job."

He relaxed his arms. "What's so bad about that?"

"Keep in mind, these were only images, impressions that came to me, but it seemed the job was located," she hesitated, trying to recall, "near Waco . . . or Fort Worth."

"In other words, not Fort Davis." His eyes hard, glassy, he studied her. "What are you trying to say?"

"My intuition tells me to not rush into marriage this August, but to wait until February like we'd planned. It's only—"

"You really know how to put a damper on things, don't you?" Turning, he ducked out through the tent's flaps.

Angela quickly changed clothes and joined him. Gently running her fingertips along his arm, she turned him toward her. "Kio, I'm sorry. I didn't mean to upset you, but call it a dream, a vision, *something* tells me we should wait six months. Like we'd planned."

A smile nagging at the corner of his mouth, he put his arms around her. "If you're that stubborn, I guess I can wait another six months." He looked into her eyes. "But I miss you. Fort Davis is lonely. I'd really like you with me."

"Me, too," she looked up at him, "but when the time's right."

He gave her a silly grin. "Yes, dear."

She playfully punched his arm. "Stop!" Her cell buzzed. Reaching for it, she read caller ID. "It's Tulah." Then on speaker, she asked, "What's up?"

"Doctor West called. He and his team will be here at ten. Want to join us?"

She caught Kio's eye, and he gave her a thumb's up. "Wouldn't miss it!"

"One other thing. Mom and Dad need us at the winery by one. With Kio here, will that still work?"

"We thought he could take the tour with me." Again, Angela glanced at him, and he nodded.

"Good idea," said Tulah. "We'll meet you at the cabin at ten."

Just as they finished feeding Frank and putting out feed for Kitz, Tulah and Clay arrived with Doctor West and two of his grad assistants. Again, Angela led them to the cave. After moving aside the rocks and securing the rope, the seven of them descended.

The team carried trowels, paint brushes, bamboo scrapers, folding rulers, and a transit, measuring and recording as they descended. When their headlamps lit the cache of bones, Doctor West gave a low whistle.

"I believe you've found a bone sink. We'll excavate to be certain, but with just a cursory glance, this has all the earmarks of having been a sink hole at one time. Animals entered easily but then could not escape."

"Look how all the bones are oriented, Doctor West." Clay pointed to them. "They all seem to be facing in the same general direction."

Nodding, Doctor West explained to his assistants. "There's a theory that widespread flowing water not only distributed bones, but caused them to lay perpendicular and parallel, relative to the flow of the water." Pointing, he said, "See how these long, thin bones are all parallel, while femurs, skull, and the bigger bones are perpendicular? Think how after a rain, all the little twigs are aligned in the same direction as the water flow. Same thing here."

"Are you saying this happened during *The* flood, Noah's flood?" Her eyes wide even in the low light, Tulah studied him.

He shrugged. "*A* flood, or more likely, a series of floods. Without further research, it's speculation, but I believe various flash floods first drowned these animals and later redistributed their remains in the patterns you see."

Wearing rubber gloves, the team began examining artifacts and photographing the area. They took soil cores and measurements using GPS and GIS equipment.

After they had documented and measured the area, Doctor West picked up the tusk to examine it more closely. Again, he gave a low whistle. "What a find."

"What's going to happen now?" Clay watched his professor's face.

"I'm going to speak to a friend about excavating here. He works with the Waco Mammoth National Monument."

"I'm not familiar with it." Angela shook her head.

"The site's relatively new. It was designated a National Monument in 2015 after the fossils of a camel, saber-toothed cat, twenty-four Columbian mammoths, and several other mammals from the Pleistocene Era were unearthed there."

"Time is an important aspect," said Clay. "How fast could a dig be put together?"

Raising his eyebrow, Doctor West inhaled deeply. "Your guess is as good as mine. Even if this site garners a lot of attention, it takes months to get the gears of government and academia in motion."

Clay exchanged a glance with Tulah before asking, "Three days is unrealistic?"

Doctor West sympathetically shook his head. "It takes longer to complete the paperwork. We're talking two to three months. At a minimum."

"What about the grant money you mentioned you need 'to burn this fiscal year'?"

Professor West's smile dissolved as he led them a step or two from the grad assistants. In a whisper, he said, "I think I can convince the university to expend enough funding to lease the land—at least long enough to perform exploratory excavation."

Tulah looked from the professor to Angela. "Someone's offered to buy this land. My parents have three—"

"Two." Angela pressed her lips together in a grim, pale line.

"Two days to make a decision."

"Then the sooner I talk to the department, the better." Professor West glanced at his watch

Using his cue, Angela and Tulah both checked the time.

"Yikes, by the time we get cleaned up we're going to be late for work." Tulah caught Angela's eye. "I'll drive."

Angela glanced at Kio. "Do you want to come with me—"

"Actually, how 'bout I drive Kio to the winery after we finish up here?" Clay looked from Angela to Kio.

"Sure." Kio nodded. "Works for me."

In between customers and tours, Tulah tried to fill her parents in on Professor West's plans.

"A bird in hand," said Mrs. Bankhead, her raised eyebrow completing the adage.

Before Tulah could answer, several customers walked into the winery.

Angela did a double take as Astin led three strangers into the tasting room.

Astin smiled as he guided his well-dressed associates toward the tasting bar. Making introductions, he gestured toward Tulah and her parents. "This is the family that owns the cabin—"

Her knee in the scooter, Kelby rolled up in time to ask, "And who are they?"

"These," Astin gave her a slow smile, "are my associates, Hank Porter, Greg Porter, and George Porter." He rattled off their names without divulging any descriptors.

"Associates?" Narrowing her eyes, Kelby gave him a snide smile. "Don't you mean AP co-conspirators?" She turned to the other men, addressing each in turn. "Hank Porter, aren't you the founder/owner of TEX-AM, the environmental company that made the environmental study for AP? George Porter, isn't your TXA

Engineering company involved with AP's water-drilling deal? And Greg Porter, doesn't Astin Starr work at your law firm? More to the point, hasn't AP made substantial campaign contributions to Hank Porter in the past?" Astin flinched. Then turning to Tulah, he gave her wide smile. "Could you introduce me to this astute young lady?"

Tulah glanced from him to her frowning parents to Kelby, and back. "This is my sister, Kelby."

Astin gave Kelby a mock bow. "It isn't often I meet such a clever young woman." He gave her a winning smile. "Where would you learn such obscure facts?"

Scowling, Kelby curled her lip, barely maintaining a civil expression. "It's amazing what you can learn online." She sneered. "Didn't a Caroline Knowles work at your law firm?"

Astin gave her an uncomfortable smile but nodded.

"She posted in a blog that everyone in the Porter law firm was 'asked' to contribute to Hank Porter's campaign. Is that—"

"A blog," Hank shrugged, "oddballs and idle ne'er-do-wells spouting off in an unmoderated forum."

Kelby straightened her spine. "Are you denying that conduit contributions were used to support Hank Porter's campaign?"

Astin exchanged a look with Hank.

"Isn't it true," she pulled a folded printout from her pocket, "that everyone in the firm was 'asked' to contribute twenty-four hundred dollars to your campaign? Wasn't it stated in a memo," she arched her eyebrow, "that anyone who could not afford twenty-four hundred dollars, would be, *and I quote*, 'reimbursed by the firm with a twenty-four hundred dollar bonus check (after payroll tax deductions) at the end of the quarter?'"

"All right, young lady." Her arm around the girl's shoulders, Mrs. Bankhead began wheeling her daughter away. "These gentlemen came to the winery to relax, not be cross-examined." Turning back to Astin and the others, she smiled hospitably. "Are you interested in a wine tasting, or would you prefer the winery tour?"

Astin gave Tulah a private smile before turning to the others. "You've got to try the tram tour of the vineyards, and then the barrel-tasting tour." He turned back to Tulah. "Will you be the tour guide?"

Angela hopped to attention. "Actually, it's—"

"No worries, Angela." Tulah met Astin's eyes in a coy smile. "I'll be happy to take this group on a private tour."

Astin grinned as he paid the four admissions. Then he checked his watch. "It's a few minutes before the hour." His eyes met Tulah's. "Think we could start a little early?"

"Sure. Why not?" She held out her hand for the tram's keys.

Angela handed them over, debating whether to remind her about meeting Clay and Kio later.

Wearing a smile, Astin turned to the Bankheads. "After the tour, the Porters and I would like to look at the property. That is, if you have no objections."

"Be our guests," said Mr. Bankhead.

Angela swallowed her grimace.

"The tour should end at five, closing time." Tulah looked from her father to her mother. "Why don't I guide them to the cabin after the barrel-tasting tour ends?"

Astin's eyes lit up. "Great idea."

"I'll catch a ride home with Clay and Kio." Angela stifled a sigh.

"Oh . . ." Tulah bit her lip. "I forgot about that."

"No problem." A smile crept across Angela's face as she got an idea. "Clay, Kio, and I can meet you there."

Tulah studied her a moment before turning toward the group. "If you'll follow me, gentlemen, the sooner we begin the tour, the sooner we can visit the property."

Her knee in the scooter, Kelby rejoined her parents and Angela as the men followed Tulah. Scowling at the men's backs, Kelby said, "Caroline Knowles had worked for the Porter law firm, emphasis on past tense."

"What happened to her?" asked Angela.

"According to this," Kelby held up the printout, "she was let go for declining Greg Porter's offer to reimburse her for making a contribution to his father's campaign. If Greg had used law-firm funds to pay back his personnel for contributions, he, his law firm, his father, and the campaign committee were all liable for violating the anti-conduit provision. Caroline Knowles knew that, so she declined. Two weeks later, she was 'asked to resign.'" She glanced at Astin's back. "They're all in cahoots. Why else would that shyster want to buy land in Barron County, two hundred miles away?"

"It's a beautiful piece of property. Why wouldn't Mr. Starr want to buy it?" Mrs. Bankhead arched her eyebrow. "And he's an attorney, not a shyster."

Kelby shook her head. "There's something fishy about this whole thing. Greg Porter's law firm works for AP, and that shys—Starr works for him. I still say he's found some loophole to buy the land in his name, using their money, with them owning the water rights."

"That's sheer speculation." Mr. Bankhead took a deep breath. "As we said, if you can come up with a better plan, we'll listen. If not, we've got one option: accept."

"What if you were offered enough money to cover operating costs at the winery . . . enough, at least, to postpone selling the land?" Angela glanced at them.

"What do you mean?" Mrs. Bankhead studied her.

Angela described what had happened at the cave. "Hopefully, Clay will have more information from Professor West about leasing it."

Mr. Bankhead glanced at his wife. "But is there time? Don't we have to give Mr. Starr an answer in two days?"

"What if you make a counteroffer to keep the water rights?" asked Angela. "At the very least, it would buy time."

"Yes!" Kelby raised her arms in victory as her parents caught each other's eye.

An hour later, Kio and Clay walked into the winery along with several other customers.

After Angela introduced Kio, she waited on the customers while Clay updated the Bankheads. She overheard them as she rang up a sale at the cash register.

"I gave Doctor West your phone number. Hope it's all right."

"Sure." Mr. Bankhead shrugged as he glanced at his wife. "We're always open to discussion."

Angela leaned over to whisper. "Did he get the funding?"

Nodding but grimacing, Clay raised his eyebrow. "I think so. We'll know more after he talks to the Bankheads, discusses that information with his department, and gets back to us."

At the sound of abrasive laughter, they all turned their heads.

As Tulah led the jovial tour group back to the main tasting room, her eyes connected with Clay's. She dropped her smile and turned back to Astin. "Let me ring up those cases for you and your friends."

She nodded silently as she tried to squeeze between Clay and the narrow entrance to the bar. When he didn't step aside, she murmured, "Excuse me."

Stepping back, Clay spoke with an exaggerated southwestern drawl. "Ma'am."

Her back to the customers, she rolled her eyes. Then forcing a smile, she turned toward the group. "Let's see, that was a case of pinot noir for you, Astin, a case of merlot for you, Hank, and a case each of the cabernet-merlot blend for you and Greg." As if she felt Clay's stare, she glanced at him over her shoulder. Then she turned back to her group. "Why don't we move down here, where we'll have more room?"

Two other customers stepped up to the wine bar. "Is there another tram tour today?"

A few minutes before closing, Angela and Tulah checked the time and looked to Mr. Bankhead.

He nodded. "Sure. One will be leaving in five minutes. Tulah—"

"Can Angela take it?" Tulah glanced from her father to Angela.

Angela shrugged. "Okay—"

"Great. Appreciate it." Reaching into her pocket, she handed over the tram keys. "Why don't you take Kio along with you?" Tulah's eyes narrowed. "And Clay."

After her shift ended, Angela and Kio rode back to the cabin with Clay. He parked next to the red convertible. "Isn't that Starr's?"

Nodding, Angela met Clay's icy stare.

Before he could respond, his cell phone rang. Clay glanced at caller ID. "Professor West."

"Good luck." Holding up her crossed fingers, Angela stepped out of the car. "Kio, why don't you help me feed Kitz? Let's see if he'll come around when you're here."

She fed Frank, but he was too busy rubbing against Kio's legs to notice. She scooped a cup of feed, and Kio followed her outside with Frank perched on his shoulder.

Scanning the area, Angela saw the yearling peeking from behind the persimmon and agarita bushes. She set down the feed and, motioning to Kio, started toward the stream.

Kio glanced over his shoulder as he followed. "He's eating."

"Good." Angela smiled. "Billy doesn't want us around when he eats." At the mention of his name, the specter appeared in their path, arms crossed, glowering. She silently shook her head.

Billy stood his ground.

"Excuse me," she said.

"For what?" Kio gave her a puzzled look.

"Not you. Billy." Wearing a wry smile, she gestured toward him with her chin.

"He's here?" Kio looked at the empty path. "Where?" As he stepped forward, he walked through the specter. Shuddering, he glanced back at her. "What was that cold feeling?"

She grinned. "Billy."

They looked up as they heard laughter floating on the breeze, and then voices.

Billy glared at her. "Who's *that?*"

Tulah, Astin, and the other three men rounded a corner and came into view.

"The group that wants to buy this place," she whispered.

"Angela, I'm glad you're back." Looking right through Billy, Tulah smiled at her. "Greg wondered if you'd mind if they peeked inside the cabin."

"No." Angela glanced uneasily at Billy. "That is, I wouldn't mind if . . ."

"If what?" Wearing a puzzled expression, Tulah watched her.

"If it's all right with . . . everyone else." Angela watched Billy become more agitated.

"Is *that* all? I'm sure it's fine with my parents." Tulah turned toward Astin and the others. "Right this way."

Angela watched Billy go before them, lifting, twisting roots in their path, tripping them.

"What the—?" Stumbling, Greg looked back at the loosened tree root.

She heard Billy laugh as he held a tree branch, letting it snap back in George's face.

"Dang it!" George adjusted his glasses. "Where'd that come from?"

Kitz ran away at their approach.

Still on his cell phone, his back to them, Clay turned as he heard Astin's shouts.

The red convertible was backing slowly down the drive.

"What did you do?" Astin gave Clay a dirty look before he ran after his car.

Doubling over in laughter, holding his sides, Billy watched as Astin and his friends chased the sports car.

Tulah looked from Clay to the four sprinting men and back again. "Did you do that?"

Putting his phone on mute, Clay shook his head. "I don't know anything about it."

"Don't lie to me! It's one thing to delay the sale," said Tulah, "but to deliberately—"

"Now wait just a darned minute! I didn't—"

"Hey! Hey! Time out!" Angela made the T sign with her hands. "Clay didn't do anything. Billy did it."

"Billy?" Clay squinted. "Oh, yeah, the resident ghost . . . really?"

Angela nodded.

Then Clay glanced at his phone. "Oh, crap. I left Doctor West on mute."

They heard him apologizing to his professor as he stepped away. Several minutes later, Astin drove up in a cloud of caliche dust. Angela looked at the cat rubbing against her legs, picked him up, and stepped back just before Astin slammed on his brakes. His tires dug into the gravel only inches from them, rolling over where Frank had been standing. Astin jumped out, strode over to Clay, and grabbing his shoulder turned him around.

"What the hell did you do to my car?"

"Whoa! Take it easy, *pal*!" Using his elbow, Clay knocked Astin's hand from his shoulder as he squared off.

"Hey, you two." Tulah stepped between them and spoke to Astin. "Long story short, Clay wasn't responsible for your car rolling away."

"Then who was?" Eyes narrowed to slits, Astin looked at them.

"Nobody." Angela stepped in. "It was—"

"An accident." Tulah took a deep breath. "Nobody was driving it. You saw for yourself. It was just coasting downhill. Maybe you left it in neutral."

Astin blinked as if considering it.

"And in the future," said Angela, holding firmly onto Frank, "I'll thank you to drive slowly on private property. You could've run over my cat." She thought of Kitz and the turtle. "Or the wildlife."

"In the future," Astin glared at her, "this will be my private property, and I'll drive however I please."

With the three men still sitting in the convertible, the car began slowly backing away, gathering speed as it rolled in reverse.

Only Angela saw Billy move the gear shift. She deadpanned. "You really do need to get that transmission fixed."

Astin scowled at her, and then took off after his car. The man in the passenger seat tried to reach the brake as the men in the back unsuccessfully strained at their seatbelts.

Angela heard Billy whooping in the distance, and she began chuckling. Her amusement contagious, Kio, Tulah, and Clay began snickering. Within minutes, the four of them were laughing.

Tulah was the first to compose herself. "We really shouldn't laugh at them. Astin's car could've crashed into a tree, or someone could've gotten hurt."

Clay's grin drooped. "He got what he deserved wheeling around in that convertible like he owns the place."

Tulah shrugged. "He practically does." Then she stood up to her full height. "Besides, he's just high-spirited, that's all."

Clay rolled his eyes. "You've got to be kidding."

"Astin's going to make a fine neighbor." Her eyes lit up. "He said he's going to make this land into a game reserve."

Angela caught her eye. "Game reserve?"

Tulah nodded. "That's what he said."

"Where the animals live in safety?" Angela lifted her eyebrow. "Or where they're hunted for sport?"

"Well . . . I suppose where they'll live in safety . . ." Tulah glanced at her. "At least, that's the way it sounded."

The other three exchanged looks.

"What?"

"I don't trust that guy," said Angela.

"You never did."

"If I hadn't picked up Frank, he would've run right over him." Angela pressed her lips together as she took a deep breath. "That doesn't sound like an animal lover to me."

Kio nodded. "It sounds like another way to make money off the land's surface, while he drills underground and pumps the aquifer dry."

"Did he happen to say anything about the water rights or whether he'd drill wells?" Clay's eyes narrowed.

Tulah thought for a moment. "He didn't say much about it . . . but he did ask a lot of questions."

"Like what?" Clay studied her.

"Oh, things like, how many gallons per minute does the well supply? And are there any options for pumping water off-grid?"

Again, the other three exchanged looks.

Tulah frowned. "What's wrong with questions like that? Any prospective homeowner has a right to know those things."

"Homeowner?" Clay sniffed. "I can't see him living here. He'd turn up his nose at the cabin. He's a prospective *buyer* just snooping around, trying to find out all he can about the water situation."

"You just don't understand Astin." Tulah shook her head. "He wants to own a piece of history."

"He said that?" His eyes narrowing, Clay watched her.

"Not in so many words, but he said he wants to own a piece of Texas."

Clay scoffed. "Yeah, its water. He wants to buy and peddle off a piece of heaven. Like Angela said, I don't trust him."

"So it's up to us to stop him." Angela swallowed a smile. "Billy's already done his part." Then she glanced at Clay. "With all the excitement of the runaway car, we forgot to ask what Doctor West had to say."

Clay's eyes lit up. "Good news." He turned towards Tulah. "He talked to your parents and the dean of his Department. Your parents agreed to the archaeological survey, and the dean agreed to transfer the funding, so they'll be reimbursed."

"That's great news," said Angela.

Tulah chewed her lip.

"You haven't said anything." Clay watched her.

Tulah took a deep breath. "I'm torn. I want my parents to keep the property, but . . ."

"But what?" Clay's tone was impatient.

"Truth be told," Tulah shrugged. "I'd like Astin as a neighbor. He's already told me to come over any time, that nothing would change."

"Don't you get it?" Clay's eyebrows bunched together in an angry scowl. "He isn't planning to live here. I don't think it's even his money. Somehow the Porters and/or AP are financing this venture. It's all about water. Buying, pumping, and selling our water. Once they siphon off the aquifer, they'll move on, leaving us high and dry."

Kio broke the strained silence. "How long will the funding last?" He rubbed his jaw. "In other words, how long can we stall the sale?"

"That's the bad news." Clay turned toward Tulah. "There's only enough money to reimburse your parents for the exploratory study, about a month's lease, according to Doctor West."

Tulah silently bit her lip, seeming deep in thought.

"That's a month's grace we hadn't had." Angela glanced at them. "Kelby said if the property was significant in some way, had archeological value, we could possibly get it listed on the National Register of Historic Places." She grinned. "Thanks to Doctor West's support, its archeological importance is now fact, not wishful thinking. This month's reprieve buys us time to get the property listed on the Register *and* write grant proposals."

"Angela's right." Grinning, Kio caught her eye and then turned to the others. "The property's been granted a stay of execution. I say this calls for a celebration. Besides, it's Saturday night."

"And it's getting late." Angela nodded. "Why don't you two join us for a campfire dinner?"

A half hour later, the four of them were lounging around an open pit fire. Angela flipped the aluminum-foil packets of fingerlings and sweet potatoes in the coals.

"I thought you couldn't cook." Kio gave her a twisted grin.

"I can't." Angela shrugged. "It's just hobo packs." She added the fish fillets to four more twelve-inch squares of heavy-duty foil. Squeezing lime juice over the fillets, she added butter and salt. After dusting them with freshly picked chives and rosemary, she folded the edges up and over to create packets, pinching the edges closed.

"It sure smells good from here." Kio's face warmed into a grin.

Angela gave him a mysterious smile. "Fancy that."

He studied her. "Have you been taking cooking lessons?"

"I've just been watching Mr. and Mrs. Bankhead. They should be chefs. I'm serious."

"They're both good cooks." Tulah nodded. "Have been as long as I can remember."

"Lucky thing I bought a bottle of Viognier from our tour guide this afternoon." Kio winked as he passed around the paper cups and opened the wine. "We'll obviously need an appropriate beverage to equal this gourmet meal."

Angela rolled her eyes. "You haven't tasted it yet. Save your opinions till after we eat." She grinned. "Though I'm sure the wine will help the flavor."

"That was a feast." His eyes twinkling, Kio gave her an admiring glance. "You never stop surprising me."

She stared back. "Why?"

"You've always made such a big thing about not cooking. That meal was delicious."

She shrugged. "I've just been watching the Bankheads." As her mother came to mind, an ache tugged at her heart. "My mother never cooked. She never had the time or inclination. I simply never learned."

"You're catching on fast." Kio leaned over to hug her. "You have a knack for it."

Wearing a self-conscious smile, Angela scoffed. "Fancy that."

"Not to change the subject, but after Mass tomorrow," Tulah turned to Angela, "how would you guys like to take in a cemetery tour?"

Clay wrinkled his nose.

"What's so great about visiting a cemetery?" Kio's brow puckered.

"It's not *just* a cemetery." Tulah flashed a winning smile. "It's costumed actors telling the stories of Fredericksley's pioneers. The cemetery's the stage where history comes alive."

"I like the idea." Angela glanced from face to face. "Who knows? We might learn something to help get the property listed on the National Register of Historic Places."

Maybe Billy will be there. It'd be good to talk with him.

"Look at those campfires lighting up the dusk." They followed Clay's stare.

Tulah chuckled. "They remind me of the Easter Fires."

"Easter Fires?" Kio looked at Angela.

Shrugging, she turned to Tulah. "What are they?"

Tulah exchanged a grin with Clay. "The original Easter Fires go back to 1847."

"The same year Billy was shot," Angela whispered to herself.

"What?" Tulah glanced at her.

"Nothing, just thinking aloud." Angela shook her head. "What happened in 1847?"

"A group of town fathers met with the Penateka Comanches to make a peace treaty."

Rolling his eyes, Kio scoffed.

"No." Tulah held up her hands. "This didn't end the way most peace treaties did with the Native Americans. It's one of the few pacts that was never broken."

Squinting, Angela cocked her head. "What's it got to do with Easter Fires?"

"I'm getting to that." Tulah took a deep breath. "John Meusebach was the German leader. Because of his red hair and flowing, red beard, the Comanches called him *El Sol Colorado—*"

"The Red Sun," said Kio.

Tulah nodded. "He and most of the townsmen met with the Comanches near the San Saba River, where they made the initial agreement. With the men gone, the women and children were left vulnerable to attack."

"At sunset, the Comanche war parties lit bonfires on the surrounding hilltops, sending smoke signals about the treaty's progress," said Clay, "but the settlers misinterpreted the fires, fearing the worst."

Tulah picked up where he left off. "According to local legend, one enterprising mother told her children a story to calm them. Recalling the German tradition of lighting 'Spring Fires,' she told them the large Easter bunnies they had seen—"

Clay grinned. "Jack rabbits—"

"The jack rabbits," nodding, she continued, "were boiling Texas wildflowers to make the dyes for the Easter eggs. She told her children to go to sleep, so the Easter bunny could hide the eggs."

"By morning," said Clay, "the men had returned with the good news about the treaty."

"But the tradition of telling the Easter Fires legend continues to this day." Tulah grinned.

Angela glanced at the campfires flickering in the gathering dusk. "It makes a great story, but I can't imagine how frightened the settler women must have been for their children that night."

Tulah shook her head. "Me, either."

"Was that all there was to making the peace treaty?" asked Kio. "Just that one meeting between the settlers and the Comanches?"

"No," said Clay. "They finalized their negotiations in Fredericksley about two months later."

"And they never broke the treaty," said Tulah.

After Mass, they met in the parking lot.

"Kio's got to drive back to Fort Davis, and Tulah and I have to be at work by one," said Angela. "Maybe we should caravan, each take our own car."

"Good idea." Clay glanced at Tulah. "You know the way. Lead on."

A few minutes later found them parked beneath ancient live oaks. Angela peered up at the robin's-egg-blue sky through the gnarled oak branches, the ball moss clinging to them like green-gray lace. They followed the crushed granite path into the cemetery, stopping at the first of the costumed actors.

Standing beside 'his' headstone, holding an antique rifle, the bewhiskered man grinned at them. "Welcome to the Tombstone Tale Trail. I'm Griff Baines, a Texas Ranger. In 1876, I rode with a hand-picked group, known as the Special Force. Our task was to bring in John King Fisher and his gang of murdering cattle and horse thieves.

"In those days, they called stolen horses and cattle 'wet stock' since the desperadoes would steal them on one side of the Rio Grande, swim them across, and then sell them on the other.

"The day we caught 'King' Fisher, as they called him, we ambushed his hideout and caught them playing poker on the porch. Before they had time to strap on their guns, we had 'em surrounded.

"We tied their feet to their stirrups and then hooked the stirrups together beneath their horses. Then we fastened their hands to their saddles' pommels and led their horses to Eagle Pass, where we threw them in jail.

"Old 'King' Fisher was a wily one, though. He never was convicted. Five years later, he was appointed a deputy sheriff in southwestern Texas." He grinned. "I'd like to thank you for your kind attention."

Smiling at the irony, the small group applauded him.

"Now, if you'll follow this path to the next stop on the tour, you'll meet one of our pioneer ladies."

The ancient path was overgrown with bluebonnets that had escaped from the grave covers and spread into the crushed red granite. The bluebonnets were so thick, the visitors had to gingerly pick their way, trying to avoid stepping on either the fragile flowers or the close-set graves.

Angela stopped momentarily to stare at the panoramic blanket of blue.

Kio caught up with her and put his arm around her waist. "Beautiful, isn't it?"

She nodded. "I've never seen bluebonnets in such profusion. They're so closely packed together, they create a blue and green pattern in the red granite. It's like an oriental carpet."

A few steps later, they came upon an elderly woman in a rocking chair, embroidering. She wore a black dress with a white lace collar and bonnet tied beneath her chin.

"Hello, everyone, I'm Helena Hirsch. I'd like to thank you for visiting me. It gets mighty lonely out here, and it's good to have company.

"Migrating from Germany, my husband and I settled here in the Hill Country. Cholera took him a few years later. To feed my daughter and myself, I opened a boarding house in town."

She held up her needlework. "Besides cooking and cleaning for my boarders, I embroidered every towel, bed sheet, and pillow slip. No short cuts, no lazy daisy stitches or French knots in my handiwork. Embroidery is art, and like many pioneer women, I not only took pride in it, it was my creative outlet.

"Now, if you'll continue to the next stop, you'll meet William Hall."

William Hall? Billy? As she approached, Angela looked at the adolescent dressed in buckskin trousers, cotton shirt, leather boots, and a wide-brimmed hat. *He can't be more than fifteen or sixteen. Billy couldn't have been that young when he was shot.*

"Welcome, everyone. I'm William Hall, a farmer, who settled a few miles from here in a cabin that still stands today. When the Comanches came to Fredericksley to sign the Meusebach-Comanche Treaty and collect their gifts, they camped along the banks of the stream behind that cabin.

"It was there that John Meusebach smoked a peace pipe with the three chiefs: Old Owl, Santa Ana, and Buffalo Hump. I recall they spread buffalo hides in a circle. The Comanche chiefs sat on one side with their warriors, while John Meusebach, his men, and I sat across from them.

"Twice they passed the peace pipe before distributing the gifts. Then the Comanches sang and danced as they beat drums made of stretched buffalo hide. Not to be outdone, we sang German folksongs and yodeled for them."

Suddenly, Billy appeared near the actor. Angela gasped as she compared them side by side.

"You all right?" Kio glanced at her.

Whispering "Billy's here," she stepped away from the group.

Billy studied the boy after he joined her. "He's half the age I was and twice as well dressed."

Wearing a crooked grin, she whispered, "Is he telling the truth? Was the treaty signed on your property?"

"Not exactly." He gave her a crooked smile. "They signed the treaty the next afternoon in Fredericksley, but the Germans and Comanches shared a camp along the stream the night before. The part about them passing the peace pipe, singing, yodeling, and dancing . . ."

"Was it true?" She glanced at him.

He nodded. "Yes, that part's true. The Honey Eaters—"

"Honey Eaters?"

He grinned. "That's what some people called the Penateka Comanches. Others called them the Wasps."

"Why?"

"They liked honey. They dipped sliced pemmican in it for a healthy snack." He paused, as if remembering. "The Comanches wore their best finery that night: porcupine quills, feathers, and paint."

"War paint?"

He shook his head. "No black paint for war or death, just colors for the festivities that night."

Smiling, she searched his face for clues. "Is there any proof, any evidence this took place on the property?"

"Maybe some arrowheads," Billy shrugged, "but nothing substantial."

Pressing her lips together, she sighed. "We need more than legends to get it listed on the National Register of Historic Places."

When the tour ended, Kio walked Angela to her car. "Think about August, will you? I'd really like us to get married sooner, rather than later."

"August to February is only six months' difference, but . . ." She took a deep breath, trying to recall her dream's images, impressions, trying to put those into words that made sense to him—and her. Frustrated at her inability to express herself, she shook her head. "I just get the feeling I'm supposed to go to, or I'll be called to Waco . . . or Fort Worth."

"But not Fort Davis." He sighed. "Give it some thought. August is four months away. A lot can happen in that time."

She gave him a crooked smile as she put her arms around him. "I love you. Kio. I just don't want to rush into anything."

"Who's rushing you?"

She cocked her eyebrow. "Yeah, who'd possibly do that?"

Smiling, he leaned down to kiss her. "See you in three weeks?"

"Definitely." She kissed him back.

Despite her lingering goodbye to Kio, Angela arrived at work early. A sullen silence met her as she walked through the office door.

"What's wrong?" She looked at them.

Wordless, Kelby wheeled toward the sink and turned on the tap. The spigot sputtered as successive gushes of air shook the pipes. Out came a trickle of murky water.

"The well's gone dry." No smile, Mrs. Bankhead spoke in a dejected monotone.

"We knew this drought was bad, but it's the first time the well's ever run dry." Mr. Bankhead stifled a sigh. "I'd no idea the water table had dropped this much."

"Without water, we can't process the wine." Mrs. Bankhead sniffed. "We can't even wash the tasting room's wine glasses."

Angela thought for a moment. "Why don't you use disposable glasses, at least for today?" She watched their expressions. "It'd get us through . . ."

Mrs. Bankhead glanced at her husband. "That's true . . . but then what?"

"I already told you." Brooke held up a forked branch. "I can water witch."

Angela squinted. "Water *what?*"

"Water dowse, water divine." Brook looked at Angela's blank stare. "I can find water without drilling for it. I've got the gift." Again she held up the Y-shaped stick. "All I need is this."

Mrs. Bankhead scowled. "It's New-Age tripe—"

"It's not New-Age, and it's not tripe." Brooke rolled her eyes. "Water dowsing has been used successfully for centuries. Even modern pharmaceuticals like Hoffman-La Roche have had dowsers on their payroll since the forties."

Mrs. Bankhead deadpanned, "It's called water *witching,* isn't it? Need I say more?" Shrugging, she spread her hands.

Brook started to argue. Then biting her lip, she stifled a sigh and began again in a reasonable tone. "It's called *witching* because European settlers used witch hazel branches to locate water. The word *witch* came from the Middle English word *wiche*, which meant pliable. Witch hazel or *wiche* hazel simply meant bendable, pliant hazel branches that lent themselves to dowsing."

Mrs. Bankhead shook her head. "Dowsing is a kind of divination, and the Bible forbids it." When Brooke started to argue, Mrs. Bankhead's eyebrow shot up. "Just a moment ago, you yourself called it water-divining. Brooke, we've had this conversation so often, I have the chapters and verses memorized. Deuteronomy 18:10: 'Let there not be found among you anyone who . . . practices divination . . .'"

"Semantics," said Brooke.

"And Hosea 4:12: 'My people consult their piece of wood and their wand makes pronouncements for them . . .'" Eyes narrowed, Mrs. Bankhead studied her daughter.

"And the Bible also states Moses and Aaron used a 'rod' to locate water." Brooke met her mother's eyes. "Wouldn't that be divination?"

Apparently stumped, Mrs. Bankhead pressed her lips together as her eyes bunched up. Then a smile broke over her face. "Numbers 20: God told Moses to strike a *particular* rock with a branch to release its water. Moses didn't locate the water. God told him where to find it. *That's* the difference. What *you* do is witchery."

"Water-witching's got nothing to do with witchery," said Brooke. "It's either a gift you're born with, or a skill you learn."

"Skill? You mean craft," Mrs. Bankhead's eyes gleamed, "witch-craft."

"Call it what you want," said Brooke, "but the facts are, the well's gone dry, and I can find water."

"You put a lot more faith in yourself," her mother stared at her, "than you do in the divine."

"Dowsing's got nothing to do with religion or witchcraft. It's a knack, a gift, and I've got it." Brooke stared her mother down. "I've made good money on the oil fields as a dowser. A water-well drilling company in Abilene hired me to tell them where to dig. Heck, I've got an eighty percent success rate." She took a deep breath as she looked from one parent to the other. "At least, let me try. What have you got to lose?"

Mr. Bankhead caught his wife's eye. When she gave a curt nod, Mr. Bankhead said, "Give it your best shot."

Brooke grinned at her father. Then after checking the time, she motioned them to follow her. "We've got a couple minutes before we open. Let's see what we can find."

They walked outside, and Brooke turned to her father. "Where's the most convenient location for a well?"

He pointed to an area behind the winery's tasting room. "The closer to the building, the easier it is to run pipe."

"Okay." Gripping both forked ends of the branch, Brooke extended her arms in front of her, palms up. Then as she steadied the Y-rod at a forty-five-degree angle, she took a deep breath, seeming to compose herself, ground herself. Holding the branch with a light touch, she began walking toward the location.

"When the branch responds," she called over her shoulder, "it'll jiggle and dip toward the ground." Then she became silent, methodically walking back and forth across the area as she searched for water.

After several hushed minutes, Angela stifled a yawn. Several more minutes passed in silence. Suddenly the branch wobbled. Brooke doubled back, retracing her steps, homing in on the exact location. When she reached the spot, the branch pointed toward the earth so hard, it vibrated, nearly wrenching itself from her hands.

"Drill here." Then wincing, she dropped the branch and grabbed her side.

"Brooke!" Mrs. Bankhead ran to her daughter and used her shoulder to prop her up.

"I'm fine." Shaking her head, Brooke waved her off. "Really. It just caught me off balance."

"Your due date's getting close." Glancing at Mr. Bankhead, her mother took out her cell phone. "Maybe we should call your husband, Noah—"

"It's not time yet," said Brooke. "We can't both afford to be off work, at least, not until the baby's actually on its way. He can't miss work for false labor."

Mrs. Bankhead grimaced. "Don't wait too long . . ."

Brooke stood up straight. "I'm fine. Really." She gave her mother a warm smile. Then she turned to her father. "That's where you'll find water. Call the drillers."

"It's expensive to dig a well, thousands of dollars—and that's if you're lucky enough to find it the first time. We can't afford any mistakes." Taking a deep breath, he rubbed his chin. "Are you sure . . ."

"You saw where that branch pointed." Brooke gave him a firm nod. Then, using her foot, she drew in the soil. "X marks the spot."

He nodded. "All right. We're putting our money on you."

Mrs. Bankhead looked at her watch. "We open in two minutes. Angela, where did you see the disposable glasses?"

"In a cupboard at the private wine bar." She held up the tram keys. "Back in a minute."

"And where's Tulah?" Frowning, Mrs. Bankhead checked her watch again.

"Here I am." Smoothing her hair into a ponytail, Tulah meandered toward them.

"Where were you?" Mrs. Bankhead's eyes narrowed as she checked her daughter's appearance.

Tulah shrugged. "Just got back from the cemetery tour."

Angela gave her a quick glance but kept her thoughts to herself.

"What's going on out here?" Tulah looked at the group.

"Help me bring back the plastic glasses," said Angela. "I'll tell you on the way." She relayed all that had happened. "Just hope Brooke knows her business."

"Me, too." Tulah took a deep breath. "My parents don't have money to pour down the drain," she caught Angela's eye, "literally."

She took a closer look. "How come you're late getting back from the cemetery?"

Tulah's eyes sparkled. "Clay and I had a few things to . . . discuss."

Angela raised her eyebrow.

"I said, *discuss*." She gave a twisted smile. "What with him helping my parents hold onto the land, it just didn't seem right to be at odds with him."

"Is that so?" Angela stifled a smile as she pointed to her lower lip. "You might want to fix your lipstick. It seems to have smeared a little . . ."

Water Witch

The dowsing rod is a simple instrument which shows the reaction of the human nervous system to certain factors which are unknown to us at this time.

– *Albert Einstein*

Wednesday after classes, Angela drove straight to the winery. As she walked into the tasting area, she saw Brooke. "I couldn't wait to find out." Angela lifted her eyebrow. "Did they find water?"

Brooke's expression was impassive. "They started digging two pits near the drill site about seven this morning."

"Pits? For what?" Angela studied her face for clues.

"When they began drilling, they had to shoot water down the drill hole to soften the soil. The overflow gushed into the pits." Brooke's lip lifted in a half smile. "Just like an old-fashioned hand pump, it takes water to get water."

"So did they hit water?"

Brooke exhaled. "I don't know. The drill bit just broke through the bedrock a couple minutes ago. I couldn't stand in the sun any longer, so I came inside."

Angela's focus instantly changed from the well to Brooke's welfare. "Are you all right?"

"I'm fine. I just had to sit down a minute." She gave a wan smile. "Go on outside and see if they've hit water."

"Can I get you anything?"

Brook shook her head. "Just let me know what's happening. I'm more anxious than anyone to find out if the site's right."

"Understandably." Nodding, Angela gave her a supportive grin. Then she went outside to find Clay standing with Mr. Bankhead, watching the men and machinery. She heard the drill's pulsating drone as it dug deeper into the earth. Dragonflies floated above the muddy overflow pits.

Shouting over the drill, she asked, "Have they hit water?"

They turned bunched, worried eyes toward her as they shook their heads.

Clay made an attempt to smile. "Not yet."

Then the foreman made a slicing motion across his throat to cut the engine. As the motor sputtered to a stop, the man listened.

Angela's ears echoed from the drill's raucous din. Still, she strained to hear along with him, not knowing what she was listening for.

The foreman made a twirling motion with his hand, and the drill operator began lifting the bit out of the well hole. After they removed the drill, the men shoved a PVC pipe into the opening.

Angela, Clay, and Mr. Bankhead held their collective breath. She glanced at their intent faces and said a silent prayer.

Suddenly, murky water trickled, and then gushed through the pipe. The foreman and his team cheered, slapping each other on the back with muddied hands.

Clay's and Mr. Bankhead's faces relaxed into smiles as the cloudy water began to run clear.

Thank you. Angela glanced toward heaven.

The foreman joined them, grinning. "You've got yourselves more than enough water to fill this tank, maybe thirty, forty gallons per minute." Then he held his head back, watching their response. "I haven't seen a gusher like this since the drought began. How'd you know to drill in that spot?"

Mr. Bankhead and Angela caught each other's eye. "My daughter water-witched it."

The foreman chuckled. "She done good. With this drought, it's getting harder and harder to hit water, especially on the first try. Tell her, if she ever wants a job, she's got one with my drilling team."

Grinning, Mr. Bankhead nodded. "I'll do that."

The foreman and his crew began shoring up the new well with gravel and cement as Angela hurried inside to tell Brooke the news.

"Guess what?!" Angela looked around the tasting room and office, but she was nowhere to be seen. Then she saw her exiting from the restroom. "They just hit water—"

Brooke looked at her with dark, tense eyes. "And my water just broke. Can you drive me to the birthing center?"

On the way, Brooke called her husband and her mother, both out of town but promising to be there as soon as possible. A quick call to Tulah let them know she was on her way back from San Antonio. As they walked into the birthing center, Brooke glanced bashfully at Angela.

"Would you stay with me, at least until my family gets here?"

"Of course. And if it helps put you at ease, this isn't my first birth." Smiling, Angela told her about Maria's preterm birth.

Brooke's grin turned into a grimace as a contraction began. Hunching over, she grasped her belly and grunted through gritted teeth.

The nurse-midwife met them in the waiting room. "I'm Janet," she said to Angela. Then she turned toward Brooke with an encouraging smile. "Let's get you in a birth pool filled with nice, warm water. It'll be just like getting into a warm bath."

Brooke gave a nervous laugh and then sucked in her breath, wincing. "Can't be soon enough."

After Brooke undressed, she donned a short, loose-fitting gown. Janet and Angela helped her into the birthing pool, where she crouched down. Janet dimmed the lights, turned on soothing music, and added six drops of lavender essential oil to the water. Instantly the room smelled less like an antiseptic hospital and more like a sun-drenched garden.

"The soft lighting and music will help you feel more in tune with your labor," said Janet, "and the lavender scent helps reduce anxiety, lighten the mood during early labor. How do you feel?"

Brooke's face relaxed into a smile. "I feel lighter. The water seems to buoy me up."

"It definitely makes it easier to move around, so you can make yourself comfortable." Nodding, Janet gave her another encouraging smile.

"Should I be in any particular position?"

"The best position is whatever helps your baby move easily through your pelvis. Rule of thumb: Keep your knees lower than your hips, but you can assume a lunge position, too. Keep one knee up and one knee down. That helps some babies descend."

Brooke's face contorted as she felt another contraction. When it passed, she reached out her hand to Angela. "I'm glad you're here."

Grasping her hand, Angela gave her a lopsided smile. "I'm not doing much. You and Janet are doing all the work."

Brooke grinned. "You're filling in for my husband, my mother, and my sisters."

"I know your father had to stay at the winery, holding down the fort, at least until they finish shoring up the well, and Tulah's on her way here from San Antonio," said Angela. "What about your husband, Mrs. Bankhead, and Kelby?"

"Noah's on his way here from Midland. Mom had taken Kelby into Austin for a dentist's appointment." Brooke gave a crooked smile. "You're my pseudo sister, at least for today." Then her grip tightened as she felt another contraction.

Janet gently rubbed Brooke's back until the spasm passed. Then she reached for another bottle of essential oil. "Just a drop of rose oil should do it." She wrinkled her nose. "Too much is overpowering, but one drop helps relax the pelvic area, open up the cervix. As you inhale the rose aroma, I want you to visualize a rose bud opening into a full flower. Visualize your cervix as that rose bud, gently blooming, gradually opening."

For an hour, the only sounds were Janet's soothing voice as she guided the visualization and the water lapping at the sides of the tub as Brooke gently rocked her hips.

Then Brooke groaned as one contraction after another overtook her. Angela grasped her hand, sensing the pain through the pressure of her grip.

When the series of contractions had passed, Janet said, "Warm water helps you cope with the pain. It's like taking a bath to soothe aching muscles." Then she reached for three other bottles of essential oil. "Clary sage helps the uterus with contractions. It also has a calming effect on the nervous system." She squeezed three drops of the essential oil into the pool.

Instantly, a woodsy, earthy scent permeated the room.

Brooke wrinkled her nose. "It smells bitter."

Nodding, Janet squeezed a drop of another essence into the warm water. "Everyone interprets scents differently, but if we mix in geranium oil . . ." She watched as Brooke inhaled deeply and her face relaxed into a smile. "Geranium's uplifting aroma helps counteract the sharper scent of clary sage. It's also said to stimulate the circulatory system."

Janet monitored the water's temperature, Brooke's blood pressure, and the fetal heartbeat. Sitting back, she smiled. "Only a few more minutes."

The contractions came closer together. Then they began to increase in strength until Brooke was nearly panting.

Janet squeezed a drop of oil on her bath pillow. "Neroli oil helps comfort you, relax your breathing. You're entering the transition phase now." After monitoring the fetal heartbeat again and gently palpating Brooke's abdomen, she smiled. "The baby's descended into the birth canal and is in position to deliver."

Brooke's eyes opened wide.

"This is it." Angela gave her hand a reassuring squeeze.

Several more pushes, and the baby's head crowned. Janet carefully loosened and unwound the umbilical cord that had wrapped itself around the baby's neck. Another two pushes, and the baby was out.

Janet lifted it from the water and put it on Brooke's chest. "Congratulations," she said as she suctioned out the baby's mouth and nostrils. "You have a beautiful daughter."

An hour later, Mrs. Bankhead and Kelby rushed into the birthing center.

After congratulations, hugs, and tears, Mrs. Bankhead looked at her daughter in amazement. "When we left this morning, we didn't have water, and we didn't have a granddaughter. What happened?"

Brooke and Angela took turns relating the story.

"You mean to say," said Mrs. Bankhead, "just as the drillers hit water, Brooke's water broke?"

Wearing an ironic grin, Kelby threw her hands in the air. "Everything's about water around here. If it's not droughts or water rights, it's water wells, water breaking, and water births." Then she hugged her sister. "Congratulations on *both* counts. You produced water and *heir* elements today."

"Water and air?" Cocking her head, Brooke squinted. "What do you mean?"

Kelby grinned. "You're the reason the drillers found water, and you delivered an heir under water. You're a water witch, and you're a mother."

Mrs. Bankhead glanced from Brooke to the birthing pool on the other side of the room. "You gave birth to my granddaughter under water?"

"Not exactly." Brooke shared a chuckle with Kelby and Angela. "I was sitting in water, and the baby was born under water. Within a second or two, the midwife brought her to the surface." She smiled. "No snorkels or scuba gear were used in her delivery."

Never breaking a grin, Mrs. Bankhead nodded thoughtfully. "What are you going to name her?"

"Actually, I'm waiting for Noah to get here before we choose her name."

"Speaking of the devil . . ." Kelby gestured toward the door. "Look what the wind blew in."

A bear of a man appeared in the doorway. The moment his eyes connected with Brooke's, he maintained eye contact until he was at her side. "Babe, I'm so sorry I wasn't here for you. I came the moment you called."

Covered with grime, he reeked of oil and sweat. Angela smiled to herself. It was obvious he'd rushed from the fracking fields straight to his wife.

Between kisses, Brooke told him about Angela's help. "It all worked out fine."

"Where's my daughter?" He looked around the room, searching for the baby, nodding absently as he glanced from person to person.

"She's getting her first bath, should be back any minute."

Noah looked at himself. "Is there a place to wash up before I meet her?"

"There's a sink over there," said Janet, bringing back the baby.

Noah never took his eyes off the mewling bundle as he scrubbed his hands and arms. After he dried himself, he walked up to Janet and held out his arms. She smiled as she carefully made the transfer. The burly man gently enfolded the baby in his arms, caressing her downy head with his calloused hands.

Then he brought the baby over to Brooke. Placing the bundle in her arms, he knelt down to be face to face with his wife and daughter. "What'll we name her?"

Brooke glanced at her mother before looking into Noah's eyes. "Do you still want to give her the name we discussed?"

Nodding, he smiled. "Sure."

Brooke looked at her mother. "We thought we'd name her Henrietta since Noah's father's name is Henry, and yours is—"

"Henrietta." Mrs. Bankhead wore a shy, surprised smile. "I'd like that."

Grinning, Noah kissed his wife. "It was my little water witch's idea."

"Water witch?" Kelby grinned. "Your 'little water witch' not only delivered a baby, she brought in a well today."

He looked at his wife. "You did? That's my girl!"

Tulah stuck her head in the door. "Did I hear there's a new member of the family?" All faces turned toward her as she walked in.

"Where've you been?" Kelby scrutinized her sister.

Tulah breezed past her. "Had to make a couple stops." She brought out a bouquet of flowers and handed them to Brooke. "This is for you, and this," she brought out a cable knit bow headband, "is for my niece."

"How'd you know it was a girl?" Kelby studied her.

Tulah smiled at Angela. "A little birdie texted me." Then she looked at Brooke. "Can I put it on her?"

"Sure." Brooke and Noah both protectively held onto their new daughter as Tulah fastened the headband. Stepping back, she appraised the baby. "She's so tiny."

Her eyes sparkling, Brooke chuckled. "What did you expect?"

"I don't know." Tulah shrugged. "An armful. Something bigger than a doll."

Mr. Bankhead walked in with Clay close behind. Glancing at the scene, he spoke to his wife. "So we're grandparents."

She smiled. "Wait till you hear her name."

All eyes turned to Brooke. "Henrietta."

His eyes sparkling, Mr. Bankhead thumped his hand against his forehead. "You mean, now I've got to contend with two Henriettas?"

While the group chuckled, Clay glanced at Tulah several times, as if trying to catch her attention, but she kept her eyes glued to the baby. Finally, he leaned in front of her, reaching out his hand to Noah and then to Brooke. "Congratulations."

Both proud parents beamed as they shook hands with him.

"It's hard to believe she's here." Noah glanced down at the baby, a look of wonder in his eyes.

Watching her husband's reaction, Brooke chuckled. "Harder for some to believe than others . . ."

"When are you getting Henrietta baptized?" Mrs. Bankhead looked from Brooke to Noah and back.

Brooke glanced at her husband before answering. "Baptists don't believe in baptizing infants—"

"Baptists don't believe in baptizing?" Mrs. Bankhead scoffed. "I never heard of any such thing. Of course, babies have to be baptized, and the sooner, the better."

Brooke took a deep breath before answering patiently. "Baptists believe in waiting until the children are old enough to understand the gospel and make a lifelong commitment to Jesus."

"You're denying your child the grace of God?" Mrs. Bankhead's lips were white with outrage. "John 3:5. Jesus said no one can enter the kingdom of God without being born through water and the Spirit." She peered at her daughter through narrowed eyes. "Acts 2:38: 'every one of you must be baptized in the name of Jesus Christ for the forgiveness of your sins, and you will receive the gift of the Holy Spirit.'"

Brooke rolled her eyes as she took another deep breath. "A certain maturity is necessary so the child understands what they're doing."

"'A certain maturity' sounds to me like an age requirement, an achievement where they're old enough to 'qualify' for baptism and salvation." Mrs. Bankhead shook her head. "Salvation is a pure gift, not something to be earned or merited. You were brought up Catholic. How can you lapse in your faith so much that you deny your own child salvation?"

Noah held up his hand. "Let's not make a moral battle out of this." Putting his arm around Brooke, he smiled at his mother-in-law. "This is a time to rejoice. Your daughter's just come through the delivery safely, and our daughter's healthy and whole. We should be celebrating, not squabbling."

Mrs. Bankhead spoke under her breath. "There should be a baptism."

"All right, if it'll help keep the peace, I'll get baptized." An amused glint in his eyes, Noah looked at his in-laws. "I'm a lapsed Baptist—never had been baptized, at least, not till now, and you're all invited."

Afterwards, they met back at the Bankheads' home, all except Noah, who stayed behind with Brooke and the baby. Mrs. Bankhead pulled the barbecued pork that had been slow cooking all afternoon, whipped together several side dishes, and invited Clay to stay for dinner.

As they sat around the oversized table, Mr. Bankhead said a prayer, and then they began to pass the dishes. "We have a lot to be grateful for," he said, "a healthy granddaughter and daughter, a well that came in on the first attempt—"

"Now if we could just settle this land issue . . ." Mrs. Bankhead sighed.

"We made a counteroffer to keep the water rights." Grimacing, Mr. Bankhead updated them. "Stall tactics, but it buys time."

"The question is," Mrs. Bankhead stifled another sigh, "how much time. With this drought, we can't afford to wait long."

"I spoke with Doctor West about the terms of the lease," said Clay. "He said it depends on funding, but the dean's agreed to transfer enough grant money to reimburse you for an exploratory study, which means a month, at least, probably two." He glanced at them hopefully.

Tulah refused to make eye contact with him, seeming to purposely look away if they happened to glance at each other.

Kelby glanced up from her plate. "Will it be enough to take the land off the market?"

"It'll buy us time in the short term, enough to pay for the new well and cover the winery's operating costs," Mr. Bankhead looked from Kelby to his wife, "but I don't know about the long haul. At this point, I don't see a way around selling the land . . . eventually."

"Grant money." Kelby wiped her fingers and mouth on the napkin. "I've been researching it online. To save the land, all we need to apply for a grant is a 501(c)3."

"Texas Mustangs is a non-profit 501(c)3." Clay caught her eye. "Can we somehow work it into the equation?"

"Maybe." Kelby's eyes lit up. "I'll research it after dinner."

"Here we have a new granddaughter/niece, and we're talking about land, grants, and non-profits." Mrs. Bankhead gave her husband a sharp look. "What about our granddaughter's baptism? Doesn't it bother anyone else that until she's baptized, her soul's in jeopardy?"

"We knew when Brooke married Noah outside the Church, there would be differences of opinion." Mr. Bankhead took a deep breath. "We can make suggestions. We can pray about it, but ultimately it's their baby and their choice."

Lips pursed, Mrs. Bankhead sighed. "And why would Noah refuse to get Henrietta baptized, yet volunteer to be baptized himself?"

Clay glanced from her to Tulah and back. "You heard him. He was never baptized. Besides doing this for religious reasons, I think he was trying to make a good-will gesture to keep peace in the family. His faith doesn't endorse infant baptism." Wearing a half smile, he added, "But he knew a baptism was important to you. He's doing it for you," again he glanced at Tulah, "and the woman he loves."

Tulah stared at her plate, refusing to meet his eyes.

After dinner, as they cleaned the kitchen, Angela turned toward Tulah. "What's going on with you and Clay?"

"The truth?" Tulah took a deep breath. "I was late getting to the birthing center because I had lunch with Astin."

Rolling her eyes, Angela exhaled. "I thought you and Clay had 'discussed' a few things."

Tulah shrugged.

"You're walking a fine line, seeing two men at the same time," Angela sniffed, "one who's trying to save the family property, and one who's trying to take it."

"You mean, buy it."

Angela shook her head. "I mean, *take* the land and steal the water. I've never trusted Astin. We know he works for Agua Purificación, and intuition tells me he's using you to get them the water."

Tulah scoffed. "How can you accuse him of posing as the buyer . . . and then of using me to get the land?"

"Because that's what he's doing. I think he'll use anything and anyone to get what he wants."

Chewing her lip, Tulah seemed to wage an internal battle before meeting Angela's eyes. "I'll be honest. I'm confused. I know Astin works for the Porter law firm. I know AP is their client, but when I'm with him, I believe he really means to buy the land for himself."

Grimacing, Angela raised her eyebrow.

"I know. Even I think it's suspicious, but I believe what he tells me."

"You *want* to believe what he tells you, so you do." Angela shook her head. "I don't think you're able to be objective. Not when it comes to Astin."

"Maybe," she mumbled.

"What about Clay? Where does he fit into all this?"

Tulah shrugged.

"He seems more concerned about your family's land than you do." Angela gave her a twisted smile. "And it seems to me he's a lot more concerned about you than you are about him."

"I don't know . . ."

"As long as you've been 'discussing' things with Clay, maybe you should tell him about your interest in Astin?"

Tulah took a deep breath. "I have to admit. I'm attracted to Astin. Clay's the salt—"

"I know. Clay's the salt of the earth, and Astin's the brightest star in the heavens." Angela rolled her eyes. "You've told me this before."

Tulah's shoulders sagged. "Clay and I have a history together. That's true. It's just that sometimes I . . . *remember* it more clearly than other times. But Astin." Her eyes lit up. "I've never met anyone like him. He's told me how after he buys the land we can come over any time, that nothing will change."

Angela frowned. "You remember what Clay said about that."

"Vaguely . . ."

"He said Astin won't live there, that the Porters, AP, or both of them are behind the deal. Clay said it's all about water that Agua Purificación's going to siphon off the aquifer."

Tulah shook her head. "Astin's told me how he has plans to make the land into an animal reserve."

"Animal reserve." Narrowing her eyes, Angela stared hard at her. "Last time you said he called it a game reserve. Does he mean animal sanctuary or game reserve?"

Tulah blinked. "I don't know. What's the difference?"

"Even if he's telling the truth about being the buyer, *which I doubt*, was Astin talking about creating a safe place for animals?" Angela thought of Kitz. "Or was he thinking of pumping out the water below ground, and then doubling his income by using the land above ground for canned shoots and trophy-hunting?"

Tulah's jaw hung slack. "I don't think he's capable of that . . ."

"I wouldn't be so sure." Angela stifled a sigh as she thought of all the captive-animal facilities posing as humane sanctuaries that in fact were roadside menageries or exotic-animal breeders. "I agree with Clay. I think Astin will tell you anything you want to hear to get his hands on the land. Then he'll pump out the water, leaving you and the aquifer high and dry."

Before Tulah could respond, Kelby rolled into the kitchen. "Good news! I found a grant for a non-profit corporation."

"Really? Something where Texas Mustangs could apply?" Angela looked from one sister to the other.

"Yes," Kelby nodded, "but for the non-profit to qualify, the mustangs would need to be physically located on the property."

"That's a problem." Tulah squinted, as if thinking. "There's very little fencing around that property—"

"And fencing's expensive." Kelby finished her thought for her.

"The idea's to bring money in with the grants," Tulah grimaced, "not spend it."

"This one doesn't sound like a good fit, but it's a respectable first step." Angela turned toward Kelby with an encouraging smile. "Keep up the good work." Then she remembered Billy's story. "Here's another slant."

"What?" Kelby studied her face.

"Billy—"

"Your ghost?" Kelby's eyes lit up.

Angela nodded. "He told me the Comanches and Meusebach group camped by the stream the night before they signed the peace treaty in Fredericksley. See if you can find any evidence to support that information."

Sunday morning, they arrived at the church early, chatting in front of the brick building.

Kelby drew Angela aside. "I've found some information online about where the Comanches and Germans camped."

"Already?" Angela's eyes opened wide.

"Texas has given historical markers to two other sites connected with this peace treaty, one in San Saba County, and the other in Mason County."

"Good sleuthing, both sites are nearby." Angela nodded. "Did you find anything in Barron County?"

The girl shook her head. "Not yet, but I'll keep looking." Biting her lip, Kelby took a deep breath. "While I was online researching grants, I investigated something else, something Tulah won't want to hear."

Cocking her head to the side, Angela studied her. "What?"

"Astin Starr's married."

A honking horn drew their attention as Noah and Brooke drove up with their baby.

Angela exchanged a quick look with Kelby. "Tell me later."

Lips pressed together grimly, Kelby nodded.

Noah and Brooke led the group into church, where the preacher welcomed them with a short prayer. Then he invited them to stand at the edge of the baptism pool. As he removed his shoes and socks, he asked Noah and another man to do the same.

"This is an exciting day for Noah, so I want to thank you all for joining us. Baptism's an important event in a Christian's life. The book of Acts lists story upon story of people accepting Jesus as their Savior and then being baptized in obedience to His word.

"The Apostle Paul wrote in Romans, 'all of us who were baptized into Christ Jesus were baptized into his death.' We were buried with him, so that just as Christ rose from the dead, we too, may live a new life. In baptism, we identify with the death and resurrection of Jesus Christ. As we are immersed, the water symbolizes us dying to our old selves, and as we come up out of the water, we are raised to a new life in Christ.

"That new life is marked by three things: commitment, covenant, and commission. From this day forward, Noah is committed to Christ. Compare this to a wedding ceremony, where a person publicly commits the rest of his or her life to following Jesus, for richer, for poorer, through thick and thin.

"In baptism, you enter a covenant, a relationship with Christ, becoming a part of the body of Christ. You're also commissioned. Every follower of Christ is called to be Jesus's salt and light, to make the world a better place."

The preacher looked from one to another. "Today Noah is being commissioned to use his strengths, weaknesses, time, treasure, and talents for the Kingdom of God. Noah is here before you as one testifying to a changed life in Christ."

The preacher grinned at him. "Now for a 'dry run.' First, I'll ask you a series of questions. Then Bob and I will each take one of your elbows and dunk you." He beamed. "Are you ready?"

Tight-lipped, Noah seemed uneasy, but he nodded.

The three men waded down the steps into the pool. From their goosebumps and blue-tinged lips, the water seemed cold.

"Noah, is there anything you'd like to share before you're brought into the fold?"

Silently, he shook his head, visibly shivering.

"Noah, have you accepted Jesus Christ as your personal savior, and do you believe He died for your sins?"

His hands clenched in prayer at his waist, just above the water line, Noah said, "Yes."

"And is it your desire today to make that belief public by being baptized?"

Noah mumbled through chattering teeth. "Yes."

"Then it's an honor and a privilege to baptize you in the name of the Father, the Son, and the Holy Spirit." With those words, the preacher and his assistant took hold of Noah's elbows, bowed him over backwards, and submerged him in the water.

Noah came up sputtering, arms flapping, as he splashed water over the spectators and involuntarily pulled the preacher and his attendant into the baptismal pool. When the three men regained their footing, they were drenched and shivering, but grinning. Rudely awakened by sprayed water droplets, the baby began crying. The spectators wiped splattered water from their arms, faces, and glasses, but everyone was smiling.

After a moment, the preacher recaptured his composure. "Thank You, God, for Noah's faith and his step of obedience in his walk with You. Please continue to guide and direct this man as he seeks to follow Jesus. Use his life as a witness to friends and family to draw others to Christ by the difference they see in his life."

Brooke smiled proudly as an attendant led Noah, dripping but grinning, to a dressing room.

After congratulating Noah outside the church, Kelby pulled Angela and Tulah aside.

"We're late. The winery's opening in fifteen minutes." Tulah's tone was impatient. "What?"

Kelby took a deep breath. "I did a background check on Astin—"

"You did *what?*" Her voice rising, Tulah gave Angela a sharp look, and then scowled at her sister. "Can't either of you give him a break? The benefit of a doubt? Yes, I know he works for the Porters and AP, but—"

"Astin's married." Kelby swallowed.

Tulah's face blanched. She blinked, processing. "What?"

"I said—"

"I heard what you *said!*" Her outraged sigh sounded like a low growl. Then her eyes narrowed to thin slits. "Prove it!"

Kelby handed her a printout of a newspaper item. Highlighted were the words, *Mr. and Mrs. Astin Starr were spotted at the Houston Winter Gala. Astin Starr, executive director of the Texas Environmental Foundation, leads the foundation in its quest to balance long-term conservation with sustainable usage. Mrs. Starr wore an original Oleg Cassini, a Charmeuse gown sprinkled with Swarovski crystals and enhanced with a sweetheart neckline and empire waistline.*

Crumpling the paper, Tulah turned on heel and strode toward her car, calling over her shoulder. "I'll see you at work."

When Angela arrived at the winery, she saw Tulah sitting in her car, cell phone in hand. She opened up the tasting room and began to set up for the afternoon visitors. Singled-handed, Angela struggled to keep up with the demand as customers began arriving. She peeked out the window and saw Astin's red convertible parked next to Tulah's. Even through the windshield, she could see they were having a heated discussion.

"Miss," called a man, holding a bottle, "we'd like this merlot. Can you help?"

Angela saw a line of three other customers behind him. "Yes, sir."

She hurried back to the cash register as another group of people at the wine bar waved for her attention. "Can we get some service?"

Smiling through gritted teeth, Angela nodded. "Be right there." *Tulah, hurry up.*

A half hour later, Tulah strolled into the winery. Her eyes were red, but she was smiling.

Angela motioned toward the cash register as she divided her time among three groups of wine tasters.

There wasn't time to talk until Tulah's parents came in an hour later. During a lull, Angela whispered, "What happened?"

Tulah grinned. "The newspaper article was about his parents, Mr. and Mrs. Astin Starr . . . senior."

Angela wasn't sure whether to be glad for her or angry. "That's good news for you, but next time, please have your spats with Astin *after work*. I was swamped in here."

"Definitely." Tulah gave her a hug. "Thanks for covering for me."

When Angela returned to the customers, she thought it through. *Maybe Tula's convinced of Astin's innocence, but I'm not so sure.* During her next break, she called Kelby.

"That newspaper article about Astin Starr, was it the only item mentioning a wife?"

"It's the only one I've found . . . why?"

Angela relayed Tulah's conversation. "This makes me curious. Think you'd have time to run a search on him?"

"It'd be my pleasure." Kelby gave a dry laugh. "Incidentally, a newsletter just came in from the Fredericksley Alliance. I'll forward it to you, but here's the gist. The bad news is, the North Edwards Aquifer Authority granted a temporary permit to AP to pump two hundred-ninety million gallons of Trinity Aquifer water each year—"

"What!" Angela scoffed. "I thought they're the group that claimed how fragile the Trinity is, how slow it is to recharge."

Kelby sniffed. "The Trinity's low already, yet our well and most of our neighbors' wells depend on it. The good news is, concerned citizens formed the Barron Trinity Protection Association to oversee the aquifer. Based on legal grounds of North Edwards incorrectly governing this permit's grant, Barron Trinity just filed objections to them."

"That's the first good news I've heard in this water war." Angela shook her head. "How does AP manage to manipulate the groundwater conservation districts?"

"Persuasive lawyers and deep pockets." Kelby drew in her breath sharply. "Uh-oh."

"Now what?"

"I just googled Mr. and Mrs. Astin Starr and got fifty-nine hits."

"Any photographs?" asked Angela.

"Searching." Angela heard typing in the background. Then Kelby said, "Found five images. Two are definitely of an older couple, but I recognize Astin in the other three, all with the same woman."

Angela clicked her teeth. "Now what?"

"Wait."

Angela squinted. "For what?"

"I just forwarded the photos and links to my sister. Let's see what happens next."

Monday, when they returned to their San Antonio apartment after school, Tulah collared Angela. "Got a minute?"

"Sure." Angela sat on the sofa as Frank jumped on her lap.

"Do you know about the photos Kelby sent me?"

Uncertain how much to disclose, Angela silently nodded.

"Astin told me he's never been married, but he and the woman in these prints had lived together." She caught Angela's eye. "*Past tense*. He said she's no longer in the picture."

Angela's eyebrows shot up. "Doesn't cohabitation equate to common-law marriage in Texas?"

"That's what I thought, but he said no." Tulah held up her fingers as she made her points. "He said, 'Texas needs three things to recognize a common-law marriage. In addition to living together as husband and wife, the couple has to agree to be married and, at least once, tell others they're married.'"

"Sounds like a sleazy shyster response." Frowning, Angela sniffed. "Let me guess. He never 'agreed to be married'?"

Tulah glanced down, avoiding her eyes.

Angela shook her head. "If I were you, I'd consider the door closed on Astin, and I'd stop pounding on it to open."

"But he wasn't married."

Angela took a deep breath. "Legally, whether or not he was—or is—married is something for the courts to decide, but this man's devious. When you asked him about the first newspaper article, and he—"

"Those were his parents." Tulah's eyebrows met as she rushed to defend him.

"Maybe so, but it opened a dialogue. That would've been the time to mention his 'significant other' if he'd wanted to be honest with you. Instead, you had to hear it from Kelby. I hadn't trusted

Astin before. Now, I wouldn't touch him with a ten-foot pole."

Tulah grimaced. "You just don't understand him."

Resisting the urge to roll her eyes, Angela stood up. "Okay. Follow your conscience. I'm done wasting my breath. With finals the week after next, my internship starting, and the first draft of my water-issues paper due, I've got enough on my mind."

Angela smiled at Tulah as she and Frank retreated to her room. She opened a textbook, trying to study, but images of Kitz and the turtle kept coming to mind. *What will happen to the wildlife if Astin buys the land and confiscates the water for AP?*

Prioritizing, she sat in front of the keyboard and began writing the water-issues essay. *If I put my thoughts on paper, maybe it'll clear my mind enough to concentrate on the finals.*

> In legal jargon, the Rule of Capture is a law of non-liability. It contends that landowners can pump as much groundwater from beneath their land as they wish, and no one can do anything about it. The law sets neighbor against neighbor, residential area against industrial, agricultural consumption against environmental. In this semi-arid region, water translates to power and profit.
>
> A private company, Agua Purificación (AP), recently moved into a Barron County 'white zone' to capitalize on the antiquated Rule of Capture. Rather than use the rationale for the law's enactment, e.g., the water necessary for a family and its livestock, AP has found a legal loophole. It plans to pump 5.3 million gallons per day from the already stressed Trinity Aquifer to supply water to fast-growing, master-planned communities.
>
> A 'white zone' is defined as an area that is not managed by any regulatory entity. Outside the boundaries and jurisdictions of two interrelating, but not overlapping, conservation districts, AP

plans to drill their wells *through* and *below* the Edwards Aquifer into the underlying Trinity Aquifer, legally bypassing all jurisdiction. AP can pump the aquifer dry, leaving homeowners, business-owners, and wildlife to suffer the consequences.

Because the rules governing Texas's water were drafted before geologists understood water flow, groundwater and surface water are bound by two separate laws. Texas is a dual-doctrine state that recognizes both riparian and prior-appropriation doctrines.

The riparian doctrine allows water rights to landowners along rivers and creeks. Surface water rulings were introduced during the Spanish settlement of Texas, over two hundred years ago.

Groundwater is subject to the Rule of Capture that springs from the English common law rule of 'absolute ownership,' which the Texas Congress adopted in 1840. As a result, Texas water law has earned the dubious moniker of the 'law of the biggest pump.' Texas courts have consistently ruled that landowners have the right to pump all the water they can from beneath their land, regardless of the effects on other wells.

The legal opinion in Texas assumes all sources of groundwater are percolating water, moisture that seeps into the ground, versus subterranean rivers flowing beneath the land. As a result, the landowner is presumed to own underground water until it is proven that the source of the water supply is actually a subterranean river.

Subterranean river. Angela blinked, processing. Could there be *a subterranean river* flowing beneath the Bankheads' property? She texted Kelby with an idea.

Holey Water

The drops of rain make a hole in the stone,
not by violence, but by oft falling.
– *Lucretius*

That Friday at the Bankheads' dinner table, Kelby grinned mischievously. "I did a little research about groundwater and underground rivers."

Tulah looked up from her plate, her eyes narrowing. "What for?"

"Background information on the property." Kelby smiled blandly. "The Edwards Aquifer stores water in underground lakes and rivers."

"Is that so?" Her father glanced at her as he reached for the butter.

"The entire Hill Country is one big karst," said Kelby.

"A what?" Mrs. Bankhead looked at her.

"A karst area," said Noah, quickly swallowing a mouthful of food, "is basically a landscape with limestone beneath it, so it has lots of underground sinkholes and caves."

Kelby nodded. "It forms as underground water dissolves limestone to create caverns, where the water can flow and collect in pockets."

"How does water dissolve rock?" Mrs. Bankhead glanced doubtfully at her glass of water.

"Carbonic acid," said Kelby. "As rain passes through the atmosphere and then trickles through the soil, it accumulates enough carbon dioxide to form a weak carbonic acid."

Noah picked up the thread. "But it's strong enough to dissolve the limestone's calcium carbonate."

Mrs. Bankhead nodded.

"In layman's terms," Noah, grinned, "water dissolves rock."

Swallowing a smile, Kelby winked at him. "Anyway, the point is, this area's crisscrossed with veins of water. In theory, a river could be running three to seven hundred feet right beneath our feet."

"Interesting concept, but why are you bringing up the subject?" Mrs. Bankhead arched her eyebrow.

"The timing," said Angela, turning toward her. "While I was writing my water-issues paper, I learned Texas's legal opinion about groundwater. It assumes all groundwater is the result of rain seeping into the land, not subterranean rivers flowing beneath it."

Tulah crossed her arms. "So?"

"So," said Kelby, "a landowner legally owns all the groundwater . . . unless you can prove the water source is a subterranean river." Triumph gleamed in her eyes. "If we could prove there's an underground river flowing beneath the land—"

"Astin couldn't pump a drop more water than for personal use." Finishing her thought, Tulah coldly surveyed her sister.

Kelby lifted her shoulder. "It could be Astin, or it could be the Porter law firm or AP. Whoever buys the land wouldn't be allowed to pump water on a commercial scale."

Tulah scoffed. "What makes you think there's a river running underneath us?"

"This area's karst," said Kelby, "limestone pockmarked with caves, sinkholes, faults, fractures, and underground passages. We know two aquifers—"

"The Edwards and Trinity," interjected Noah.

"Both lie below our feet, but at separate levels. No one completely knows all the watercourses or their flow patterns. It's a complex, underground drainage system." Kelby grinned. "When you're dealing with unknown factors, anything's possible."

Tulah shook her head. "Don't forget. There's a stream flowing aboveground not a mile from here. What makes you think there'd be an underground stream, too? Wouldn't one cancel out the other?"

"Not necessarily." Noah shook his head. "In karst landscapes, rivers can slip in and out of sinkholes at different points, flowing into underground caverns and connecting with springs and other streams that eventually rise again to the surface as artesian wells or rivers. Then when the water plunges through a sinkhole or flows over a porous limestone bed, the river runs dry because the water's been absorbed through the limestone into the caves below."

"And the process starts all over," said Kelby. "Surface water doesn't rule out the presence of groundwater. It's better to say surface water transforms into groundwater and then back again."

"It's not magic," Brooke smiled, "just hydrology. In fact, this whole area's fed by a web of hydro lines. Every river, stream, creek, and spring within the aquifers' area is a hydro line."

"If there were that much underground water, we wouldn't have to worry about a drought." Mr. Bankhead gave them a wan smile. "Nor would we have to sell our land to keep our heads above . . . water, proverbially speaking."

Everyone smiled but Kelby, whose mouth turned down in a grimace. "We have a drought. We need water, and shysters are buying up land to sell groundwater back to us at inflated prices. We need natural gas, and frackers are wasting precious water drilling through shale to sell us cheap gas, but at what cost to the environment?"

"Now, wait just a minute." Taking a deep breath, Brooke glanced at Noah. "Don't equate one with the other."

"Whether we're talking about water or gas, it's a few opportunists cashing in at everyone else's expense." Her arms crossed, Kelby challenged her. "Tell me how it's different."

"For one thing," said Brooke, "water's the basic necessity of life. Companies like AP that twist the laws to pump aquifers on a commercial scale exploit the public. When they cause neighboring wells to go dry, those speculators deprive folks of their homesteads, livelihoods, and *life,* just to turn a profit."

Kelby scowled at her sister. "And that's different from fracking, *how?*"

"Fracking doesn't deprive anyone of anything." Again, Brooke glanced at Noah. "It's a means to keep the US energy independent."

"Doesn't deprive anyone of anything?" Kelby scoffed. "Fracking impacts the entire environment. Besides affecting land use and water consumption, what about water contamination, air emissions, noise pollution, and potential earthquakes?" Shrugging, she gestured with upraised palms. "Hello!"

Noah shook his head. "Fracking's usually done a mile or more beneath the surface. It's not likely to affect water sources just a few hundred feet below ground."

"Weren't we just talking about how aquifers occur at different levels?" Kelby raised her voice. "Blasting through one or several levels to get at another level could easily cause contamination. Water could drain out. Gases could seep up. Look at that town in Pennsylvania."

"Centralia," said Mr. Bankhead.

Kelby shot him a grateful smile. "A mine fire's been burning underground since 1962. Even if, and I do mean 'IF,' fracking operations are properly installed and sealed, over time, pipes corrode and leak. Benzene and methane were recently found in contaminated water wells in Wyoming. Who wants flammable water taps?" Nearly shouting, she met Noah's eyes. "How can you say fracking doesn't affect groundwater?"

The baby woke with a lusty cry.

"Okay, discussion's over." Brooke lifted the baby from the portable crib "Now that you woke Henrietta, I'm officially calling this debate closed." She arched her eyebrow. "Just keep in mind, fracking employs a lot of people and feeds a lot of families . . . including ours."

The next morning, after Brooke, Noah, and the baby left for west Texas, Angela and Tulah met Clay at the cabin. Doctor West and his team arrived minutes later, and they began hauling their equipment to the cave.

The professor chatted with them as they walked. "Until recently, archaeologists rarely excavated in wet caves."

Clay glanced at him. "Why's that?"

"Cave mud can be so elastic, it's difficult to dig and impossible to screen for artifacts. Until they developed new field methods in the nineties, archaeologists ignored water-logged caves."

"Water-logged?" Tilting her head, Angela gave him a puzzled look.

"That's right." Doctor West nodded. "When we were here last week, we discovered there's a muddy base of caliche and silt beneath the top layer of bones. The deeper we dug, the wetter and denser the mud became. We also discovered a trickle of water in one of the tunnels."

"Tunnels." Angela mentally replayed her excursion into the cave. "I never noticed any tunnels."

Clay shrugged. "This is the first I've heard of it."

"Once we began excavating," said Doctor West, "we unearthed a slight opening surrounded by damp soil. It proved to be a tunnel filled with silt deposits. As we dug deeper, we found a seep or tiny spring that saturated the lower sediment layers, creating densely compacted mud. Once we dug through that barrier, we saw a partially blocked passage." His face softened into a smile. "A tunnel, actually what seemed to be a bifurcated tunnel with a second passage leading off to the right."

"And you saw a trickle of water?"

The professor nodded. "As we shone our light through the opening, we saw its reflection in what appeared to be a narrow trickle of water."

Recalling Kelby's words, Angela caught Tulah's eye. "Are you thinking what I'm thinking?"

Tulah nodded. Then she turned to Doctor West. "Is there any chance this passage could lead to an underground river?"

His eyes lit up as he considered the idea. "Possibly. This area's riddled with interconnecting caves and passages. The tunnels would need to be excavated and explored to state anything conclusive, but since it's a karst cave, the likelihood does exist."

When they reached the cave's entrance, Angela couldn't help but notice the progress they had made. "You've widened the access. Now we won't have to dive head-first to get into the cave." She took a deep breath, recalling how claustrophobic that had made her.

"And we constructed this covering to keep out the elements, animals, and curious." After pointing to a wooden structure his team had moved aside, he grinned at Angela. "Now you can step into the cave, not nose-dive."

Besides their headlamps, carbide lamps helped light their way. Angela marveled at the details she could see in the brighter light. "I can't believe all the changes you've brought about in such a short time."

When they reached the cave floor, Professor West picked up the mammoth tusk with gloved hands and held a lamp close to it. "Look at this scrimshaw."

Angela saw delicate lines incised on the mammoth ivory. Subtle cross-hatching described form and movement. She looked up at his face.

"Is this a carving of a horse?"

Smiling, he nodded.

"Who made this artwork?" She wanted to touch it, run her bare fingers over the subtle etching, but held back, afraid the oils from her skin would damage it.

"Without radiocarbon testing in a lab, this is only a preliminary guess, but I'm relatively confident a Clovis-era forager created it."

Angela's eyebrows shot up. "So you're talking how many years ago?"

"Again, without carbon dating, it's pure conjecture, but this could be as old as eleven thousand years."

Giving a low whistle, Angela glanced from Tulah and Clay back to the professor. "I don't know what you're thinking, but this certainly seems like an amazing find to me."

Doctor West nodded. "At the risk of sounding presumptuous, I agree, but I don't have the final word. The use of any gift to the archaeology department is up to the office of the provost, the dean, the faculty, and a donor-approved advisory board. Of course, I'll make all the assertions." He held up the tusk. "This being my most persuasive argument."

"If that etching is a horse," asked Tulah, "wouldn't it prove horses were in North America prior to Christopher Columbus's Spanish horses?"

Doctor West glanced at the tusk's artwork. "If this scrimshaw portrays a Pleistocene North American Equus, that would be substantial proof."

Her eyes sparkling, Tulah turned to Clay and Angela. "This could help reclassify mustangs as native North American wildlife, not as feral or introduced animals. If that happens, mustangs couldn't be rounded up or slaughtered anymore. The Endangered Species Act would protect them, just like it does the desert tortoise or grizzly bear."

"Really?" Angela cocked her head. "How?"

"Two key questions define an animal as a native species." Clay held up his fingers as he counted. "*One*, where did it originate, and *two*, did it evolve along with its habitat? This find might prove the mustang qualifies on both counts." He glanced at the tusk before meeting their eyes. "It's priceless, not only for establishing this land's historical importance, but for proving mustangs are native to Texas and must be protected."

Two weeks later, Angela began living in the cabin fulltime. After the spring semester ended, she started her part-time internship at the Enchanted Rock State Natural Area, working at both the park and winery. When time permitted, she helped Kelby write grant proposals.

Saturday evening after dinner, as she and Kelby were researching potential grant sources, Angela looked up from her computer. "What was the name of the foundation Astin's father heads?"

The girl shrugged. "Something about the environment. Give me a second. I'll find the article." She ran a search and read from the screen. "It's the 'Texas Environmental Foundation,' and he 'leads the foundation in its quest to balance long-term conservation with sustainable usage.'"

Nodding to herself, Angela took a deep breath. "I thought the name sounded familiar. Listen to their mission statement. 'Our Environmental Conservation Program protects critical ecosystems. We collaborate to create lasting change in how land and freshwater ecosystems are managed.'" She turned toward Kelby. "Sound like a good fit?"

"Definitely!" The girl's eyes lit up gleefully as she gave an evil laugh. "It's perfect, especially the part about Astin senior being the means to counteract Astin junior's plan."

Sharing a grin with her, Angela clicked links and read from the grant resources page. "'We want you to succeed. Interact with our foundation staff to create a grant that solves problems and stimulates discoveries. Under the guidance of our grant team, we will assist you with documents and templates to help you develop your grant.'"

"Wow." Kelby was silent a moment, seeming lost in thought. "This could be the answer. Not only would they give us grant money, they'd help us write the proposal."

"Don't count your chickens . . ." Angela arched her eyebrow. "There's still the minor, insignificant part about the foundation liking our idea. Listen to this. 'When there are shared goals, we will work together to design a grant.'"

"Shared goals . . ." She looked at Angela. "How can we phrase our grant request to have 'shared goals' with the foundation?"

"According to their mission page, they 'seek to achieve their goals by funding approaches that result in protecting critical ecosystems.'" Angela thought of her promise to Billy. *Protect the water*. Then she caught Kelby's eye. "Isn't that what we're trying to do? Save this land from being mined for its water and turned into a canned-hunt ranch?"

"That," said Kelby, "*and* get the land listed on the National Register of Historic Places. *And* get funded by Doctor West's archaeological department. *And* get the 501(c)3 grant for the mustangs." She took a deep breath and blew it out. "We're taking on a lot of applications and proposals. Do you think we're biting off more than we can chew?"

Angela sighed. "Grant writing is labor-intensive. I agree, but look at it this way. The more we apply for, the better our chances. If we apply for three grants, we triple the odds of one of them funding us."

Nodding, Kelby pursed her lips together. "We've got to do all we can to save this land."

Save the water. Again Angela thought of Billy, Kitz, and the turtle. "With all these projects, let's do a sanity check."

"Okay."

Angela held up her thumb. "Grant money would pay your parents for the research on their property." She held up her index finger. "That income would postpone them having to sell the land to save the family business."

Kelby nodded.

Angela held up another finger. "Holding on to the land would protect the water."

"For now . . ."

"I know." Angela grimaced. "It isn't the answer, but it's a stop-gap measure till we find a solution."

"Girls," called Mr. Bankhead. "Bob Anderson just called."

Kelby glanced at Angela and then called back, "From Anderson Realty?"

"Come into the kitchen a minute."

When they were all assembled, Mr. Bankhead said, "Mr. Starr has made a counteroffer to our counteroffer, as well as increased his earnest money and his offer price."

"He's serious about buying this land." Mrs. Bankhead caught her husband's eye. Then turning toward Kelby, her eyes became somber. "How are your grant proposals going? Have any of these paid out?"

When Kelby did not answer, Angela spoke up. "You knew Doctor West was trying to get his funding extended."

Mrs. Bankhead nodded.

"I was saving the good news for dinner, but the funding came through." Angela held up her phone. "Clay texted me. Doctor West got another two-month's extension, enough to reimburse you for an exploratory study through June."

Mr. Bankhead mumbled, "He did?"

Angela nodded, hoping what she said next sounded confident. "I'm sure by then, at least one of our grants will come through."

Kelby glanced at her parents. "We've got a lot of irons in the fire."

Mrs. Bankhead appraised her daughter before turning toward her husband. "Speaking of irons, I still say strike while it's hot. Accept Mr. Starr's more-than-generous counteroffer."

Inhaling, Mr. Bankhead bit his lip as he seemed to weigh the information. Finally, he turned toward his wife. "With the reimbursement funding, we'd have enough operating cash to keep the winery going, at least until July."

"Then what?" Mrs. Bankhead's eyes bunched up. "Don't forget. Kelby's starting UTSA next year. We'll need her tuition money."

"Don't sell the land on my account." Glassy-eyed, Kelby said, "I've got one small scholarship. Maybe I can get another. Besides, I can get a job to cover the rest of the tuition."

Wearing indulgent smiles, both her parents studied her.

Mrs. Bankhead asked gently, "What about all the other expenses?"

"I'll make do . . . do whatever it takes to keep that land." Kelby swallowed hard. "Just please don't sell that land because of me." She cleared her throat. "I couldn't forgive myself."

Her parents glanced at each other. Then Mrs. Bankhead nodded. "We've got until July to think about it."

When they returned to Kelby's room to continue the hunt, Angela smiled at her. "As long as we're researching grants, who says we can't expand our search to find you another scholarship?"

The next morning, Angela watched the sun come up over the stream with Billy and Kitz. She listened to the birds calling to each other, singing their morning chants. Looking through the trees, she saw the sky change from amethyst to fuchsia to a rosy gold.

Then she turned from the heavens to Billy. "It's like being in church."

He smiled. "How so?"

She analyzed it a moment. "The sunlight between the trees is like looking through stained glass windows. The bird songs are the prettiest hymns I've ever heard, but most of all, it's the sacred hush at dawn. It's as if nature herself is saying a prayer of thanks for the new day."

He nodded. "There's a peace here, a peacefulness I've never felt anywhere else."

Kitz sat at her feet, flicking his ears, listening. Mallard ducks swam near the other shoreline, keeping their distance, yet seeming to join in their quiet reflection.

"I can understand you wanting to stay here." Angela whispered her thoughts, not wanting to break the spell. "If there's a heaven on earth, this must be it."

Suddenly, they heard laughter. Her ears perking, she gave Billy a perplexed look. Kitz scrambled to his feet, the mood broken.

Then they heard several men's voices and a woman's. "Is that Tulah?" Again she looked at Billy, but he had disappeared. Kitz vanished soundlessly into the underbrush. Angela momentarily thought of hiding herself, but after listening, was sure it was Tulah's voice.

"When we were kids, we used to fish from this point." Tulah's tone was nostalgic. "Caught my first bass here."

A minute later, Tulah, Astin, and the three Porters came into view, carrying a cooler and fishing gear.

"Good morning." Angela purposely spoke loudly, announcing her presence, her 'ownership.' Her smile was an unconvincing afterthought.

"Angela!" Hand on chest, Tulah gasped. "You surprised me."

"Really?" Her tone was cool.

Recovering, Tulah gave a nervous laugh. "What are you doing here?"

"I live here." She shrugged.

Tulah pointed toward the cabin. "Yeah, but—"

"And you're just in time to join us for mimosas." Wearing a smirk, Astin pulled a carton of fresh orange juice, a bottle of prosecco, and a bottle of vodka from the cooler. Then he turned to Tulah. "Where are the glasses?"

She came to attention. "In my backpack." She hurriedly unzipped the pouch, brought out five plastic glasses, and smiled as she presented them. "Here you go."

Her fingers interlaced over her chest, Angela curled her lip. "Thanks, but sunrise is a little early for me to start drinking."

"But the perfect time to catch fish." Astin turned toward Tulah and the Porters. "Isn't that right?"

Tulah agreed with a ready nod. "The fish are jumping."

Raising her eyebrows, Angela heaved a silent sigh. *They're not the only ones jumping.*

Astin popped the cork of the prosecco, filled a glass, added a splash of OJ, and handed it to Tulah with a smirk. "Milady."

He then poured liberal amounts of vodka into four glasses and added a splash of OJ. "Help yourselves to screwdrivers, gentlemen." Holding his glass aloft, he turned back to Tulah. "To the prettiest angler I've ever seen."

The three men chuckled as they lifted their glasses to Tulah and downed the contents.

While they got out their fishing tackle, Angela called Tulah aside. Gesturing toward the men with her chin, she asked, "What do you think you're doing?"

Tulah shrugged as she sipped her mimosa. "Being neighborly."

"Kelby, Clay, and I are doing everything in our power to prevent the sale of this land, and you." Angela scoffed. "You're fraternizing with the enemy."

Tulah smirked and tossed down her drink. "I swear, you're as naïve as Kelby." Sneering, she put on a coy smile. "I'm running with the big dogs now."

Angela pressed her fingers between her eyes, trying to stave off the sudden headache. Glancing at the four men, she then peered at Tulah. "You lie down with dogs, you get up with fleas."

Her eyes cold, Tulah turned away and wordlessly began walking back to Astin.

Angela sighed. "Sorry. That was out of line."

Tulah kept walking.

"Look, I'm driving to church and then to the winery." Angela forced a wry smile. "Would you like to ride with me?"

"Thanks, I'm otherwise occupied." She sneered.

Angela nodded, suppressing a sigh as she started back to the cabin. "Then I'll see you later."

"Maybe." Tulah shrugged as Astin refilled her glass.

One of the Porters cast across the stream, narrowly missing the ducks and getting his line caught in the trees. "Dang it!" He tried pulling at it from different directions, but it was tangled. Cursing, he cut his line. "I just bought that lure."

When he began adding a new triple-hook lure to his line, Angela stopped in her tracks. "I hope you're going to retrieve that hook and line."

The man scoffed. "Why?"

"Because they're hazardous to every animal that comes by." Angela took a deep breath. "They see something shiny, and they think it's something to eat."

Shrugging, he finished fastening the new lure. Then ignoring her, he cast again and began reeling in the line, slowly trolling the bait through the water.

Angela made a mental note of the hook's whereabouts. Rather than argue, she decided to retrieve it after work. Then she paused to watch the four men fly-fishing from the stream's bank, chattering, laughing as Tulah played barmaid on the sidelines, refreshing their drinks, watching, but not really part of party.

"Next time," Astin called to Tulah, "put a little 'Irish' in it."

So much for a heaven on earth.

Angela looked for Tulah at Mass but did not see her. Nor was she at work when Angela opened up the winery. After customers began arriving, Angela tried calling and texting her, but Tulah never picked up or responded.

A half hour later, the Bankheads arrived. "Where's Tulah?" asked Mrs. Bankhead.

Reluctant to snitch, Angela simply said, "She hasn't texted or called me."

Mrs. Bankhead left a message on Tulah's cell. A half hour later, she got a call back.

A half hour after that, Tulah showed up at work, unkempt, smelling of fish and alcohol.

Mrs. Bankhead took one look at her daughter and rushed her into the office. "You're no help to us like this. You're drunk. Sleep it off on the couch. Your father and I'll deal with you when we get home. Ephesians 5:18, 'Don't get drunk on wine, which produces depravity. Instead, be filled with the Spirit.'"

At closing time, Tulah was sitting up but hungover. "Got any aspirin?"

Angela fished in her purse for the container as Tulah's mother studied her. "Can you drive?"

"Yeah, I'm fine." Tulah tried to stand up, but wincing from the headache, slumped back down.

"I'll drive her home," said Angela. "She can leave her car here tonight."

Mrs. Bankhead grumbled something under her breath. "Angela, go on. Take off now. We'll clean up." Her smile was wan. "Appreciate your holding down the fort . . . again."

In the car, Angela turned toward Tulah. "What happened?"

She sighed. "I didn't have any breakfast. Then I had the mimosas. Then I was thirsty, so I drank orange juice, but Astin said it needed a little 'Irish.'" Groaning, she leaned her head against the window and fell asleep.

When they arrived, Angela helped her into the house. "Do you want me to put on coffee?"

Again, Tulah groaned. "No, I just want to sleep." With that, she slumped onto the sofa.

Angela covered her with the comforter and drove back to the cabin.

After feeding Frank, she took a scoop of feed out to Kitz, but he was nowhere around.

That's odd. He's always here waiting when I get home, as if he has an internal clock.

Then she remembered the fishing line and hook snagged in the tree. *I doubt they cut it down. Better get it before something tries to eat it.*

She met Kitz on the way to the stream. Something flashed in the sunlight. "What's that?" She tried to hold his head still to see, but he kept turning away. Finally, Angela saw the three-pronged lure hooked in his lip.

"No!"

She tried to unhook one barb, but as she moved one, she dug the second deeper into his lip. The third hook pointed in the opposite direction, and she was afraid it would catch his bottom lip, pinning his lips together.

She tried time and again, but every movement made him squirm from pain. Finally, she tried calling a veterinarian. She left message after message, but on Sunday night, no one was in the office.

Again and again, she tried to pull out the hooks, but nothing worked. Apparently too sore to take any more, Kitz grunted and pulled away. After one last tug, he ran away.

"Kitz! No, I'm sorry. Come back!" She followed after him, catching up by a rusted barbed-wire fence.

As if Kitz knew what he was doing, he latched the third hook on a strand of rusty barbed-wire and pulled back, tugging harder and harder, until the hooks tore through his lips.

Close to tears, Angela wiped his bleeding mouth with a tissue. Then she put her arms around his neck, trying to comfort him. "Kitz, I'm so sorry this had to happen to you."

She thought of the irresponsible sportsman and shook her head. *Leaving his fishhooks dangling from a tree for curious animals to skewer themselves . . .* She shook her head. *It's unconscionable.*

That's what Astin and his crew do, dig their hooks into something beautiful, and entangle everyone and everything in their schemes.

She recalled the stream earlier that morning, the peacefulness as the day had dawned over its sparkling water. Astin and his crew had fouled its purity, its serenity. *They take the water and pollute it.*

She remembered how Tulah had sneered at her as she sipped the mimosas. How she had skipped church, forgotten to show up at work, and had to be helped home. *Fleas. Astin and his 'big dogs' just take, take, take. All they give in return is fleas.*

When Kitz's mouth stopped bleeding, Angela wrapped the bloody tissue around the three-pronged fishhook and put it in her pocket. Then she walked him to the stream and carefully rinsed his lips. Afterwards, she waded across the shallow water to retrieve the cut line, still tangled and dangling from the tree. *At least, nothing else can swallow or get tangled in this fishing line.*

The next morning, Kelby came to the breakfast table wearing a big smile.

Angela had to ask. "What're you grinning about?"

"This." She handed Angela a printout.

After skimming it, Angela grinned back. "Congratulations!" Then she turned toward the rest of the people at the table. "Long story short, Kelby won a grant for Texas Mustangs."

"That's the good news." Kelby's smile faded. "Not that it's bad news, but there's a requirement for this grant. The mustangs have to be housed on the property . . . which means fencing it and building a shed."

Angela thought of the sagging barbed-wire Kitz had used to tear the fishhooks out of his mouth. Still fuming about the abandoned tackle, she took a deep breath.

"Kelby," said her father, "that's a lot of work to fence the property, put up a shelter, and move the horses."

"Especially," said Mrs. Bankhead, "since we're selling the property—"

"But it's leased until July. You said you weren't going to sell it!"

"We said we'd *think* about it." Mrs. Bankhead glanced at her husband. "Your father and I feel fencing, building a shelter, and hauling the mustangs are a lot of work for nothing."

"It's not for nothing. It's just the beginning." Kelby's eyebrows met in a V. "Besides, it won't cost you a thing. This grant funds the materials . . . *and labor.*"

Her parents looked at each other. Finally, Mr. Bankhead sighed. "If it means that much to you, and you've got the money . . ." He glanced again at his wife. At her nod, he said, "Go ahead. Even if it's only for a few months."

The next morning, a crew of laborers began digging postholes in the caliche soil and putting up cedar fence posts not far from the cabin.

"What's going on?" Billy wore a puzzled expression.

"They're moving the mustangs here."

"Horses here?"

She nodded with a twisted grin.

"I've missed them." He gave a contented sigh. "It'll be good to have horses on the property again."

Within the week, the property's perimeter was fenced in, and a lean-to shed offered protection from the Texas sun.

"Cross fencing's next," said Kelby. She and Angela watched on the sidelines while Tulah and Clay unloaded the mustangs.

"Why?" Angela took her eyes off the horses to glance at her.

"We need to rotate the pastures," said Clay as he led one of the mustangs from the trailer, "or the horses won't let the land rest."

Angela squinted. "I'm not following."

"Instead of one big enclosure, cross-fencing separates the land into smaller sections. It keeps the horses on one section until they've eaten all the grass. Then we move them to a second to let the first recover. By the time they've eaten all the grass in the second section, the first will be green again." His thumbs hooked in his belt loops, Clay grinned at her.

"Makes sense." Angela looked to Kelby again. "But does the grant cover cross-fencing?"

Shaking her head, she gave a wry smile. "Back to the grant proposals again."

"Have you heard anything from the Texas Environmental Foundation?"

"Yes, I forgot to mention it." Kelby's eyes lit up. "They requested more information about the stream. It seems they're very interested in streamflow and streamgaging."

Angela thought for a moment. "Not that I'm familiar with those terms, but it sounds like they want to measure the water's current."

Kelby nodded. "They're sending two people to measure it with what they called 'the bucket' method."

"Sounds high tech." First deadpanning, Angela then smiled. "What are they going to do, see how fast a bucket fills with water?"

Kelby's eyes lit up. "Exactly."

After unloading the horses, Clay, Kelby, and Tulah left. Angela waved goodbye. Then she and Billy walked around the penned-in pasture with Kitz following behind.

While Billy admired the mustangs, he glanced at Angela. "Like I said, it's good to have horses again."

Nodding, she grinned as the Appaloosa approached them and began nuzzling her hand.

"You mooch." She laughed as she rubbed its velvety nose, feeling its soft, warm breath on her fingers. "What makes you think I have any treats for you?"

The horse gave a low whinny.

Taking a baby carrot from her pocket, she fed it to the mare on her open palm, the way Tulah had taught her.

"I'm seeing a lot of changes around here," Billy said slowly. "Fencing, horses, scientists working in the cave, but what about the water? What are you doing to save the stream?"

"It's *all* about protecting the water. If the owners don't come up with funding, they'll have to sell this land."

Billy stood to his full height. "I'm the owner."

Pursing her lips, she gave him an exasperated smile. "The *current* owners. If we don't come up with funding, you'll have new owners that will shrivel the stream to a mud puddle and drain the aquifer dry." She gestured toward the horses. "We got a grant—"

"Grant?" Wearing a puzzled expression, he cocked his head to the side.

"Money. As a nonprofit rescue, by housing the horses on this land, we're eligible for more grants, more money." She pointed in the cave's direction. "The scientists are leasing the land while they do research. Because of these two incomes, the current owners can hold onto the property until July."

"July? That's just a few months away."

"Hopefully, this'll buy us time to find more funding." Angela hunched her shoulder. "It isn't cheap protecting land from speculators."

Billy grimaced. "Neither the land, nor the water that flows on and below it."

Mr. Bankhead looked up from his breakfast coffee. "We made another counteroffer to Mr. Starr to keep the water rights." He grimaced. "Still stall tactics, but it'll buy time."

"But the question *still* is," Mrs. Bankhead stifled another sigh, "how much time? With this drought, we can't afford to delay selling the land too long. Even with the new well, the winery barely has enough water to meet production."

"I was researching vineyards and wineries," said Kelby. "One study said it takes twenty-nine gallons of water to produce one glass of wine." She arched her eyebrow. "Is that the best use of water?"

Tulah snickered. "We might want to lose the 'Save Water Drink Wine' bumper stickers for the Water-to-Winery."

"That study was based on outmoded European vineyards," said Mr. Bankhead. "The average U.S. grape grower produces about four times that yield. Our methods use a fraction of that water usage."

"Even cutting it in half," Kelby raised her eyebrow. "It still takes about fourteen, fifteen gallons of water to produce one glass of wine."

"Is that using water wisely?" asked Angela.

"We dry farm, which means we don't irrigate," said Mr. Bankhead.

Angela frowned. "You irrigate—"

"With gray water, *reused* water. That's the biggest saving in water usage." Mr. Bankhead gave her a patient smile. "Plus we recycle any water we use to clean the barrels and fermentation tanks. Not a drop's wasted."

"Vineyards and wineries are mentioned in the Bible," said Mrs. Bankhead. "Even Jesus drank wine."

"I'm not challenging the morals of drinking wine." Kelby looked at them. "I'm questioning the water usage in its production." Her eyes twinkled. "Not everyone can turn water directly into wine."

Angela glanced at the Bankheads. "Kelby does bring up a good question. Are vineyards sustainable?"

"Our goal," said Mr. Bankhead, "is to match the use of water to wine production, one to one, a gallon of water to a gallon of wine.

We're close. Currently, we're using about three gallons of water for each gallon of wine."

"But despite conserving water, we barely have enough to meet production." Mrs. Bankhead studied her daughter. "You're researching ways to save the property." She shook her head. "Without rain, or a miracle, we'll have no choice but to sell it, not if we want to keep our heads above water financially."

A subdued silence followed. Angela glanced at the others around the breakfast table, but no one looked up from their plates. The only sounds were silverware on china and toast being buttered.

She forced a cheerful smile. "Clay, Tulah, and I are meeting with Doctor West this afternoon. Maybe he'll have some good news."

Kelby looked up and gave her a grimace that nearly passed for a smile.

Tulah stiffened but said nothing.

"Cold water to a thirsty throat," said Mrs. Bankhead, "such is good news."

Angela caught her eye. "That sounds biblical. Is it?"

She nodded. "Proverbs 25:25. The Bible's full of water imagery. Water's mentioned in the first chapter, second verse of Genesis. Water not only sustains our bodies, it's a metaphor for our spirits. It's compared to new life in the New Testament. John 4:14, 'The water that I shall give will become a spring of water within, welling up for eternal life. In Jeremiah, Yahweh's called the fountain of living water and the hope.'"

"Hope." Kelby's eyes lit up. "Maybe we'll hear some good news today from Professor West." Her mouth lifted in a half smile. "Got to have hope."

Angela spent the day inside the Enchanted Rock State Park's office, answering questions and providing maps. After work, she rushed home to feed Frank and Kitz, and then hurried to the cave before the team left.

Tulah, Clay, and Doctor West were just surfacing when she arrived.

"Good, you're still here." Angela caught her breath. "How's the research going?"

Grinning, Clay held up what looked like the gills of a huge, fossilized mushroom.

She studied its indented ridges. "What is that?"

"A mammoth tooth." He held it out for her to touch.

Her eyes opening wide, she ran her fingertips lightly over the ridges of its cracked, calcified surface. "You found that here?"

Clay nodded. "Doctor West was just telling us about a Japanese group of scientists that's predicting the birth of a baby mammoth."

Angela's eyes opened wider. "What?"

"The technology exists," said Doctor West. "Scientists continue to better understand the roles of genome parts. It's only a matter of time until we see live woolly mammoths for the first time in four thousand years."

Puzzled, Angela squinted. "But isn't the question *how?*"

"Quite a few frozen mammoths have been extracted from permafrost. It's conceivable their nuclei could be implanted in an Asian elephant's egg cells. Then the elephant would act as a surrogate mother."

"Why Asian elephants?" Angela cocked her head to the side.

"They're genetically closer to mammoths," said Doctor West, "than African elephants."

"But you said the mammoth tusk we found could be as old as eleven thousand years." Angela narrowed her eyes.

"That's right," he said. "In fact, carbon dating proved it this past week."

"Then why did you say we might see live mammoths for the first time in *four* thousand years?"

Realizing the disconnect, he nodded. "Although mammoths stopped roaming in Texas ten to eleven thousand years ago, woolly mammoths lasted on Wrangel Island in the Arctic Ocean until four thousand years ago—"

"The point of all this," said Clay, "is mammoths are a hot topic right now. That new Waco Mammoth National Monument is showing an interest in this cave."

"More a collaborative *awareness* between Baylor University and the Waco Mammoth Foundation," said Doctor West, "than an interest, but this cave is getting a lot of attention."

"Will that attention translate to funding?" asked Clay.

The professor drew a deep breath. "That's more difficult to answer. The wheels of academia churn slowly." He smiled. "But our team has been making good progress."

"Really?" Angela looked at them. Though Tulah seemed preoccupied, Clay's and the professor's faces were animated.

"I'd mentioned that once we began excavating," said Doctor West, "we unearthed two tunnels filled with silt deposits and what appeared to be a narrow trickle of water."

She nodded.

"The team had a break through, *literally*," he smiled, "and we were able to explore the passages. The first tunnel had collapsed just a few yards in from where we'd dug, but the second tunnel goes on for a minimum of several hundred feet, possibly much farther."

"Will you be able to explore it?" Clay watched his response.

Doctor West shrugged. "If we had time and were professional cavers, possibly." He grinned. "We saw tantalizing evidence of more *Mammuthus columbi* and *Equus simplicidens* farther into the tunnels."

Squinting, Angela glanced at Clay for a translation.

"Mammoth and horse bones," he whispered.

"And I've saved the best for last. The office of the provost, dean, faculty, and the advisory board have all agreed . . ." Doctor West paused, beaming proudly.

Angela watched Clay's eyes light up. Holding her breath, she crossed her fingers.

"To extend funding through July thirty-first!"

Silence.

"Well," said the professor after several soundless moments. He looked from one stunned face to another. "Say something."

Hesitant to show her disappointment, Angela tried to be tactful. "The month's extension certainly will help." She glanced at Clay and Tulah for moral support. While Tulah wore a distant smile, Clay chewed his lip, seeming lost in thought. Sighing, she pushed on solo. "We were hoping for a longer-term arrangement."

"That's still not out of the question," said Doctor West, "but the academic world isn't like the private sector. Going through the proper channels, submitting the paperwork, and having it signed, reviewed, and approved by each and every stakeholder—all that takes time."

Which is running out. Angela nodded, but kept her thoughts to herself.

Seeming to regain his composure, Clay shook his professor's hand. "Thanks for your help. It's not that we're ungrateful." As he held up the mammoth tooth, he gave a dry laugh. "I guess we'd hoped you could put the bite on them."

Doctor West smiled sympathetically. "You were hoping for news you could sink your teeth into." Then his smile twisted cynically. "But sometimes, you have to be realistic and bite the bullet."

Clay helped the research team carry their equipment while Tulah paused by the stream.

Angela watched her shoulders slump as she leaned against a cypress. "What's on your mind?"

Tulah flinched as she woke from her reverie.

"That's what I mean," said Angela. "You've been so distant, so out of it lately . . . ever since Sunday."

Tulah's half smile and sniff passed for a laugh.

"What's going on?"

Tulah took a deep breath, as if gathering her thoughts. "If I tell you something, will you think I'm crazy?"

Angela laughed. "I already think you're crazy."

The ice broken, Tulah smiled. "Maybe I am." Her expression thoughtful, she glanced at the greenery beside the stream, as if looking for something.

Angela sat on her favorite rock overlooking the water. "What happened?"

"Last Sunday, after you left, as I was drinking the mimosas—"

"And the screwdriver."

"Actually plural, screwdrivers, something came over me."

"Yeah." Angela raised her eyebrows. "It's called a drunken stupor."

Tulah grimaced. "I wouldn't call it a stupor, but I did fall asleep—"

"You mean, pass out?"

"If you're going to be nasty, forget it." Turning, she started to walk away.

"Sorry," Angela gave her a sheepish smile. "What were you about to say?"

Taking a deep breath, Tulah slowly walked back. Peering at her, as if debating, she finally sat down. "What does Billy look like?"

Giving a nervous laugh, Angela did a double take. "Why?"

"I think I saw him, heard him." Tulah stared hard at her. "It's the only thing that makes sense."

Angela's eyes narrowed. "Describe him."

"He wore a blue chambray shirt and faded jeans and had a thick shock of dark hair . . . and his eyes were a haunting pale, pale blue. Like ice."

"That's Billy." Angela laughed to herself. "How did you see him?"

"It's not so much I saw as dreamt him." Tulah shrugged her shoulders. "It must have been a dream, yet he seemed so real."

"When you're asleep—or drunk—your guard's down. Your subconscious is more . . . receptive." Angela cocked her head, listening. "Did he say anything?"

Tulah nodded. "Can't recall the exact words, but basically he said to stand up for myself."

Angela remembered how Tulah had seemed the ignored girlfriend waiting in the wings, relegated to barmaid, and watching, wanting to be included. She also recalled how Tulah had placed Astin's ambitions above her family's or her own.

"Billy told me to assert myself, speak up."

"What'd you say?"

Tulah grimaced. "I told him I didn't want to seem insecure, needy. I wanted Astin to think me worldly, so I let things slide when he didn't . . . show respect. Billy told me nothing's worth losing my self-respect. He said, if I didn't speak up, tell Astin how I felt, bitterness could overtake me," she glanced up, "the way it's consumed him."

Angela nodded as she digested that information. *So bitterness is the reason he hasn't moved on.* She turned toward Tulah. "Let me guess what he said. Don't be your own worst enemy. Don't let Astin take advantage of you."

"Pretty much." Grimacing, Tulah nodded. "Then he lectured me on how a lady doesn't 'dally with the bottle.'"

"Good for Billy." Angela arched her eyebrow. "He had the nerve to say what the rest of us should've Sunday."

"I thought I was rubbing elbows with the movers and shakers, but they were just *bending* their elbows with me, while I refreshed their drinks . . ." Tulah glanced down. "Probably laughing up their sleeves at me the whole while."

Angela pressed her lips together, mentally agreeing. "Sounds to me like Billy's opened your eyes."

Tulah nodded. "And he said something else."

"What?"

"He said I shouldn't 'settle for something shiny but shoddy.' I should value substance, not arrogance, not Astin but—"

"Clay?" Angela caught her eye.

Tulah nodded. "He said Astin's like a fish lure, gleaming in the sun, but hiding fishhooks that could rip me apart inside."

When they met for dinner, Tulah told her family about the lease's extension.

Kelby's eyes lit up. "That gives us all of July to get grants."

Mrs. Bankhead caught her husband's eye but said nothing.

As Angela reached for a tortilla, she glanced at Kelby. "Another month's grace. Have you heard anything more from the foundation?"

She nodded. "They emailed their revisions this afternoon. I'll make their changes, follow up on their suggestions, and email the updated proposal after dinner."

"They're really being helpful." Angela smiled as she held up her crossed fingers. "Hope the grant comes through—"

"And . . . in time." Mrs. Bankhead stifled a sigh.

As Angela and Tulah walked through the pasture after dinner, they couldn't help but notice the ground. Cracks had formed in the parched soil two inches deep. Instead of walking on level land, it was like stepping from one raised paver to another. Tufts of brittle grass crunched beneath their shoes. A sunburnt brown instead of bright red, Turk's Caps buds withered on the stalks, too scorched to bloom.

Tulah shook her head. "I don't ever recall it being this dry this early."

Angela looked at the yellow leaves wafting from above. "Though it's June, the trees are already starting to shed their leaves. We need rain."

A rescued mustang whinnied, and they looked up.

Clay waved to them from the shelter as, brush in hand, he pointed to two more tied horses. "I've already picked their feet. Grab a brush, and we can finish grooming them."

Tulah chose the horse beside his. Angela swallowed a smile as she walked to the Appaloosa tied at the other end of the corral. While she curried its mane and tail, she watched Tulah and Clay's body language. Too far away to hear their banter, she could see them smile, catch snippets of laughter. By the time she finished brushing the Appaloosa, she saw Tulah and Clay saddling up their horses.

Tulah called to her. "We're going for a sunset ride."

Angela called back. "Do you want me to feed the horses?"

Tulah shook her head. "We'll feed them when we get back. Just leave the corral gate open for us."

The next night at dinner, Tulah refilled her water glass. "The governor just signed a bill letting Texas use gray water as another drinking water source."

Her father shook his head. "It doesn't seem that long ago 'gray' was a four-letter word when it came to water."

Tulah grinned. "I guess new technology makes reused bathwater clean again."

"Reused bathwater is a step in the right direction," said Kelby, "but toilet water's the issue. With all the excreted prescription drugs being flushed into the sewers, the water-purification systems can't filter out the chemicals or hormones."

Tulah gave her a blank stare. "What?"

"You heard me." Kelby nodded. "During a 2000 geological survey, scientists gathered data from thirty states. Even back then, drugs contaminated over a hundred American streams and rivers."

Angela glanced at her. "What kind of drugs?"

"Everything from antibiotics, contraceptives, and hormone replacements," Kelby gestured with her hands, "to painkillers and psychiatric meds. Eighty percent of the water samples showed contamination."

Tulah shrugged. "So what?"

"So what?" Kelby's eyes opened wide as her voice rose. "Studies have linked birth-control hormones in our waterways to reduced fertility in all species."

Tulah grimaced. "Facts can be skewed to support any findings."

Kelby shook her head. "Scientists placed cages of male minnows in isolated, northern Minnesotan lakes. Within three weeks, most of the males were feminized to the point they had trouble reproducing."

"That's fish," said Tulah, "not humans."

"Estrogen flushed into our water messes with reproduction. Even in tiny amounts. Even in remote lakes. I hate to think of the concentrations in major waterways."

"So fewer fish reproduce." Tulah shrugged. "Big deal."

"Don't you get it?" Kelby sighed. "Fish are the canaries in the coalmine. It's not just fish with lowered sperm counts. It's every species. A 2013 report showed feminization in wildlife mirrors increased male infertility, genital defects, and testicular cancer—*in humans*. It's epidemic, and its cause is in the water. *Peed drugs*."

"If it isn't one thing with you, it's another." Tulah rolled her eyes. "If you're not fighting for water rights, you're worried about water pollution. Water this, water that."

"Water's critical," said Kelby.

"I'm not saying it isn't, but *infertility?*" Tulah scoffed. "What are you going to tell us next? You get it from sitting on toilet seats?"

Kelby started to answer, bit her lip, took a deep breath, and started again. "Three generations after contact with contraceptive hormones in the water, fish have trouble reproducing. With declining reproduction rates in industrialized countries, doesn't it make you wonder if there's a connection?"

"Water's a symbol of life, fertility. Deuteronomy 8:7-8," said Mrs. Bankhead. "'The Lord your God is bringing you into a fertile land—a land that has rivers and springs, and underground streams gushing out into the valleys and hills; a land that produces wheat and barley, grapes, figs, pomegranates, olives, and honey.'"

"Drinking hormone-laced water isn't life-giving. It's a slow drain." Kelby studied her glass of water. "Gradual death."

A few days later, Angela hurried to the cave after work, hoping to speak with Doctor West.

"I'm glad for the continued research through July," she said, "but the Bankheads want to sell this land. Without a long-term commitment, that'll happen next month. Do you think the funding will continue?"

"This cave's a treasure trove of *Mammuthus columbi* and *Equus simplicidens,* with tempting indications of more in the tunnels."

She peered into his eyes, trying to read what he wasn't saying. "But . . ."

"It's the anthropological slant that attracts funding."

Relieved, she smiled. "You've already found that in the artwork on the mammoth tusk. Wouldn't that be—"

He shook his head. "It's a marvelous piece in itself, but without context, some way to anchor it to this area, some evidence that Paleoindians worked it *here*, its significance is diminished to the point it doesn't prove anything. It's an anachronism, out of time, a duck out of water."

She gestured toward the cave. "But you found it in this cave."

"It could've been washed here through ancient floods. Without concrete proof the Paleoindians occupied this particular site, there's no framework for its classification, no context."

Taking a deep breath, she tried not to show her disappointment. "What kind of proof would you need?"

He shrugged his shoulders. "A stockpile of Folsom or Clovis points—"

"Arrowheads?"

He nodded. "Those or glyphs, pictographs, something concrete that'd tie the artwork to Paleoindians living in this area."

"They've found pictographs on cave walls nearby." She glanced up hopefully. "Maybe something will turn up in the tunnels you found."

"Possibly." He grimaced. "But all that takes time . . . which translates to having enough money to fund *the finding of new evidence* to create new funding . . ."

She nodded slowly. "A vicious circle."

After Angela fed Frank and Kitz, she walked to the corral. While Tulah and Clay finished grooming the horses, she told them about her conversation with Doctor West.

"So finding an etched mammoth tusk and a cave full of ancient bones isn't enough?" Clay pushed back his hat.

Angela grimaced as she shook her head. "Apparently not."

Pausing, brush in hand, Tulah sighed. "I'd hoped that tusk carving would prove horses had been in North America long before Christopher Columbus arrived." Her smile was wistful. "It'd be great if mustangs could be reclassified as native wildlife."

Nodding, Clay caught her eye. "Tell Angela the good news."

Tulah's face lit up. "Kelby won another grant for Texas Mustangs. It's not very big, but it's enough to cross-fence the pastures and build a hay shed—"

"And buy hay." Taking off his Stetson, he wiped the sweat from his brow as he studied the pasture. "Without rain, the land can't support these mustangs. They're eating a round bale of hay every other day."

Angela glanced at the soil. If anything, the cracks appeared deeper, wider. The few remaining patches of grass were brown and dry. Even her untrained eye could see there wasn't enough to feed the horses, but she forced a bright smile. "I'm glad the grant came through. Kelby might still be confined to crutches, but it hasn't slowed her from finding grants online."

A car horn blared in four shrill bursts, breaking the evening quiet.

Whinnying, the horses reared up and pulled back on their ties, nearly trampling Tulah and each other in their hurry to escape.

"Whoa! Whoa!" Clay and Tulah sprang into action, trying to calm the horses and retie their lead ropes.

Still wide-eyed with fear, the mustangs responded nervously, prancing, pawing at the dry soil.

A minute later, Astin pulled up in a cloud of dust.

Clay stomped toward him. "Don't you know better than to honk your horn around horses?"

Wearing a simper, Astin smoothed his lapel. "I'm used to well-trained thoroughbreds, not wild horses."

Clay's eyes narrowed to slits. "What do you want?"

"To help." Astin's eyes found Tulah's, and his sneer broke into a smile. "Rumor has it you'd moved your non-profit rescue. Now that I see you have, I'm here to offer my services *pro bono*." Turning back to Clay, his smile returned to a sneer. "As I'd promised."

"Thanks, but my sister's handling the paperwork." Tulah coldly appraised him as she found her tongue.

Turning his full attention toward her, Astin visibly turned on the charm. His eyes twinkling, they homed in on hers as if she had a secret, and he knew what it was. "I'd be happy to give it a legal review. Consider it a personal favor."

Lifting her chin, she stared him down. "Thanks, but that's not necessary."

Astin took a step closer. "Perhaps you'd like to review the paperwork together . . . over dinner."

"Like I said, we don't need your help."

"You heard her." Clay stepped between them. "Your 'services' aren't needed."

Astin raised his eyebrow. "I'd toyed with the idea of letting your non-profit lease the land after I buy it." He glanced at the new fencing and corral. "But if you still feel there's nothing to discuss . . ." His offer dangling like a carrot, he looked past Clay and spoke directly to Tulah.

She took a deep breath. "This land isn't yours to lease."

"It will be soon enough."

Tulah eyed him coldly. "Not if we can help it."

All eyes turned to her. Surprised, Angela lifted her brow but kept her thoughts to herself.

Astin blinked. "If you recall, you're the one who asked for my help. What prompted this about-face?"

A smile playing at her lips, she glanced at Clay. "Call it a change of heart." Then, her eyes narrowing, she turned back to Astin. "Now, if you'll excuse us, we have a lot of work to do."

He blinked again, glanced at Clay, sniffed, and began walking back to his convertible. Hand on the door, he turned back with a sneer. "Don't say I didn't give you every opportunity." With a dry laugh, he got into his car, revved the engine, and tore down the caliche road in a cloud of dust.

Again, the horses whinnied, reared up, and pulled back on their ties, but this time, Tulah and Clay were prepared.

After they had calmed down the horses, removed their halters, and turned them out to pasture, Clay turned to Tulah. "Did you mean that?"

"Mean what?" She looked up into his eyes.

"That part about a change of heart?"

"Rule of Capture." Nodding, she gave him a shy grin. "Water's not the only thing you can catch."

As Clay bent to kiss her, Tulah noticed Angela and blushed. She cleared her throat as she straightened her spine. "Why don't we see if Kelby can use our help writing grants?" Then she turned toward Clay with a smile. "Would you like to stay for supper tonight?"

Following dinner, Kelby, Tulah, Angela, and Clay worked on finding, writing, and editing grants until midnight. It became a ritual. After work, after feeding the horses, they met for dinner and then researched or wrote grants until they couldn't keep their eyes open.

"The Texas Environmental Foundation grant is the biggest fish." Using crutches to get around, Kelby handed them each a printout. "If we win this grant, the land will be made into a conservancy. With the stipend for being caretakers from that, Mom and Dad will have the money they need to keep the business going. Best of all, the water will be safe from shysters and speculators."

They sat around the dining room table, staring at the papers Kelby placed in front of them.

"Each 'chapter' is a separate part of the grant," said Kelby, "meeting a particular prerequisite. The Project Abstract is the most difficult. It's a concise summary of the entire grant, on one page. The Statement of Need describes the issue and the population it'll serve." She smiled at them. "You get the idea."

Tulah looked up at her sister. "How many 'chapters' are we reviewing tonight?"

"Besides what I mentioned, there's the Program Description, References, Goals and Objectives, Timeline, Proposed Budget, Evaluation, Staff and Organizational Information, Appendix of Letters of Support, and the Efficacy Study—"

"Efficacy Study?" Wearing a puzzled frown, Tulah looked up.

"Remember when they sent two people to measure the streamflow with the 'bucket' method?"

Tulah nodded.

"They recorded the streamflow and streamgaging in the Efficacy Study." Kelby grinned. "Let's hope it was effective."

"What's the Staff and Organizational Information about?" Clay glanced at her.

"Ten pages long, it basically says caretakers will live on site. A stipulation for the nonprofit becoming a conservancy is that it requires round-the-clock surveillance, twenty-four seven."

"Oh, darn." He deadpanned. "You mean someone will actually have to live in that vacation getaway?"

"Yup."

"A fate worse than death." Clicking his teeth, he grinned. "Are you taking volunteers?"

Kelby arched her eyebrow. "Don't forget the ghost."

"Billy?" Clay shrugged. "Haven't heard much about him lately. Did he leave?"

Tulah glanced at Angela before turning toward Clay. "He's keeping an eye on us."

"He doesn't seem as bound to the cabin anymore," said Angela, "but he's still keeping watch."

"Maybe we should list Billy as the on-site caretaker." Clay chuckled. "It'd keep the budget down."

Everyone laughed but Angela. *How lonely Billy must be.* Sniffing, she shook her head.

"What?" Kelby glanced at her.

"I was just thinking." Angela took a deep breath. "Billy's been bound to that land for a hundred and seventy years. If we can win this grant, have the land made into a conservancy, and protect the water . . . maybe he'll be freed, be able to move on."

"If that's the case," Kelby finished handing out the paperwork, "we'd better get moving on these reviews. The deadline's midnight tonight."

When It Rains, It Pours

Bad is never good until worse happens.
– DANISH PROVERB

Saturday morning, Angela brought only a scant handful of feed for Kitz. As Billy had recommended, she had cut back his feed a little each day, gradually weaning him off human dependence. Looking at his spikes, she smiled. He was a survivor, growing into a fine buck, integrating into nature, back where he belonged. She wanted to reach out and feel his antlers' velvety smoothness, but she realized the less human contact, the better for him. *Was it only three months ago they were downy, little nubs just barely poking through?*

With a parting glance, she started along the stream path in what had become a morning ritual. She would sit on her favorite rock, watching the sun come up over the stream, connecting with nature, communing with God. It steadied her course for the day. When Kitz finished his breakfast, he would join her, usually sitting by her feet. Most days, Billy quietly appeared, seeming to enjoy their trio's wordless communication.

With less grain to eat, Kitz joined her sooner than usual, but with that exception, the day seemed no different than any other. Angela sat down on her rock, cross-legged, watching the sky turn from a dusky blue to a pale violet, to a luminous, rosy glow.

She took a deep breath, filling her lungs with the fresh morning air. A breeze wafted the earthy scents of horses and fresh hay.

Early blooming Mexican sage released its perfume. She glanced at the shrubs' downy white and purple flowers and inhaled again. Breathing in the morning, she released all tension. *Like trees taking in carbon dioxide and releasing oxygen.* She smiled, glancing at the majestic cypresses that lined the stream. *How long have these trees stood here like sentinels, guarding the water, refreshing the air?*

"They were nearly this large when I moved here a hundred and seventy years ago. God knows how old they are."

Angela flinched. "Billy, I didn't see you." She took another deep breath, this time to shake off the surprise. Then she studied him. "I don't recall you talking about God before."

"Sure I have, lots of times." He frowned. "I must've."

She shook her head. "I can't ever recall you mentioning Him before."

"Either way," shrugging, he grimaced, "there's something you've got to see."

His tone made her sit up. "What?"

"Follow me."

Five minutes later, they arrived at the cave site. Angela gasped involuntarily. The protective covering had been jimmied off. Prehistoric bones lay scattered around the opening.

"It's worse inside," he said. "Much worse."

Looking at the destruction before her, Angela hated to think what they had done to the fragile cave. "Vandals?"

He shook his head. "Hired guns." His eyes narrowed. "I've seen their kind before."

Angela's eyes opened wide, recalling what Billy had told her about the rancher hiring a gunman to shoot him. "Who do you think's behind it?"

"The one with the car."

"Astin?" Her eyebrow shot up.

"He paid them."

She took a deep breath, relieved Tulah had stopped seeing him, but angry they had not anticipated the level of his deceit. She mentally compared Astin to the rancher who'd hired Billy killed. "Some things don't change."

"Water is power." Billy leveled his eyes at her. "Some people stop at nothing to get it."

"The most precious substance on earth," she whispered. "Water."

Angela raced to the Bankhead home.

Tulah ushered her in with a smile. "You're just in time for breakfast."

Angela took a deep breath. "Something's happened—"

"Angela," called Kelby, hobbling toward her on crutches. "You haven't heard the good news!"

Anxious to share her own news, Angela forced a charitable smile. "What is it?"

Kelby's eyes glistened. "We're finalists for the Texas Environmental Foundation grant!"

"That's wonderful. Congratulations!"

"Close isn't the same as winning," cautioned her mother. "Don't get your hopes too high."

"True," Angela winked at Kelby, "but it's a great start."

"You were about to tell us something." Tulah studied her.

Nodding, Angela reported what had happened at the cave.

"No!" Kelby's eyes widened.

Tulah pulled out her cell phone. "I'm texting Clay."

Clay arrived a half hour later, just after they finished breakfast.

"They're predicting thunderstorms." Mrs. Bankhead called to them as they scrambled out the door. "Give yourselves extra time to get to work this afternoon. After this drought, the roads will be slick with all the accumulated oils."

Before they reached the cabin, a light drizzle had started falling. By the time they arrived at the stream, a gentle but steady rain dripped down on them from the trees' leafy canopy.

Tulah hunched her shoulders against the shower. "We need the rain—badly—but why does it always happen at the worst times?"

In the few minutes it took to jog to the cave entrance, the steady rain had become a deluge. Glad to escape its driving force, they rushed into the cave, barely glancing at the scattered debris outside the entrance. As their eyes became accustomed to the gloom and glare from their headlamps, they glanced around the cave.

Though the bones had been a jumbled mass before the vandalism, the flood waters had left a uniformity in their alignment. Now, everything had been upturned, thrown about, or purposely crushed.

"What have they done?" His jaw slack, Clay stared at the destruction. "Now that the bones' layers have been disturbed, there's no context for their study. Their geologic record, their history's been stolen."

"Will this interfere with Doctor West's research?" Angela watched his body language.

Taking a deep breath, he shrugged. "It'll definitely hinder it, limit it."

"Will it mean the end of funding?" A grim twist to her mouth, Tulah's expression reflected her disappointment.

"I don't know, but it can't help." He shook his head. "The bones were gradually deposited into their positions over thousands of years. Now that they've been strewn about and kicked apart, there's no context for the time periods involved."

"Who did this?" Tulah looked to Angela.

Grimacing, she repeated what Billy had told her about the hired thugs.

"What is wrong with people?" Tulah stifled an angry growl in her throat. "How can people purposely destroy something of unimaginable historic value?"

"Because *one*, they're paid to do it, and *two*, it's worth something on the black market." Even in the dim light, Clay's expression was bitter. "Check out 'fossils for sale' on web sites and eBay. Mastodon tusks sell in the high five figures."

"What?" Tulah gave a guttural roar of frustration.

In the quiet that followed, they heard a gurgling sound.

"What's that?" Angela looked at them. Then she felt something at her feet.

Thick, muddy water was rising where they stood. Within seconds it had covered the soles of her shoes, was saturating her canvas sneakers, and had begun cascading down the entrance to the cave.

"We've got to get out of here!" Clay took the lead, scrambling hand over foot up the slippery cave floor while thick, muddy water continued to pour down the entrance, covering them with a cold, slick sludge. "Hang on to my belt," he called to Tulah. "Angela, hang on to Tulah's belt." He coughed and spat out muddy water. "We've got to keep moving."

They struggled against the murky slime that was now surging through the cave entrance. They lost traction on the slick footing as an increasing torrent of mud forced them backwards.

When Angela saw them slipping farther and farther down the slope, she began to worry. "This is an uphill battle—literally," she shouted. "We're losing ground."

She said a mental prayer to fight the sudden panic. *What if we're trapped down here? What if we can't get out, and we drown?*

Suddenly Billy appeared, gesturing toward the back of the cave with his arm. "This way."

"We'll be trapped." Angela breathed deeply, trying to squelch her claustrophobia.

"What?" called Tulah.

"I know another way out." Billy's eerie blue eyes leveled with hers. "Trust me."

Angela tugged at Tulah's belt. "We can't get out this way," she shouted. "Billy's showing us another route."

Once they turned around and stopped fighting against the muddy flow, its force slid them back into the cave on a mud-covered waterslide.

"There's a tunnel," said Billy.

Following his lead, Angela nodded and gestured to the others. She looked at the rising water, now up to her ankles. Pushing aside bones as they sloshed through the soggy mud, they slowly made their way to the back wall. Three feet up, they saw the hole the research team had dug.

"Climb through," said Billy.

Angela nodded as she felt the water sucking at her shoes. It had risen several inches in a matter of minutes.

She stepped up and over the ledge as she ducked her head. "At least, the height of this passage will delay water flowing into the tunnel."

"For a while . . . if the water's force doesn't push through the opening's base." Tulah's stern voice reflected her concern.

Angela shuddered but kept her thoughts to herself.

After they were all through, Billy gestured. "This way."

When the tunnel diverged, Billy led them through the right channel. As Doctor West had said, a tiny tickle of water ran alongside it in a well-worn trench.

"Is this tunnel leading back toward the cabin?" asked Clay.

Angela repeated Billy's answer. "Not far from it. The exit's near the arroyo."

She took a deep breath, relieved there was an escape. Then it occurred to her. "An exit near the arroyo . . . that's a dry riverbed, a seasonal stream, isn't?"

"Yup," said Tulah. "When it rains, water gushes through there fast enough to wash away a car."

Angela arched her eyebrow. "If water's rushing through the arroyo, our 'exit' is actually the entrance for water flowing into this tunnel." She looked at Billy. "Right?"

He grimaced. "Not if we hurry."

With that, they went as fast as their headlamps' scant light allowed. Then something caught Angela's eye. Stooping for a closer look, she saw it was a pottery shard and took a quick picture, documenting its position.

"Even if the vandals ruined the original cave, this is proof of human activity." She picked up the shard and tucked it in her pocket. "I'll give this to Doctor West when we see him."

The silence that followed echoed Angela's thoughts. *That is,* if *we see him.*

"Hurry." Billy shook his head. "We don't have time to dawdle."

They pushed on faster, tripping over rubble and more bones.

Then Angela heard a rushing sound. "What's that?"

"An underground river," said Billy, "part of the Edwards aquifer."

The closer they got, the louder the rushing sound became. Then Angela felt something at her feet. She looked down and saw black water seeping, then pooling, then beginning to flow past her feet as the trench overflowed. She caught Billy's eye.

"It's seeking its own level, the underground river," he said. "Once we pass the gap where it flows into the aquifer, the tunnel begins to rise. Until then, we're on a downward slope. Be careful the water doesn't drag you with it."

Angela repeated his message, then swallowed hard. As they began running, the water kept rising, and the current became stronger.

"The entrance to the aquifer is just ahead. There's a narrow ledge between the wall and the opening. Hug the wall to your left."

Nodding, Angela passed on Billy's information. The water sucked at her shoes and dragged at her feet, slowing her progress.

"Hurry," said Billy. "Hurry."

They slogged through the water, each step like walking in quicksand. When the rushing noise began sounding like a waterfall, Billy turned toward her. "Step sideways, hugging the wall with your back."

Again she passed on the information, demonstrating. The next moment, the suction at her feet and calves became overpowering.

"Hold hands," Billy said, "but keep going. Don't stop, or it'll drag you down with it."

Edging their way step by step, they made slow progress along the ledge. The roar of the cascading water echoed and rang in the tunnel, drowning out everything but Tulah's scream. As she lost her footing, she lurched forward, pulling on Angela and Clay.

Their reflexes reacting, they gripped Tulah's hands until she regained her balance. For a split second, while her headlamp pointed down into the abyss, Angela saw the water gushing fifty, a hundred feet below. They heard the splashing and roar of the swirling water.

"Keep going," urged Billy.

Gulping air, Angela struggled to control the urge to let go, stop fighting. The water's force was overwhelming.

"Don't stop now. This is the worst. Keep going. You're almost there," said Billy.

Angela nodded as she used the last of her strength shuffling sideways along the narrow ledge. The power of the surging, tumbling water was so strong, each step required all her will, all her might. One step, then another, then another.

Then the next step did not feel as difficult, nor did the next. With a sigh of relief, she realized she was past the chasm. "Keep going!" She screamed against the water's roar as she pulled Tulah and then Clay to safe ground.

Gasping for breath, Angela tried to regain her strength.

"Don't stop," Billy warned.

"But we're past the danger." Angela gave him an exhausted grin.

"This danger." He shook his head. "If you notice, the path has already begun to rise. You'll be walking up an incline until we reach the exit."

Angela's jaw dropped. "The arroyo."

"Hurry," said Billy. "You have to get to the exit before water fills the riverbed and rushes through this passage to the aquifer."

"Come on." Angela grabbed Tulah's hand and started pulling.

Tulah pulled away, slumping against the cave wall. "I can't."

"You've got to." Angela pointed toward the way out. "If we don't hurry, water's going to start pouring down our only escape route. We'll be trapped like rats."

Nodding, Tulah stepped away from the wall.

Angela gasped.

"What?" Tulah's eyes widened.

Angela pointed at the cave wall. "Pictographs." Wanting to touch the ancient artwork, tangibly connect with the people who had drawn it, she instead reached for her phone and took a picture.

"Go," said Billy. "*Go now!*"

Using the flashlight feature of her phone, Angela began leading them out of the tunnel at a faster pace. The extra light from her phone let her see her footing as she picked her way between rubble and bones. She saw another pottery shard, but she pressed on, racing against the clock.

Smiling to herself, she patted the pottery shard in her pocket. *Now we have a human connection: pottery and pictographs. This should ensure funding.* Her smile drooped. *If we make it out.*

As she scrambled up the incline, it occurred to her. *The aquifer. It's not rainwater that's seeped in. Its source is a river, an underground river. This is the proof we need. Neither Astin, the Porters, Agua Purificación nor anyone else can ever use the Rule of Capture on the property.*

The incline started getting muddy, slowing their uphill climb. Angela shot Billy a panicked look.

"This is only rainwater that's softened the soil, but hurry. The arroyo can turn into a raging river in minutes."

Then Angela began to see a thin line of faint light. "Is that it?"

"Yes," Billy said, "hurry."

As they scrambled up the incline, the light became stronger, but it appeared as a thin line.

"Are we going to be able to squeeze through there?" Trying to will away her claustrophobia, she glanced at Billy.

"Yes." He hesitated. "I think so . . ."

Her heart began pounding as she raced toward the light. When she needed both hands to climb the last few vertical feet, Angela put away her cell phone, and hoisted herself up, clutching one ledge until she felt a foothold on the next. Climbing hand over foot, she reached a narrow ridge between the riverbed and a low overhang of rock.

She lay horizontally. Limb by limb, she inched her body through the slender gap, scratching her arms and legs against the sharp rocks above and below.

Once out, she breathed deeply, gulping in ozone-scented air as the rain pummeled her. She held out her hand to Tulah, helping her through the narrow passage. *If it's this tight for us, how's Clay going to squeeze through?*

For several minutes, Clay struggled. Angela and Tulah tried to help him, but their tugging seemed to hinder more than help. Finally, Clay squeezed through, ripping his shirt in the process.

Billy shouted. "Get to high ground *now*."

Angela looked for footholds on the slick rocks as raindrops blinded her. They scrambled to a rocky ledge, several feet above the water.

"Keep climbing," said Billy.

Bending their heads against the driving rain, the three climbed from perch to perch until they stood on level ground, overlooking the steep embankment.

"Look." Angela pointed to a road with a bridge crossing the arroyo.

Tulah nodded. "That's Hall Road, just a mile or two from the cabin."

Hearing a roar, they looked upstream and saw two moving targets about to intersect. A wall of water and debris raced toward them along the dry riverbed as the red convertible dashed toward the bridge at breakneck speed.

"Astin!" Angela screamed against the wind, but her words were drowned out before they left her lips.

Apparently thinking he could outrun it, Astin sped up, trying to cross the bridge before the flood reached it.

From their vantage point high above the river bottom, they watched a tsunami of water, uprooted trees, refrigerators, and what looked like the framework of a garage slam into the bridge. Crumpling like wet cardboard, the bridge gave way, joining the onslaught of debris. The water lifted Astin's sports car and carried it along sideways.

His windshield wipers going, he turned on his hazard lights as his red car bobbed along on top of the wall of wreckage and mud. Angela almost smiled at the macabre comic relief.

"I can't stand by and watch him die." Clay started toward the edge.

"No!" Tulah grabbed his arm.

"He'll be killed if I don't help him."

Tulah took hold of his shoulders. "You could be killed if you do."

"Or both of you." Angela glanced at Billy, silently watching the drama unfold.

Minutes passed as the water and debris surged toward them. At one point, Angela lost sight of the car as it was sucked under. Grimacing, Billy shook his head.

Then at a narrow point in the arroyo, two uprooted trees snagged against the canyon walls. Debris piled up behind it, causing a temporary dam. Clay saw his opportunity and ran toward it.

"No!" Tulah screamed, but he either could not hear or would not listen.

Tulah ran after him through the driving wind and rain as Angela followed close behind.

Clay tentatively stepped on the nearest log, testing it. When it held beneath his foot, he began inching sideways toward the makeshift island of debris. Precariously perched against the roof of the floating garage, the front end of Astin's car was above water, while the tail end was mired in muck.

As Clay balanced himself against the wind and unstable debris, he edged his way forward until he connected with the car door. He pulled, but its bottom half was wedged against driftwood and broken furniture. The convertible top had been nearly torn off. Water filled the car up to the dashboard, while Astin slumped over the steering wheel.

Poised on top of the jammed debris, Clay pulled and yanked until he finally wrenched Astin from the car. Then he took off his belt, slipped it beneath Astin's belt, and half-dragged, half-carried him across the log dam to safety.

As Angela and Tulah helped him pull Astin to higher ground, Clay shook his head. "He didn't move a muscle. He was dead weight."

Angela grimaced as she met his eyes.

With a thunderous roar, the surging water dislodged the two uprooted trees. The river of debris tore through the temporary dam, splintering the trees as it ripped them apart.

The water gushed down the arroyo, scraping against the high canyon walls and overflowing its banks. Wreckage began swirling clockwise around their exit. Angela watched as water streamed into their tunnel, seeking the aquifer.

Another few minutes, and we'd have been drowned.

Angela looked for Billy to thank him, but she saw him talking to Astin. Blinking against the driving rain, she looked again. Astin lay motionless on the shore, yet a more translucent version of him stood beside his body, seriously listening to Billy.

Tulah pushed them out of the way. "Have you forgotten? I was a lifeguard at the pool last summer."

She began giving Astin the kiss of life. Nothing. He made no move, gave no response. She listened for a heartbeat, grimaced, and then resumed the mouth-to-mouth resuscitation.

Meanwhile, Angela heard Billy lecture Astin. "Do you have any idea how self-centered you've been? You saw how Clay risked his life for you, and now how Tulah's working to save you. Wake up."

As Billy finished his harangue, Astin began breathing on his own. Immediately his cough reflex started.

Cheering, they rolled him on his side as he coughed and vomited water.

Clay walked back to the Bankheads' house for his pickup, while Angela and Tulah stayed with Astin, huddling under a ledge from the driving rain. Because the bridge was out, they had to take the long way to the Fredericksley hospital.

The rain came down in sheets of driving water. Even with the wipers going full-speed, it was like looking through waxed paper. Lightning struck so often, it sounded like fireworks. At one point they thought they saw a funnel cloud, but the sky was too dark to be sure.

Radio reports warned listeners to boil their water, stay clear of low-water crossings, and evacuate to high ground, especially anyone along the Blanco River. Early reports estimated between three and four hundred homes had been destroyed in Fredericksley, many of them washed away.

Clay drove while Astin dozed in the passenger seat. In the back, Angela and Tulah kept trying to call the Bankheads, but the lines were jammed.

As they crossed the Blanco River, they were stunned by the devastation. Only one of the bridge's four lanes remained open. Tree limbs, slick mud, debris, and dead fish covered the other three.

"To have risen above the bridge, the water must've been forty feet high." Clay talked to them through the rearview mirror.

They glanced at each other.

"What's the normal depth of the Blanco?" asked Angela.

"Less than six feet."

They looked below as they crossed the bridge. Instead of centuries-old cypress trees, they saw stumps, the treetops having been snapped off several feet above ground. As the debris had rushed past, it had scraped the bark from the remaining stumps, leaving them looking like freshly peeled logs.

They saw cement slabs where houses had stood just hours before. Instead of manicured lawns leading to the water, debris was piled ten feet high on both sides of the river in both directions as far as they could see. An overturned car lay ten feet from the swollen shoreline.

Lawn mowers, picture frames, and clothes driers had perched in the tops of the few trees still standing. Stripped naked, their leaves, branches, and bark had been scoured off.

Tulah shook her head. "Some of these trees were saplings when Columbus sailed to America. Now they're gone."

With a sinking heart, Angela prayed the stream's cypresses had been spared.

The radio reported the Red Cross had begun setting up temporary headquarters in the Community Center, and the National Guard had been called out. As the rain began subsiding, they heard the buzzing whap-whap-whap-whap of the helicopters overhead searching for stranded survivors.

Entering Fredericksley, the tourist town looked more like a war zone than a vacation destination. Boxes, lampshades, and small pieces of furniture floated in the water-filled streets. Stalled cars cluttered the road as water swirled around them.

After delivering Astin to the hospital, they drove through water up to the truck's hubcaps to reach Tulah's family at the winery. Though the Bankheads were safe, the flood had trapped them.

Water had wedged their car between two live oaks. The power was out, and the cell-tower exchanges had been so busy, they could not call for help.

By the time they got back, they were exhausted. Clay stayed overnight with the Bankheads. Angela walked home, but it was too dark to see if the storm had done any damage to the property. With a sigh of relief, she saw Frank was safe, and the cabin was dry.

The next morning, Angela woke from a nightmare, feeling stiff, sore, and vaguely uneasy. It took a moment to remember why. Then it all came back to her. The flood. The cave and tunnels. Astin. The stream. *The stream! Did its cypress trees survive?* Recalling the destruction she had seen when they had driven across the Blanco, she knew firsthand how floods destroy not only the trees along waterways, but people's homes, people's lives. Generations, centuries would have to pass before the stream's cypress would reach their pre-flood size.

Pulling on jeans and a T-shirt, she fed Frank and grabbed a handful of feed for Kitz. *Did he survive the flood?*

As she walked outside, she saw tree limbs downed by the wind, but no trees had toppled. "Kitz," she called. She set down the feed and called again, but he did not appear. Praying he was hiding and not harmed, she checked on the mustangs. Her favorite Appaloosa nuzzled her hand as the others neighed softly.

She called to Kitz again, and then began walking toward the stream. Bits of tree branches and leaves were strewn like confetti. The farther she walked, the worse the damage. More and more limbs had been blown down. Then she began noticing splintered stumps, where the treetops had been ripped off by high winds and scattered like pick-up sticks.

She took a deep breath, hoping the cypress trees along the stream had been spared, but the mounting destruction left little hope.

Then she felt something touch the back of her thigh. With a gasp, she turned around to see it was the yearling.

"Kitz!" Rubbing his head, she breathed a sigh of relief. "Thank God, you're safe."

As they continued toward the stream, Angela began seeing the flood's high-water marks on the tree trunks. Debris hung from the live oaks' lower branches. Then she saw splintered tree limbs. Finally, she saw the sheared cypress trees. Twisted and torn off by high winds, they lay where they had fallen. Ancient sentinels hundreds of years old, they had become their own wooden coffins.

Twenty feet wider than usual, the stream was still swollen, raging. Even her favorite rock was buried beneath its dark, roiling water. Feeling light-headed, she leaned against a tree trunk and then immediately recoiled. It was wet, muddy. She strained her neck for a better view, looking up at the high-water mark above her head. *Glad we weren't caught here in the flash flood.*

Then she heard a bawling, bleating sound. Kitz perked his ears and started nosing through the underbrush. Buried beneath several cypress fronds was a small fawn crying like a lamb. Meh, meeeh.

Billy appeared, his mouth downturned in a grimace. "His mother didn't survive."

"Poor little thing." Angela wanted to comfort him, but she did not want to imprint on him. She turned toward Billy. "What do you suggest?"

He pressed his lips together. "Hopefully, he's old enough to browse."

They watched Kitz sniff the fawn. Bleating, it stood on its legs and tried to emulate the yearling.

"Without his mother to mimic, maybe he'll watch what Kitz does and follow his lead."

Despite the destruction all about them, the leggy fawn brought a smile to her lips. She looked at his spotted brown coat, tiny face, large, brown eyes, and perfectly proportioned legs and hooves. Unable to resist, she leaned over to gently pet his bristly coat. He was the size of a tall cat, and her hand covered half his back.

Connecting with him, she realized his coat was soaked, and he was shivering. When he did not resist, she lifted him with both hands, hugging him to share her body warmth.

Billy raised his eyebrow, and she responded with a sheepish grin. “Just for today. I promise it will be ‘hands off’ after he’s warm and dry.”

Cold, probably exhausted, the fawn lay docilely in her arms as she surveyed the swollen stream. Gone were the stately cypress trees. In their place were peeled stumps ten feet tall, naked witnesses to the devastation. Muddy water flowed swiftly over their lopped-off treetops.

Angela shook her head. “When it rains, it pours . . .”

“So much drama. What ever happened to a gentle rain?”

The Rainbow After Rain

God's illumined promise.
– Henry Wadsworth Longfellow

They were finishing dinner when they heard a knock at the door. Finally off her crutches, Kelby ran to answer it.

They heard a man's voice and then turned to see her ushering Astin into the dining room.

"Sorry for the intrusion," he said, "but I wanted to deliver this in person." With that, he turned toward Kelby and handed her a letter.

She looked at it. Then knitting her brow, she looked up at him.

Astin smiled patiently. "Go ahead. Read it."

Kelby read the envelope's return address. "It's from the Texas Environmental Foundation." Again she gave him a quizzical look. "I know your father's its executive director," Kelby's eyes narrowed, "but why would you—"

Astin swallowed a grin. "Open it and find out."

Kelby slowly unfolded the letter as she kept suspicious eyes trained on him. Then she read aloud. "The Texas Environmental Foundation is pleased to announce its award to the nonprofit group, Texas Mustangs . . ." Her eyes wide, wondering, she gazed at him as a check fell from her hands.

Angela grinned. "Don't keep us in suspense."

Astin retrieved the fallen check. "Not to steal your thunder, but . . ." He turned toward Angela and the family, still seated around the table. "The Texas Environmental Foundation has awarded Texas Mustangs a grant to develop your family's land into a conservancy." He handed Mrs. Bankhead the check.

"What?" Mrs. Bankhead stared without seeing.

"Basically the funding's to preserve the stream and aquifer's ecosystems—"

"What?" Mrs. Bankhead spoke without hearing.

Astin smiled. "It's an easement to prevent land fragmentation—"

"Why are you hand-delivering this?" Kelby watched Astin through narrowed eyes. "I thought you wanted the land for yourself."

He took a deep breath. He started to speak. Then he swallowed and started again. "Let's say I had an 'a-ha' moment." He shyly turned to Tulah. "I never thanked you for saving my life."

She shook her head. "Don't thank me. Thank Clay. He's the one that risked his to save yours."

Pressing his lips together, Astin nodded. "I plan to."

"I still don't understand why *you're* hand-delivering this." Kelby peered at him.

"You know my father's—"

"Yes," Kelby persisted, "but what do *you* have to do with it?"

"I volunteer with the foundation . . ."

"So . . ." Tulah met his eyes.

"So," he shrugged, "I happened to put in a good word . . ." Then he glanced at Mr. and Mrs. Bankhead. "I didn't mean to interrupt your dinner. Just wanted to deliver the good news in person."

Finding her voice, Mrs. Bankhead stood up. "Won't you stay for dessert—"

"Thanks." He shook his head. "I have to finish packing."

"You're moving?" Mrs. Bankhead blinked. "Why?"

Astin gave her a wry smile. "Let's say finding an underground river beneath the property changed its dynamics." He turned toward Tulah. "Thank you again for . . . everything." Then he nodded to the group. "I'll see myself out."

They sat in thoughtful silence several moments after the door shut.

Mrs. Bankhead glanced again at the cashier's check and then handed it to her husband.

"The answer to our prayers," he said softly.

Kelby read through the two-page letter. "There's a string attached . . ."

"What kind of string?" Tulah glanced at her.

"Nothing we didn't know about." Kelby shrugged. "According to the Staff and Organizational Information clause, caretakers will have to live on site. A stipulation to becoming a conservancy is round-the-clock surveillance, twenty-four seven."

The group looked at each other.

"For now, Angela lives there." Tulah glanced at her. "Which reminds me. You'll need to become a member of the Friends of Texas Mustangs." She turned toward her family. "But then what?"

Mr. Bankhead held up the check. "If the good Lord can provide this, He can find a caretaker."

Mrs. Bankhead glanced from the check to her husband. "Mr. Starr is such a gentleman."

The three girls stared at each other.

"What a shame he's moving." Mrs. Bankhead glanced at Tulah.

Tulah gave her a half smile. "It does seem he's turned over a new leaf—"

"Am I the only one who heard him?" Kelby glared at her.

"What?" Tulah blinked.

"He even admitted it. Finding the underground river changed the property's dynamics." Kelby scoffed. "Don't you get it? He, the Porters, Agua Purificación, nobody can tap the aquifer from this property."

"Why not?"

"Because the groundwater's source is an underground river. They can't pump a drop more water than for personal use." Finishing her thought, Kelby coldly regarded her sister and then turned toward her mother. "He isn't 'a gentleman.' He's a businessman, who knows when to cut his losses."

"He said he's responsible for getting the grant," said Mrs. Bankhead.

"He knew whoever bought the land couldn't pump water on a commercial scale." Kelby rolled her eyes. "That property no longer serves his or AP's purposes. Since he couldn't profit from it, he had nothing to lose by making a 'noble' gesture."

"He still did a fine thing." Mr. Bankhead nodded. "Whatever his reasons."

Kelby stifled a sigh.

As they cleared away the dishes, Angela whispered to Tulah. "Looks like you're not the only one Billy counseled."

Tulah paused on her way to the kitchen. "What do you mean?"

"Billy talked sense into you when you were dead drunk, and he talked sense into Astin when he was clinically dead."

"How do you know it was Billy, who changed his mind?"

Angela grimaced. "I saw him."

"I think something else changed him." Tulah's eyes twinkled.

"What do you mean?"

"When the flood swept Astin under, I think he was baptized in its waters." Squinting, Tulah pressed her lips together. "In a way, it was like he was born again."

Angela arched her eyebrow. "It's true Astin had no heartbeat when you began giving him mouth-to-mouth resuscitation." She thought a moment before smiling. "Born again . . . maybe it was rebirth, at that."

Two weeks later, Doctor West surveyed the cave's wreckage. "If the vandals hadn't pried off the entrance cover, the flood wouldn't have done so much damage. It'll be weeks before the cave floor dries enough to work inside." Shaking his head, he sighed. "Even then . . . I have my doubts."

Angela looked at the sludge-coated bones and the cave's interior, encrusted with mud. "This section contained so much silt, the water turned it into a quagmire." She glanced at the others before facing him. "We followed one of the tunnels and discovered another entrance. That passage has a rock floor, not silt, so it's not as muddy."

"Maybe you could explore that area while this dries." Clay watched his response.

Sighing, Doctor West gave an indifferent shrug. "Maybe."

"And," Angela grinned, "we found signs of human habitation."

Doctor West's eyes opened wide as she handed him the pottery shard and showed him a photo of its location on her phone. "Did you see anything else?"

Angela gave him a twisted smile. "We were running for our lives, so there wasn't time to investigate, but we did see pictographs on the walls." She showed him that photo.

"And more broken pottery," said Clay.

Angela and Tulah nodded in agreement.

Doctor West took a deep breath as he stood up straight. "This opens up more possibilities." Then his forehead furrowed. "Regrettably, I'm not sure the funding can continue."

Her mind moving faster than her mouth, Angela stuttered. "But . . . but you'd said if you had concrete proof Paleoindians occupied this place, you'd have a framework for its classification. A context." Taking a deep breath to collect her thoughts, she tried not to show her disappointment. "What more proof do you need?"

He shrugged his shoulders. "I'd have to see the pictographs to determine their timeframe. Even if they fit into the same chronological period as the tusk etching, it would require reams of paperwork to document. And the time to fill out all the grant applications and other paperwork."

"What if I fill out a rough draft of the paperwork?" asked Angela. "Complete as much information as I can and then turn it over to you?"

She mentally tallied her time commitments: part-time job at the winery, part-time internship at the park, and writing the water-issues paper for graduation. Plus, helping Kelby find scholarships and volunteering to feed the mustangs. *It's all right. I can manage.* "What do you say?"

Doctor West raised his eyebrows. "You're determined to help, aren't you?"

"Yup." Angela nodded.

He smiled. "How can I say no?"

Angela turned toward Tulah and Clay with a grin.

"But," Doctor West continued in a guarded tone, "first I'll have to evaluate the glyphs. If, and I do mean *if*, they fit into the same time period as the tusk, then, by all means, have at the paperwork."

"Funding would help," Tulah shook her head, "but it's not critical. We've been awarded a grant to conserve this land." She glanced at Clay shyly. "We talked it over, and we'd like your research to continue, with or without financing."

The news brought a wry smile to the professor's face. "That's a generous offer, but there are other aspects to consider besides leasing the land. For instance, equipment and student stipends."

"We have an ulterior motive." Tulah grinned self-consciously. "We're hoping your study can prove mustangs are native wildlife, not barnyard escapees."

The professor nodded thoughtfully. "Paleontological opinion and molecular genetics support your belief that the horse is native to North America. But for this to be valid research, all participants must remain impartial. Neutral." He swallowed a grin. "That being said, I'll do my best to validate your theory."

Tulah looked at him cautiously. "Is that a yes?"

Doctor West laughed. "It's as close to a yes as I can give you." Then he turned to Angela. "Starting the grant paperwork would be a tremendous help."

The three of them walked Doctor West to his car. As they waved goodbye, Angela noticed something glittering on Tulah's hand.

"What's that?" Catching her hand mid-wave, Angela studied it and then looked up in wonder. "An engagement ring?"

Nodding, Tulah grinned.

"When did this happen?" Angela looked from Tulah to Clay and back.

"Last night." Tulah glanced up into Clay's face and smiled.

"Congratulations!" Hugging her, Angela asked, "When's the big date?"

"The first Saturday in August." Clay grinned as Angela hugged him.

"It's going to be a busy week."

"Why's that?" Head cocked to the side, Tulah glanced at her.

"School ends the following Friday."

"The summer's going so fast." Shaking her head, Tulah looked from Clay to Angela. "Save some time between working two jobs and writing papers and grants." She grinned. "I want you to be my maid of honor."

After Tulah and Clay left hand-in-hand, Angela began walking toward the stream. Within a few minutes, she felt Kitz playfully bunt the back of her calves.

"Hey, you." She scratched his head between the two velvet spikes.

The newborn fawn stood behind Kitz, close, but just out of her reach. Except for the day they found him, she had never touched him. She smiled, glad he was wary.

"Good, you're keeping your distance from humans—and growing. You're losing your spots." Then she sighed. "Kitz, I've got to stop touching you. You're growing into a buck, and you shouldn't bunt me, either. People won't understand you're playing. They'll think you're being aggressive. Besides, you've got a sidekick to keep you company now."

She felt an ache in her chest, knowing that was the last time she would ever feel Kitz's bristly fur or velvet antlers.

When she arrived at the stream, the effect was almost as powerful as the first time she had seen the devastation. Tears stung her eyes. Swallowing hard, she wiped them away.

"Spilt milk," she said under her breath. "No sense crying over spilt milk."

"Why are you crying?"

Surprised, she looked up to see Billy. "The beauty, the centuries it took the trees to grow to this size . . . it's all gone."

"Stumps and downed trees help nature, too. It's renewal, rebirth, life from death."

Angela stared at him. The sunlight seemed to shine right through. "You look different. Less solid."

He nodded thoughtfully. "I feel different, less committed, less connected to this place."

"Why's that?"

"Thanks to your efforts—and your friends'—the water's safe . . ."

"Water," Angela thought aloud, recalling their first conversation, "the most precious substance on earth."

Nodding, Billy smiled. "The source of life. Life, which is why I'm going away." His smile was wistful. "As you say, moving on."

Again, Angela felt an ache. Kitz and now Billy. She thought of her adopted mother, and tears filled her eyes again.

"Why are you crying?"

"Everything that means anything to me leaves . . . dies, moves on, or grows up." She glanced at Kitz, and then she noticed the fawn's fading spots. She looked at the cypress stumps and logs. "Or it's destroyed." She glanced back at Billy. "I just feel so . . . alone."

He shook his head, but he seemed fainter, more transparent.

"You're young. You have your whole life," he gave her a wry smile, "life ahead of you, and you're not alone. You'll always have me. I'll be a thought, a prayer away."

"Billy . . .?"

Like a flame, he flickered and was gone.

"Billy!" She looked around.

All she saw was the stream. She watched as a turtle climbed onto one of the half-submerged cypress logs and began sunning itself. *Wonder if that's the turtle we saved from the road?*

A woodpecker made a hammering sound as he drilled into one of the tree stumps.

She recalled Billy's words: "Stumps and downed trees help nature, too. It's renewal, rebirth, life from death."

While she gazed at the water, a duck and her fluff-ball ducklings swam past. Kitz and the fawn took a drink as a fish jumped in the water, creating a tiny wake of concentric circles slowly floating toward her.

She thought of Tulah and Clay getting married. She thought of Kio. She thought of the future. *What do I do after graduation?*

She watched as a hawk swept down for a sip of water. Never stopping, it continued on its way. Frogs began singing from the lily pads across the shore, and crickets chirped as the sunlight began to fade. One of the horses neighed in the distance.

When the sun's last rays reflected on the stream, she heard birds calling to each other from the remaining cypress trees. An owl hooted.

She glanced at her watch, then stood up and stretched. "Goodbye, Billy," she whispered to the shadows.

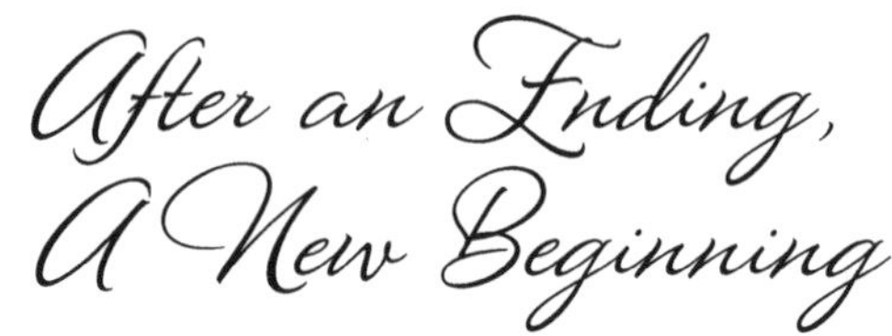

After rain, there's a rainbow.
After a storm, there's calm.
After the night, there's a morning,
and after an ending, there's a new beginning.

– *Unknown*

As Tulah and Clay dashed for the mustang-drawn carriage, all the wedding guests but Kelby threw rice.

"Rice makes birds' stomachs swell." She frowned.

Smiling, Angela shook her head. "That's an urban myth Ann Landers, Martha Stewart, the Simpsons, and who knows how many others spread." Grinning, she added, "Look it up on Snopes." Then she smiled at Kio, remembering when she had told him the same thing.

He returned her smile. "Sounds like we'll be dodging rice at our own wedding soon."

Caught off balance, Angela did a double take. With the flood, grant paperwork, and Tulah's wedding preparations, she had not had time to think about her own wedding.

"Oh, look!" Kelby turned Angela to face the bride and groom in the elegant, white coach. "My sister's going to throw her bouquet."

As Tulah tossed it, Angela leapt up, but a moment too late. Tipping it with her fingertips, the bouquet changed course, sailing overhead to the woman behind her.

Kelby moaned sympathetically. "I thought you had it."

"It should have been yours." Kio caught her eye. "You're the next bride."

"Not necessarily." Angela blinked, processing. "Who knows? Maybe that woman's wedding is next week."

"You're graduating next week." Kio gave her a warm smile. "Then we're getting married."

She stifled a sigh. "We've discussed this. Several times. I thought we'd planned to wait until February. Valentine's Day."

"That was when you'd planned to graduate in December." Kio's brow wrinkling, he gave her a quizzical smile. "Don't you want to get married sooner, not later?"

Not really. Not until February. She took a deep breath, searching for the right words.

"Come on, you two," said Brooke. "You're going to be late for the reception. Ride with us."

When they walked into the restaurant, Angela caught her breath. She felt they had been transported to a shabby-chic barn, replete with linen-covered wooden barrels for tables and curly willow branches garnished with flickering tea candles for centerpieces. An arch made of driftwood and wildflowers filled a wall, and the ceiling was strung with twinkling, vintage garden lights and garlands of flowers in shades of rose and ivory.

While they toasted with Water-to-Winery sparkling wine, first the bride and groom, and then the bride and bridesmaids gathered beneath the arch for photos.

Tulah, her sisters, and Angela all wore tooled, buff leather cowboy boots, gifts from the bride. They posed in their boots and dusty rose, tea-length dresses, laughing among themselves, glad to be part of Tulah and Clay's big day.

Just as the fiddler began warming up, Angela watched Astin saunter in from the bar. Never taking his eyes off the bride, he crossed the dance floor, stopping inches in front of her.

Tulah's smile evaporated. As the party's laughter dwindled, Clay straightened his spine and stepped between Astin and Tulah. "This is a private wedding. Invitation only."

"I'll just be a minute."

Clay took another step toward Astin. "I thought you'd left town."

Astin sneered. "Just passing through, heard about the wedding, and wanted to pay my," he gave Tulah a smug grin, "respects."

Then dropping the smirk, he bit his lip and held out his hand to Clay. "Actually, I wanted to thank you for saving my life," he glanced at Tulah, "both of you, and wish you luck."

Eyes narrowing, Kelby studied him. "You're not on your way to Kerrville by any chance, are you?"

He gave her a begrudging grin. "How did you guess?"

Kelby sniffed. "Instinct tells me you're part of the 'temporary water permit' scam."

"Scam" He grimaced. "I prefer the word 'opportunity.'"

Kelby turned toward the others. "AP's found *another* loophole. They've applied for a new temporary permit to siphon three million gallons annually from the Trinity Aquifer. Problem is," she glanced at Astin, "the well's been inoperable for years—and never had been used for agricultural irrigation as the application claims."

"It filled a pond."

"A recreational pond," said Kelby. "The Barron Trinity Protection Association has its eye on you."

Astin pretended to tip his hat to her. "That may be true, but ever since the flood, the rivers and streams have been flowing. The aquifers are recharging. Without the drought to remind people of water's worth, nobody's going to care whether or not one temporary water permit goes through . . ."

Kelby gave a frustrated sigh. "Temporary permits can be grandfathered in to become permanent permits. It's another loophole."

"You and I know that." He smiled unpleasantly. "But not the general public. Now that the drought's over, most people have lost interest."

Kelby's eyes narrowed to slits. "That's what ruins the aquifers. Not greedy corporations, but apathy. Good people standing by, doing nothing, while shysters and crooks—"

"One way or another, one *well* or another, AP will get the water it's contracted to supply."

Clay stepped closer, his mouth twisted in disgust. "You've had your say. Now can you see your way out, or do you need an escort?"

Sneering at him, Astin sniffed. "Apologies for my intrusion . . . and cordial felicitations." He raised his glass in a toast, set it down without drinking from it, and then strode out.

"Sorry he barged in." Clay put his arms around Tulah. "Don't let that shyster ruin our wedding day."

Eyes only for her new husband, she smiled up at him. "Not a chance."

"Congratulations!"

All eyes turned toward the voice. The newlyweds smiled as Doctor West walked up and handed them a letter.

"What's this?" Clay looked from him to the letter and back.

The professor grinned. "It confirms that the university's funding went through for the excavation, thanks to Angela." Turning toward her, he winked. Then he turned back to the couple. "Thought it might make a good wedding gift."

Opening the letter, Clay held it out for Tulah to read.

Her eyes opened wide. "It makes a great wedding gift." Leaning over, Tulah kissed Doctor West's cheek. "Thank you."

He chuckled. "Don't thank me. Thank Angela. All I did was toss in an archaeological phrase or two, and the application was good to go." He turned toward her with a smile. "If you ever want a job as a grant writer, let me know." Pausing a moment, he put his finger to his lips. "In fact, there's a contract opening in Waco. If you're interested, I'll put in a good word for you."

Angela caught her breath as she recalled the dream at Enchanted Rock. She glanced at Kio before turning back to Doctor West. "A contract in Waco . . . for how long?"

"The fall semester," he smiled, "but the contracts are often extended."

Grinning, she glanced again at Kio. "That would take us into the new year." Before he could answer, she turned back to Doctor West. "We'd planned to marry in February."

"Or before." Kio's forehead puckered.

"The timing's perfect. I'll talk to the director Monday morning," said the professor. "When would you be available for a phone interview?"

"Monday," shrugging, she grinned, "anytime."

"Thinking positively, how soon can you start?"

Angela blinked, processing the turn of events as she mentally checked her schedule. "Classes end Friday . . ."

Doctor West gave her a bright smile. "They've been needing a grant writer for months, but they only received permission to hire recently. *Assuming the interview goes well*, could you start the following Monday?"

"I think that might work—"

"Good! Then it's settled."

"Well . . ." As she considered the details involved with a move, Angela began backpedaling. "But I don't have an apartment or . . ."

"There's plenty of student housing and extended-stay hotels nearby. One of my grad students will email you a list." Doctor West smiled. "Then it's settled."

"Well . . ."

"Is there a conflict?" Doctor West studied her. "You don't have another offer, do you?"

"No . . ." Angela looked uncertainly at Kio.

He grimaced. "Do what you think's best." Stifling a sigh, he frowned.

"My internship's ended," she said, thinking aloud. "Kelby's helping out at the winery now. School's nearly over—"

"And Angela's moving out of the cabin since we're moving in after our honeymoon." Tulah grinned at Clay, then turned to the others with a wink. "I think that's the real reason he married me. The cabin."

"That and another reason or two." Chuckling, Clay kissed her. "Plus there's the grant's stipulation. Caretakers have to live onsite."

Smiling, Doctor West turned back toward Angela. "So with no other job prospects and nowhere to stay, what are you going to do?"

She took a deep breath and glanced at Kio, trying to read his mind.

Spreading his hands, he shrugged. "Do what you feel's best."

With a nod, Angela turned to the professor. "*Thinking positively, and* IF *the interview goes well*," she grinned as she crossed her fingers for luck, "what time should I start next Monday?"

Kio and Angela found a quiet corner at the wedding reception where they could talk and share a glass of sparkling wine. Wearing a mysterious smile, Kio handed her a small box.

"What's this?" Her eyelashes fluttered.

"Your graduation gift . . . a few days early."

"Technically, I graduate Friday, but the commencement ceremony isn't till December." She grinned at him as she opened the box. Then when she saw the blue topaz, she gasped. "Is this the stone you found at the stream?"

He nodded. "Had it cut and polished into a pendant."

"It's beautiful." She smiled, remembering the April day he had found it.

"Hope you wear it at our wedding as the 'something blue.'"

"You found it where Tulah and Clay had carved their initials into a tree. Now they're married." Tilting her head, she flirted with him. "Did that inspire you?"

Never taking his eyes off her, he gave her his slow, personal smile. "I noted the parallels."

As she held up the pendant to the flickering candlelight, she gasped. "And it's the Lone Star cut—"

"Just like your mother's earrings."

She glanced up at him with a smile. "You remembered." Then she handed him the necklace, swept her hair off her neck, and turned her back to him. "Put it on me?"

He fastened the clasp and turned her toward him. His eyes soft, dewy, he said, "Don't take that job in Waco. Let's get married. Move to west Texas with me."

She grimaced as wisps of the dreams floated through her mind.

Flinching, he pulled back his head to look at her. "What?"

"Call it a vision or the answer to prayers, God showed me what I had to do the night we camped at Enchanted Rock." She hesitated, trying to recall the details. "It was only images, impressions, but the dream showed me being offered a job near Waco . . . or Fort Worth." She gave a frustrated sigh. "It's too coincidental to ignore."

"In other words, you want to go to Waco, not west Texas with me." His eyes hard, glassy, he studied her. Then exhaling, his shoulders sagged as he spread his hands. "It was just a dream, Angela. Nothing more."

"Okay, call it intuition." She bit her lip. "Something tells me not to rush into marriage this August. Let's wait till February. Like we'd planned. It's only—"

"Six months, I know." He stifled a sigh.

"Valentine's Day." She leaned into him. "It'll be romantic."

Unconvinced, he grunted.

Angela stared into his eyes. "Graduation to marriage shouldn't be a race."

He pressed his lips together as if collecting his thoughts. "These past few months, I've had time to think, and I'm ready to make a commitment." He peered at her. "What I don't understand is why you're reluctant."

She shook her head. "Not *reluctant* . . . just not *ready.*" She gestured toward Tulah and Clay with her chin. "They renewed their love, when the timing was right." She looked across the room at Brooke. "This spring, her baby was born." She turned back to Kio. "After Astin drowned and was resuscitated, it was as if he was born again." She gave him a crooked smile. "At least, for a while."

"What are you getting at?" Kio's eyes looked bunched: troubled and frustrated.

"Renewal, birth, and rebirth."

His shoulders slumped. "I'm not following."

"I feel an energy. I feel expectant, like a new life's about to begin." She took a deep breath. "I don't know how to express it, just that I feel an excitement, like something's going to happen."

"You're graduating. Of course, you're excited." He smiled gently. "It's a brave new world out there."

"Not exactly what I meant," she laughed, "but you get the idea. I want a new perspective on life. I want to try new things, experience this world, be a part of it."

Raising his eyebrows, he blinked, seeming to reflect. "And I want just the opposite. I want less to do with it." He gave her a shy grin. "I hadn't planned on mentioning this, but I went on a retreat in San Angelo. The topic was 'In This World, But Not of It.'" He shrugged. "It made a lot of sense."

"A secluded life isn't the answer." She shook her head. "We can't hide from the world. Developing our talents, finding our calling is part of life's challenge. We learn. We grow. Then we contribute, give back."

He swallowed a smile. "Why do I get the feeling I'm losing this round?"

"Life's a smorgasbord, and I want to taste it." Gesturing toward the buffet line with her chin, she grinned at him. "Let's eat."

The End

But wait!

There's more…

Reading Group Guide for
Holy Water: Rule of Capture

1. Why is the title, *Holy Water: Rule of Capture*, significant? Why do/don't you like it? What would you have named *Holy Water: Rule of Capture?* Is the title a clue to the theme(s)?

2. Did you enjoy Holy Water: Rule of Capture? Why/why not?

3. What do you think *Holy Water: Rule of Capture* is essentially about? What is the main idea/theme of *Holy Water: Rule of Capture?*

4. What other themes or subplots did *Holy Water: Rule of Capture* explore? Were they effectively explored? Were they plausible? Were the plot/subplots animated by using clichés or were they lifelike?

5. Were any symbols used to reinforce the main ideas?

6. Did the main plot pull you in, engage you immediately, or did it take a chapter or two for you to 'get into it'?

7. Was *Holy Water: Rule of Capture* a 'page-turner,' where you couldn't put it down, or did you take your time as you read it?

8. What emotions did *Holy Water: Rule of Capture* elicit as you read it? Did you feel engrossed, distracted, entertained, disturbed, or a combination of emotions?

9. What did you think of the structure and style of the writing? Was it one continuous story or was it a series of vignettes within a story's framework?

10. What about the timeline? Was it chronological, or did flashbacks move from the present to the past and back again? Did that choice of timeline help/hinder the storyline?

11. Was there a single point of view or did it shift between several characters? Why would Bartell have chosen this structure?

12. Did the plot's complications surprise you? Or could you predict the twists/turns?

13. What scene was the most pivotal for *Holy Water: Rule of Capture*? How do you think *Holy Water: Rule of Capture* would have changed had that scene not taken place?

14. What scene resounded most with you personally—either positively or negatively? Why?

15. Did any passage(s) seem insightful, even powerful?

16. Did you find the dialog humorous—did it make you laugh? Was the dialog thought-provoking or poignant—did it make you cry? Was there a particular passage that stated *Holy Water: Rule of Capture*'s theme?

17. Did any of the characters' dialog 'speak' to you or provide any insight?

18. Did the quotes at the beginning of the chapters 'set the tone' for the subsequent action? Which ones? How so?

19. Have you ever experienced anything that was comparable to what occurred in *Holy Water: Rule of Capture?* How did you respond to it? How were you changed by it? Did you grow from the experience? Since it didn't kill you, how did it make you stronger?

20. What caught you off guard? What shocked, surprised, or startled you about *Holy Water: Rule of Capture?*

21. Did you notice any cultural, traditional, gender, sexual, ethnic, or socioeconomic factors at play in *Holy Water: Rule of Capture?* If you did, how did it/they affect the characters?

22. How realistic were the characterizations?

23. Did any of the characters remind you of yourself or someone you know? How so?

24. Did the characters' actions seem plausible? Why/why not?

25. What motivated the characters' actions in *Holy Water: Rule of Capture?* What did the sub-characters want from the main character and what did the main character want from them?

26. What were the dynamics between the characters? How did that affect their interactions?

27. How did the way the characters envisioned themselves differ from the way others saw them? How did you see the various characters?

28. How did the 'roles' of the various characters influence their interactions as sister, coworker, friend, wife, mother, daughter, lover, and professional?

29. Who was your favorite character? Why? Would you want to meet any of the characters? Which one(s)?

30. If you had a least-favorite character you loved to hate, who was it and why?

31. Was there a scene(s) or moment(s) where you disagreed with the choice(s) of any of the characters? What would you have done differently?

32. If one of the characters made a decision with moral connotations, would you have made the same choice? Why/why not?

33. Were the characters' actions justified? Did you admire or disapprove of their actions? Why?

34. What previous influence(s) in the characters' lives triggered their actions/reactions in *Holy Water: Rule of Capture?*

35. Did *Holy Water: Rule of Capture* end the way you had anticipated? Was the ending appropriate? Was it satisfying? If so, why? If not, why not, and what would you change?

36. Did the ending tie up any loose threads? If so, how?

37. Did the characters develop or mature by the end of the book? If so, how? If not, what would have helped them grow? Did you relate to any one (or more) of the characters?

38. Have you changed/reconsidered any views or broadened your perspective after reading *Holy Water: Rule of Capture?*

39. What do you think will happen next to the main characters? If you had a crystal ball, would you foresee a sequel to

Holy Water: Rule of Capture?

40. Have you read any books that share similarities with this one? How does *Holy Water: Rule of Capture* hold up to them?

41. What did you take away from *Holy Water: Rule of Capture?* Have you learned anything new or been exposed to different ideas about people or a certain part of the world?

42. Did your opinion of *Holy Water: Rule of Capture* change as you read it? How? If you could ask Bartell a question, what would you ask?

43. Would you recommend *Holy Water: Rule of Capture* to a friend?

Recipes

One cannot think well, love well,
sleep well, if one has not dined well.
– VIRGINIA WOOLF

FRIED BLACK-EYED PEAS

8 ounces dried black-eyed peas
1 cup vegetable oil
1/4 cup brown sugar
1/2 teaspoon salt, or to taste
1/4 teaspoon paprika

Soak peas in salted water overnight. Rinse. Bring 1 quart salted water to a boil. Add peas and simmer 20 minutes or until tender. Drain thoroughly and pat dry. Heat oil in a skillet, Sauté the peas in small batches. Drain on paper towels. Combine the sugar, salt, and paprika. Sprinkle the mixture over the peas. Stir to coat, and serve warm. Serves 4.

Campfire Hobo Packs

Ingredients for Sweet Potatoes

4 small sweet potatoes
4 Tablespoons sour cream
2 Tablespoons chipotles in adobo, minced
4 teaspoons brown sugar
1 Tablespoon paprika, or to taste
salt and pepper, to taste
4 teaspoons butter

Wrap each sweet potato in a square of heavy-duty foil. Place on the coals, turning every few minutes with tongs until tender. Except for the butter, combine the remaining ingredients in a paper cup.

Using tongs, remove the sweet potatoes from the fire and unwrap. Slice each sweet potato lengthways and top with a pat of butter. Divide the sour cream mixture among the potatoes, spooning over all, and serve. Serves 4.

Ingredients for Fingerling Potatoes

8 fingerling potatoes, sliced, divided
4 teaspoons butter
salt and pepper, to taste

Wrap in four squares of heavy-duty foil. Place on the coals, turning every few minutes with tongs. Serves 4.

Ingredients for Fish Fillets

4 fish fillets, cod, salmon, etc.
Juice of 1 lime
Salt, to taste
4 pats butter
4 teaspoons fresh chives, minced
1 teaspoon fresh rosemary, minced

Wrap in four squares of heavy-duty foil. Squeeze lime juice over the fillets. Salt them and add a pat of butter to each. Sprinkle with freshly picked chives and rosemary. Fold the edges up and over to create packets and pinch the edges closed.

Place on the coals, turning every few minutes with tongs until tender and fish flakes easily. Serves 4.

About the Author

Dr. Karen Hulene Bartell, author of Lone Star Christmas, Angels from Ashes: Hour of the Wolf, Christmas in Catalonia, Sacred Gift, Belize Navidad, Sacred Choices, Sovereignty of the Dragons, and others, is a best-selling author, motivational keynote speaker, IT technical editor, wife, and all-around pilgrim of life. She writes multicultural, offbeat love stories steeped in the supernatural that lift the spirit.

Born to rolling-stone parents who moved annually, Bartell found her earliest playmates as fictional friends in books. Paperbacks became her portable pals. Ghost stories kept her up at night—reading feverishly. The paranormal was her passion. Wanderlust inherent, she enjoyed traveling, although loathed changing schools. Novels offered an imaginative escape. An only child, she began writing her first novel at the age of nine, learning the joy of creating her own happy endings. Dr. Bartell lives in the Texas Hill Country with her husband Peter and her 'mews'—five rescued cats.

Connect with Karen

WEB SITE: WWW.KARENHULENEBARTELL.COM

WWW.FACEBOOK.COM/KARENHULENEBARTELL

TWITTER.COM/KARENHULENEBART

GOODREADS AUTHOR PAGE: KAREN_HULENE_BARTELL

DON'T MISS THE REST OF

The Sacred Journey Series

BY KAREN HULENE BARTELL

SACRED CHOICES

BOOK I OF THE SACRED JOURNEY SERIES

by Karen Hulene Bartell

An inspirational love story.

Centered on self-growth, *Sacred Choices* weaves together the lives of three resilient women. Ceren is a newly-married and pregnant professor who learns her husband is a bigamist who urges abortion. Judith, Ceren's colleague—an older, more worldly professor and pro-choice advocate—provides counsel based on her experiences. Judith's sister Pastora, a nun, provides the voice of reason. Written for, by, and about women who have had or are considering abortions, *Sacred Choices* is Ceren's journey—from her positive pregnancy test, through her decision whether or not to have an abortion—to an uncanny conclusion.

Sacred *Choices* has an offbeat charm steeped in the supernatural. The protagonists' search for the answer to whether it is the Aztec goddess Tonantzin or Our Lady of Guadalupe who has been revered for the past 500 years is interrupted by a giggling, young girl, who appears only to Judith. Is she a figment of Judith's imagination, a vision—or could she be an angel, as Pastora believes? Set near Mexico City and incorporating present-day Hispanic and ancient Aztec beliefs, culture, and cuisine, *Sacred Choices* deeply celebrates the triumph of the spirit.

SACRED GIFT

BOOK II OF THE SACRED JOURNEY SERIES

by Karen Hulene Bartell

Everyone is gifted, but some never open their package.

Spirits are everywhere for those privileged to see. Angela Maria Brannon, the adopted baby from *Sacred Choices*, has a sacred gift. Her connection with the Aztec goddess Tonantzin and Our Lady of Guadalupe empowers her to see ghosts. At first, people think her having 'imaginary friends' is cute, but at school she's branded 'different' and learns to conceal her special skill.

On her eighteenth birthday, Angela opens herself to communication with the afterlife. Using her sacred gift, Angela spurs those around her to recognize their potential by resolving deep-rooted pain. Traveling San Antonio's River Walk and Mission Trail she encounters eerie apparitions and wraiths. Kissed by the divine and grazed by the ungodly, Angela is proof there's "more in heaven and earth than is dreamt of."

SG

READ A FREE CHAPTER AT
www.Pen-L.com/SacredGift.html

LONE STAR CHRISTMAS

BOOK III OF THE SACRED JOURNEY SERIES

by Karen Hulene Bartell

Deep in the heart of Texas, the miracle of Christmas brings hope, but darkness threatens this joyful season.

As December 25th nears, San Antonio prepares with twinkling lights, riverboat caroling, and frosty nights. The air is fragrant with Mexican hot chocolate and homemade tamales. But Maria, seven months pregnant, abandoned, and losing hope, encounters a darker force in the air.

Recently released from jail, her boyfriend Mal wants her back in his life, but he doesn't travel alone. Latched onto him are a dark angel seeking revenge and a demon destroying him with meth. When she meets José—considerate, spiritual, and protective—he's a gift, the answer to her needs. But is he the answer to her prayers?

Obsessed with Mal, can Maria escape his grip and fight off the evil forces at work?

Will this Christmas be a celebration of life for Maria—or a deadly failure?

READ A FREE CHAPTER AT
www.Pen-L.com/LoneStarChristmas.html

ALSO BY KAREN HULENE BARTELL:

CHRISTMAS IN CATALONIA

A simple trek through Spain becomes a life-changing journey through fear and hope.

On an obligatory walk along Spain's Camino de Santiago before her marriage day, Gwen Alton's trek becomes a life-changing journey through ghosts, fear, and hope, and the beginning of a life-long pilgrimage.

READ A FREE CHAPTER AT
www.Pen-L.com/ChristmasInCatalonia.html

Belize Navidad

Follow your star or follow the crowd?

Belize Navidad is Christmas magic in a tropical-isle setting. This one warms the heart as it chills the spine, with nods to *A Christmas Carol* and *The Gift of the Magi.*

FIND IT AT YOUR FAVORITE BOOKSELLER OR AT
www.Pen-L.com/BelizeNavidad.html

Angels from Ashes: Hour of the Wolf

True love is like a ghost. Many believe in it, but few encounter it.

Chloe Clark stumbles on both but, burned by romance and riddled with low self-esteem, she's unable to recognize true love when it finds her. Agreeing to care for her great-aunt Edwina, she travels to Door County, Wisconsin. There she meets Hud, a charismatic Menominee Indian man, who initiates her in sunset cruises on Lake Michigan, the aurora borealis, his tribe's Wolf clan, and the importance of faith, family, and love.

At her great-aunt's antiquated house, Chloe learns of her family's roles in the tragic Peshtigo Fire of 1871 and the miracles at the Our

Lady of Good Help Shrine. Things get frightening when she accidentally summons the spirits of two restless relatives who begin manipulating her emotions.

Faced with the still-unsolved murder of her great-aunt's sister at age fourteen, an ongoing family feud from six decades before, and a vengeful phantom, Chloe must help her ancestors find peace to be freed of their grasp. Can she realize that peace and find true love with Hud?

Dear Readers,
If you enjoyed this
book enough to review
it for Goodreads, B&N,
or Amazon.com, I'd
appreciate it!
Thanks, Karen

67868750R10156

Made in the USA
Lexington, KY
24 September 2017